The Bones Will Tell

A Skye Cree Novel

VICKIE McKEEHAN

beachdevils
PRESS

The Bones Will Tell
A Skye Cree Novel
Copyright © 2013 Vickie McKeehan

Published by
beachdevils
PRESS

ISBN-10: 0615862934
ISBN-13: 978-0615862934
Printed in the USA

Cover design by Vanessa Mendozzi
Wolf designed by Jess Johnson

You can visit the author at:
www.vickiemckeehan.com
www.facebook.com/VickieMcKeehan
http://vickiemckeehan.wordpress.com/
www.twitter.com/VickieMcKeehan

For Gene, who knows *all* my faults,
but chooses to love me anyway.

"If the blue meanies are going to get me they'd
better get off their asses and do something."
The Zodiac

The Bones Will Tell

A Skye Cree Novel

VICKIE McKEEHAN

Prologue

Six months earlier
Seattle, Washington

His first taste for killing happened when he was eight. On a visit to his grandparents' farm, he snared a rabbit in a trap he'd built himself. He'd taken out his trusty Swiss Army knife then and there and slit its throat right before he skinned it.

But that was twenty years ago. Since then he'd graduated to bigger and better rabbits. He chuckled at his own joke as he made another pass on foot, past the house where the blonde lived whom he'd been spying on for the better part of a week.

He'd already been inside her townhouse. He knew her name was Carrie Bennington and that she lived alone, except for the occasional men she brought home for pleasure and companionship, always on the weekends. He smiled. Carrie didn't have to worry too much longer about whether she would be alone or not, or how she spent her time, or how dedicated she was at her job as an administrative assistant.

Because the clock ticked and the Grim Reaper waited for Carrie like a long lost friend, or maybe it was a nice friendly labradoodle. Either way, he'd picked Carrie after she caught his eye at the marketplace and he'd followed her home. That had been a week ago last Saturday. He'd waited until that Monday morning after she left for work before he picked the lock on her sliding glass door and slipped inside. That was the first time, the neighbors none the wiser. So much for the Neighborhood Watch program.

Because he was good at climbing, athletic and lean, he didn't let things like a two-story apartment building dissuade him from getting at his quarry, not if he really wanted to get inside. He'd been a long distance runner in high school and still kept in shape. But even so, he liked to keep it simple. He preferred it when his victims had the good sense to own their own homes. Like Carrie who lived in a stylish two-story townhouse with an undersized courtyard.

He'd spent hours there going through her closets, her dresser drawers, even her refrigerator. He'd used her bathroom. After all, when the urge to take a dump hit a guy, he had to go.

Every day this week he'd spent some time in Carrie's home. He'd watched. He'd waited. That's how he knew what time she left for work each morning, what time she unlocked her front door every evening, and where she picked up men during happy hour on Friday and Saturday nights.

He knew she kept a vibrator in her nightstand, the one on the left hand side of the bed. He knew which store she'd purchased her last pair of underwear from.

It excited him that he could come and go as he liked. He touched the ring he carried inside the pocket of his hoodie, the ring he'd taken from her jewelry box, some dime-store trinket he'd known when he took it that she'd never miss. The ring kept him focused, had for a week. Not that he needed incentive or purpose to think of what he wanted to do to Carrie. But the ring was a reminder that he could come and go in her things, get inside the place where she should've been the safest whenever *he* needed or wanted.

Standing under the light from a street lamp, he watched as Carrie's bedroom light went out right on schedule. Ten-thirty. He shook his head. One thing about Carrie, she was dependable. He walked to the end of the block, sliding into the shadows of the alley behind her co-op. When he reached the six-foot fence, he took the time to stretch on a pair of gloves. He had help vaulting over the barrier by using crates he'd had the forethought to stack along the alleyway beforehand.

In the backyard, he took out his penlight. He went over to the little outdoor shed Carrie used as a greenhouse, found the metal pipe he'd spotted there a week earlier. He hefted the weight onto his shoulder and stepped to the sliding glass door. He didn't need the tool to break the glass. Only amateurs made too much noise. And he was no novice at B&E or killing. No, he had another use in mind for the heavy rod. From the inside of his pocket, he took out his mask, pulled it down over his head. He pulled out his picklock and went to work on the door he'd already breached once before.

Inside the living room, he scanned the area using the beam of light. Even though he had familiarized himself with the location of the sofa, the coffee table, the bookcase—which wall held the flat-screen television, which side of the room had the fireplace—he still took his time until his eyes adjusted. But knowing the layout made it easier for him to make his way to the staircase in short order. He managed to avoid the steps that creaked along the way up and kept to the path that allowed him the art of surprise.

When he stepped into Carrie Bennington's bedroom and stood over her sleeping form, he paused long enough to appreciate her golden hair, her soft skin, her long neck. By the time he placed his hand over her mouth it was too late. He thrilled at the terror he saw reflected in her green eyes. Not only that, but it excited him to know his face would be the last one she'd ever see.

Chapter One

Present day
Seattle, Washington

In the whole of her life Skye Cree would never get used to how brutal one human being could be to another. If given the opportunity and the motivation, man or woman could be one cruel, sick beast.

She'd taken that as fact for a dozen years or more. It's what drove her to hunt down the monsters, those who preyed on others, who set their sights on the most vulnerable and attacked, at times without reason or logic.

Skye took in the crime scene, the bedroom belonging to the young brunette lying dead on the hardwood floor not two feet away. One thing that caught her attention and stuck fast was that even though the killer had brutalized the victim, evident by the cuts all over her body, even though he'd used a knife, he hadn't been overly messy.

He'd managed somehow to contain the blood splatter so it was kept to a minimal area around the body. She also thought he'd spent some time here with the victim.

Skye considered both significant. She took a second glance around the room.

Since the victim had shared the home with her longtime boyfriend, there was plenty of evidence to indicate that. Both nightstands held the usual clutter. One spoke female with its collection of body lotions, a box of Kleenex, a bottle of water, and a few odd pieces of jewelry.

The other table held all the guy stuff, the TV remote, a pump bottle of lubricant, a stack of sports magazines, a cell phone charger, and the clock radio.

The body hadn't, in fact, been discovered until said boyfriend had flown home a day early from his business trip to Dayton, Ohio. He'd been gone three short days. During that time a killer had managed to gain entrance into the house and taken the life of Sylvia Waterston. According to the BF, the only way he'd been able to conclusively ID the love of his life was the one-carat diamond engagement ring he'd given her not three weeks earlier. The rock was still wedged on the third finger of her left hand. According to her Washington State driver's license, Sylvia had yet to see her thirtieth birthday.

From the looks of the damage to Sylvia's pretty face, her loved ones would more than likely have to opt for a closed casket.

Skye shook her head at that gruesome thought. In her mind, if a person could get used to dealing with this kind of vicious cruelty on a regular basis, she didn't believe he was right in the head.

She'd seen death before, had come close to it herself a time or two. If she counted the dreams that came to her in the night, visions that wouldn't let her be, she'd seen and experienced quite a bit in her twenty-six years. But right this minute Skye had to wonder exactly what the lovely Sylvia had done to piss someone off enough that he'd left her naked, battered beyond recognition, especially the face, and posed her on the floor for the most possible humiliation factor.

He'd taken the time to do all that while he all but set up shop in her bedroom—which meant he'd spent an inordinate amount of time admiring his handiwork—and making sure Sylvia made a statement, or rather her body did.

Skye stepped closer so she could get a better look at the red marks, the distinctive fingerprints he'd left around Sylvia's throat where he had choked the life out of the young woman with his bare hands. Had he strangled her *before* he'd taken some type of blunt object and smashed her pretty face in? Skye wondered. And when exactly had he taken out his knife and started slicing?

That determination she'd have to leave to the medical examiner. At this point, she couldn't even tell which method had ended Sylvia's life. She chewed her bottom lip and tried to figure that out for herself. She'd already taken a tour of the adjoining bathroom and hadn't spotted a visible trace of blood anywhere there. But then they were just getting started. The crime scene people hadn't yet worked their magic. No doubt they'd earn their stripes on this one.

Looking at the stone-cold, grayish corpse though, Skye began to regret ever answering the phone two hours earlier.

She scanned the room a second time, hoping to pick up…something. She'd already determined the killer had obviously enjoyed *being* with Sylvia. Skye noted he'd rifled through the woman's things because he hadn't completely pushed each dresser drawer into its slot. He'd left all nine drawers open about an inch. Each drawer was left exactly that same distance. Could the killer have obsessive-compulsive tendencies? With a gloved finger, Skye wedged open what looked like Sylvia's lingerie drawer. The sparse amount of underwear and teddies left inside said to Skye the killer had pilfered a few souvenirs to add to his war chest.

The victim's jewelry boxes had been gone through. Earrings had been paired up with the wrong mate. Which meant only one thing—he'd wanted them to *know*—it was the only thing that made sense. His intent to mix up the bracelets and necklaces had clearly been deliberate. That explained the odd pieces left on Sylvia's nightstand. He'd taken what he wanted as a memento, not to steal to feed any type of habit, but to make sure he remembered Sylvia.

Because he hadn't taken anything of value, like the diamond solitaire on Sylvia's left hand, Skye took a quick inventory. A Movado watch, not exactly worth a fortune, but something a petty thief would've keyed in on and grabbed, remained in plain view on one end of the dresser. But then a petty thief would have left a cluttered, disorganized mess behind. This guy had not. It was as if he'd wanted, no needed, to savor his time to meticulously go through Sylvia's personal items one by one. He hadn't been in a hurry.

In Skye's mind he hadn't been afraid of getting caught.

Skye crossed over to the walk-in closet. Here, designer dresses and tops had purposely been slid off the hangers to litter the floor. She couldn't help but wonder if Sylvia Waterston had known her killer. Otherwise why would a rapist even think to rummage through his victim's outfits like this, tossing them here and there? Had she invited him into her home with the boyfriend conveniently out of town and things had turned ugly between them? It was something Skye would put in her mental data bank to check later.

She turned to her friend of more than a dozen years, Seattle police detective Harry Drummond. For the first time since she'd arrived at the woman's townhome, Skye took the time to give Harry a sidelong glance to study his face, his attitude, his demeanor. The man she'd known for half her life looked tired. He'd lost weight. Puffy bags under his eyes looked as though he carried a couple of extra pounds in his face and showed a serious lack of sleep. He looked as though he'd aged ten years since she'd last seen him. How had Harry gotten that old in such a short time? Skye wondered.

Finally she wanted to know, "Why am I here, Harry? What is it you want from me? Even though the Farmer's Market's nice and all, Queen Anne isn't my usual haunt. And you know that." Skye locked eyes with Harry. Her violet eyes bored holes in his. She watched him lift a brow.

Before Harry answered he couldn't help it, he took in Skye's high cheekbones, the raven-black, shoulder-length hair she hadn't bothered pulling back today. It fell around her shoulders.

He remembered the first time he'd seen Skye Cree as a twelve-year-old, a terrified little girl who had spent three days in the clutches of a sexual predator.

Now he stared at the woman with the Native American cinnamon skin, the wide mouth that never seemed to have a problem giving him hell about something. "This is number five, Skye. Within a twenty-mile radius of where we're standing. Five. Attractive. Single women. Random order. So far we've been unable to establish a connection other than the obvious. The first one had been bludgeoned to death with some sort of metal object and left a bloody mess in her bed. Two were strangled but they also had their throats slit. The last two, and now Sylvia, had additional knife wounds to the body. All of them had been raped. The DNA he left connects one guy to the first four, of that I'm certain. I'm pretty sure when we get Sylvia's lab work back this will be his fifth."

Skye angled her head, chewed the inside of her jaw. "So why haven't I heard anything about these women on the nightly news? Nada on the Internet."

"Because we've managed to cap this for the press. But after this one—" Harry's voice trailed off before he nodded his head toward the body on the floor. "I don't think it's possible."

"So let me get this straight, you've got a serial killer and you haven't yet warned the public? That isn't right." Skye rocked back on her heels and studied the windows, one on each side of the bed. She crossed over to the closed drapes, pulled the fabric back with her latex-gloved hand.

"He watched her from outside—beforehand—probably multiple times before making his move. He got inside without a problem. Your guy is more than decent at B&E."

Harry's eyebrows popped up. "There's a pry mark on the back door. It's becoming one of his trademarks. It seems this guy started out as a cat burglar and worked his way up to cold-blooded maniac. According to the neighborhood watch program there have been a number of petty thefts within a six-block area during which time he took nothing of real value, stuff like costume jewelry, pairs of panties, a few extra house keys have gone missing, insignificant items like that. Although four streets over, he did steal a couple of nickel-plated Berettas he found hidden in a portable safe, which he managed to get into by picking the lock. So far, that's about the extent of his bounty, though."

Skye gnawed at her bottom lip, thinking, considering. "Then Sylvia didn't let him in. He watched. He waited. He broke in with some skill and he surprised her while she slept."

Harry bobbed his head. "Let's step out into the hallway for a minute."

"Gladly. This is a little too much even for me."

At Harry's direction, the crime scene investigators moved in to bag and tag, collect and preserve. But once Harry got to the living room he turned to Skye and lowered his voice. "Did you pick up on anything in there?"

Skye rolled her eyes before giving him a sneer meant to mock his question. "Since when are you a believer in that sort of thing?"

Harry ignored the attitude. "How about we get out of here? I'll buy you a cup of coffee."

"Why?"

"I'm trying to make peace here, Skye. Unless you'd like me to reconsider and we remain in neutral corners for another few months. Is that what you want?"

Skye blew out a breath. "No. I don't want that. But I have to say, I was surprised to hear from you. It's been almost three damn months."

As they drifted out the open front doorway of the victim's townhome and headed into the little courtyard outside, Harry acknowledged in the only way he could. "I know…but I needed time." He scratched the stubble on his cheek where he hadn't bothered to shave. "I took Callie out to Orcas like you suggested. You were right. It's beautiful out there. We had a great five days of a long overdue second honeymoon."

For the first time Skye showed her dimples when she smiled. "Told ya. Glad you two had fun. It's about time."

Harry made a thumbing gesture over his shoulder. "There's a coffee shop two blocks that way. Feel like stretching those long legs?"

"Sure. That's how I wear out so many pairs of boots. Good thing I know a great thrift store."

Harry shot her a look. "You'll never take a dime of Ander's money, will you?"

"It's *his* money. He earned it."

Harry shook his head. "Washington is a community property state."

"Man, you are tired. Did that little part about a wedding escape you? Josh and I aren't married."

This time, Harry's mouth twitched at the corners. "Yet. By this time I'm sure Ander knows what a stubborn person he's getting with you. I'd warn him about that but I've never seen you so…besotted."

"Besotted? Where do you come up with this stuff?"

"Over the moon then where a man is concerned," Harry corrected. "And you aren't telling me Ander isn't just waiting for you to come to your senses and take that walk down the aisle with him."

Skye gave Harry a steely-eyed glance while a bead of sweat popped out over her brow at the idea of that. "He hasn't asked me yet, Harry. And even if he did, the answer would still be no way."

"Why? Does he have bad habits that didn't show up in the background check I did on him?" Harry held up his hands to explain before Skye exploded in his direction. "A purely precautionary measure at the time. I'm sure if I hadn't done it, Travis Nakota would have."

Skye knew that was probably true. Travis had been her father's best friend. When her father, Daniel Cree had been alive, Travis and Daniel had been like brothers. And since the death of both her parents in a car accident, Travis had always been there for her. At least, until the day she'd gotten shipped off to live with a nutty aunt and uncle in Yakima. But Harry's disclosure about the background check on Josh still didn't make it right. "That was so unnecessary, Harry. Josh had the perfect life before he met me."

"Did Josh tell you that?"

"Of course, he didn't. He didn't have to. I'm not blind."

"You're selling yourself short," Harry stated flatly. Thinking it best to end this topic of discussion and move on, he added, "Hard to believe Callie and I hadn't gone over to Orcas before when it's a mere ferry ride away. Has Josh taken you back out there recently?"

Skye bristled at the question. But then, just as easily as she searched Harry's face, she decided it fell under the heading of small talk between old friends and was not meant to have any connotations other than banter between longtime pals. "We spent Fourth of July weekend there."

"I'm glad you found someone, Skye. I am. If I didn't tell you that before I'm telling you now. Ander seemed…different though at the cabin that day, different than the first time I met him. I can't put my finger on it. As long as the guy makes you happy though, it's about time you had that. You deserve it."

"He does make me happy, happier than I've ever been before. We still haven't known each other all that long, Harry. I might've fallen hard and fast but it's the real thing, at least as much as I know about things like that."

"And Travis Nakota accepts this relationship?"

Skye frowned. "Why wouldn't he?"

"I don't know. I always thought Travis was a little on the overprotective side where you were concerned."

The comment struck a nerve with her. "That's weird. Josh said the same thing."

As soon as they reached the coffee shop, Harry swung the door wide so Skye could go in first. He followed her to the counter where they placed an order for two no-frills coffees. They kept the chat light until the barista handed them steaming cups which they took to the condiment bar for cream and sugar. Once they'd settled in at one of the tables, Harry got back to business. "So did you pick up anything back there?"

"You mean other than the fact your guy is one very sick puppy? He enjoys what he does, Harry. I can tell you that. A lot. But Josh could probably tell you more."

Harry caught what she'd said. His brow creased in genuine puzzlement. "That's the different thing I saw that day at the cabin last time we talked. And that means exactly what?"

Harry thought back to when Josh and Skye had disappeared for a week right after Ronny Wayne Whitfield had his throat ripped out by some type of animal, supposedly a wolf.

Harry stared long and hard at Skye, took in that stubborn set to her chin. When she said nothing, he uttered a soft, "Ah."

She'd walked right into that brick wall she thought now. A tap dance might be required to get around the truth. "I wouldn't say it's new, exactly." She'd have to learn to keep her trap closed from now on around Harry. Unlike the way things had been in the past, full disclosure was not a good idea or an option. She backtracked to purposefully downplay her comment. "Since I first got together with Josh, for some reason, the man's interested in what I do. But you probably knew that already. Josh is a smart guy with skills you could use. He brings a lot to the table as far as investigative tools are concerned. That's why he offered up his programming skills to find the whereabouts of all those girls shipped off to foreign destinations. If he could help track down the phony manifests used in human trafficking, the guy's an asset any day of the week."

Harry picked up his cardboard cup, sipped through the opening on the plastic top. "I guess we'll have trouble getting past this, won't we?"

"It doesn't have to be that way. But the ball's in your court."

"Okay, I'll level with you. I know you have some sort of gift for finding people in trouble. No doubt Josh's methods are more conventional than yours." He raised a hand to stop her from responding so quickly.

But instead of tossing out a pithy reply, Skye offered up a poker face. She'd play out the hand now and let Harry have his false impressions. So she listened as he got to the point.

"I've tried to wave this off. I admit I was skeptical in the beginning. You know that. But…over the last couple of months, I've decided to accept the fact you refuse to share how exactly you do whatever it is you do." He ticked off three names. "Ali Crandon. Hailey Strickland. Erin Prescott. All found alive after a few days of captivity after getting snatched in broad daylight by sexual predators. There's no way you got that lucky...without some…vibe, some psychic ability…or something else entirely."

Skye wasn't about to admit the "something else entirely" amounted to having a Nez Perce spirit guide in the form of a silver wolf named Kiya. Even though lately, Kiya belonged more to Josh than to her, it didn't make for a simple conversation over coffee. "Harry—"

"I'm not finished. Just be quiet a minute and let me finish what I have to say. Because of that and more, I know you have something extra that works. Not sure what it is. Not sure I care. But whatever it is I want to make good use of it. There's no better time than the present, no better case than this one. I've already contacted the FBI about this sick son of a bitch. Their profiler got back to me after the fourth woman. I'll share what I have from them because I want you onboard with this, Skye, full out with the approval and sanction of the department. We're slowly getting to the point where we're grasping at straws on this one."

"But you said you have his DNA."

Harry nodded. "That we have. But it doesn't do us a damn bit of good without a hit, which we don't have…yet. The department isn't willing to sit back and wait either. You have a knack and I need you to put it to good use to help me catch this guy before he kills twenty. Hell, maybe he's already reached double digits for all I know and we just haven't connected the bodies from other jurisdictions yet. If bringing you into this means I also have to deal with Josh Ander, then so be it. But I'm about to stick my neck out with my captain and the department on this entire thing…in a big way. I'll take some flak for it." He wouldn't admit he'd already taken a considerable amount of razzing from the other detectives after what had happened last spring on his own beat.

The entire incident had haunted him for the better part of three months. It stuck in his craw like a pill that refused to go down right. The fact that Skye Cree and her partner, Josh Ander, had been the ones to pull off a miracle almost caused him to resign from the force. The two of them had managed to put an end to a human-trafficking ring operating in Harry's own backyard—without any help from him.

They had found and rescued six young girls ranging in age from ten to sixteen who otherwise would've ended up dead or destined to a life of servitude in the sex-trade industry. There were some things better left out of the public domain. In Harry's opinion, one that he'd spent a considerable amount of time stewing about for the past two months, Skye's and Josh's involvement topped that list.

And when she rolled her eyes at him from across the table, he added, "You have my word, though, that if you use anything out of the ordinary to get results this time, I'll keep it to myself. That's a promise."

Hearing that, Skye sent him a dismissive stare. "I need a little more assurance than that, Harry. I don't want to get blindsided and hung out to dry by the press. If they should catch wind of—"

Harry didn't let her finish. "They won't. I'll see to that." But when she continued to bore holes in him with those deep violet eyes, he decided to lay all his cards out on the table and level with her. "Okay, I admit there have been some rumors floating around. But that's all they are, Skye. The media's convinced you had something to do with finding those girls and that the department, specifically me, covered up the whole thing."

Harry pointed a finger at her. "We both know that isn't true. And yet, what I do know is this. You and Josh were somehow able to locate the whereabouts of those missing girls in that warehouse. I have no idea how you did it. I'm not sure I care anymore. But I know you two were there that day, Skye. Not for public consumption, I know." Harry paused to take another sip of the steaming brew, looked at Skye over the rim.

When he set his cup down, he went on, "I've been a good, clean cop for more than twenty-five years, Skye. For the first time in my career you gave me pause to question that. Right or wrong, well, mostly wrong, you took the law into your own hands that day and we both know it. I understand why you did what you did. How you dragged a man like Ander into your 'cause' is anyone's guess."

When he saw those violet eyes narrow, the irritation flare, he knew she was about to spit fire at him. So Harry held up his hand. "Don't bother with that temper of yours. We're going to start over here, Skye, with a clean slate. You can thank my wife for that the next time you see her. We're going to do this by the book though. Except for your ability or whatever it is you and Josh bring to the table to get the job done, I don't want details. I won't ask troublesome questions and demand answers. What I care about is getting results."

Right this moment, he had a serial killer who needed to be his main focus. That was all he cared about now, not some wedge he'd had a difficult time putting behind him. The extraordinary woman sitting across from him was a resource he didn't intend to disregard any longer, no matter how much his cohorts gave him grief about it. But he needed to make sure there were no slip-ups this time. No misunderstandings about the rules.

"I admit I should've listened to you. You tried to tell me about the human-trafficking problem. There, I said it. Happy now? Whitfield had been in the sex-trade business for years, off my radar in Tacoma—doing God knows what right under my nose for years—I'm not proud of that. I had to come to terms with that, Skye. Or I wouldn't be sitting here."

"You wanted to quit?"

"I did. And this sick bastard I'm dealing with now is one of the reasons I didn't. But in order to come to terms with what happened at the warehouse, I choose to think of it like this. You did what you did out of a sense of justice. That day you were my partner when you walked in there to take care of business. I guess maybe you and Ander both were. You got the job done while I—refused to listen—if not for you and Ander those girls might've never seen the light of day again. You think that fact hasn't kept me up nights? Well, think again, because it has. I almost turned in my badge. If you and Ander hadn't shown up when you did, I shudder to think where those girls might be right now, how they'd be forced to live."

"Which I still have no intentions of confirming or denying," Skye muttered when she finally got a word in.

"I know you don't. And it doesn't matter to me."

"Do you mean that, Harry? Because when I looked down at my phone this morning, I'll be honest, I almost didn't pick up. I hadn't heard from you since that day at the cabin. I was pretty sure there was no salvaging our friendship."

That's one of the reasons it was Harry who made the first move. He stretched his arm across the tabletop, patted Skye's hand. "So how about it? Will you help me catch this son of a bitch, Skye? You'll get the usual consultation fee from the department."

"See to it the money goes to The Artemis Foundation and you've got yourself a deal."

Harry nodded. He'd expected no less from Skye Cree. "I'll be happy to arrange that."

She flipped Harry's hand over and grasped it tightly in hers. "Then you have yourself a couple of consultants. Because Josh is in this thing, too. For the long haul. And trust me, Harry. You won't be sorry you added Josh to the mix."

Chapter Two

The Artemis Foundation had found a home in the same upscale high rise in downtown Seattle where Ander All Games had their corporate offices.

It had not been Skye's first choice. At first, she had resisted what she termed "palatial digs" inside a "too-fancy" address. She would've felt much more comfortable locating The Artemis Foundation in a little bungalow near her current studio apartment. In fact, she preferred it that way.

But since Josh and his business partner, Todd Graham, owned the building, the two men didn't actually charge the foundation rent. And once Josh had dangled free space, even forever-frugal Skye Cree had recognized a tipping point. Because she respected a healthy bottom line, especially for her own non-profit organization, *free* was the one thing she couldn't ignore.

So she'd opted for the smallest office space in the posh building and squeezed The Artemis Foundation into a nine-hundred-square-foot afterthought of a suite on the third floor.

The gaming headquarters might have taken up the proverbial executive floors at the top but the square footage she'd agreed to "lease" was ample room for a one-woman operation. And right now, that's exactly what it was.

Skye didn't have a staff, although her friends had offered to volunteer their time and services whenever the situation called for it. Lena Bowers, a widow and honorary aunt figure Skye had relied on in the past, was the perfect go-to person to direct traffic. Lena was good with people. And the woman had recently taken in a stray off the streets. Lena now had temporary custody of one feisty teenager named, Zoe Hollister. Zoe, a former runaway whom Josh and Skye had encountered living a hand-to-mouth existence now ate regular meals, wore clean clothes, had a roof over her head. If Skye wasn't mistaken, Zoe even had a trip to the mall planned to shop for new clothes for eighth grade in the fall. Thanks to Lena, Zoe had been given a chance to end her life of living out of a cardboard box.

Another tried-and-true friend, Velma Gentry, a waitress at the Country Kitchen, where Skye had worked right out of high school, had agreed to help in a pinch. Velma could be counted on to put her considerable customer service skills to work— skills she'd honed for more than thirty years waiting tables. Skye believed Velma would make an excellent coordinator when it came time for the foundation to go into crisis-mode.

And it would happen. One thing Skye knew for certain: a sexual predator couldn't change his habits. Sooner or later, he'd go after a kid, either male or female. Sometimes it didn't matter which. Because of that, the foundation had to be in ready-mode. It was Skye's job to make sure they had an effective game plan.

For reinforcements on that score, Skye relied on Travis Nakota, the man who had been like a father figure to her since her own parents had died when she was thirteen. If only she could have spent that time living with Travis instead of in Yakima where she'd been shipped off to live with religiously fanatical Aunt Ginny and Uncle Bob, her only blood relatives.

Nothing she could do about that now though, she decided as she made her way through the swanky lobby and to the bank of elevators. Looking around at the polish and shine of the impressive thirty-story Breslin Building, as the locals called it, Skye realized Josh had known exactly which buttons to push to get her to sign on the dotted line.

She might've caved about the location and the digs. She might never have thought in a million years she'd have an "office" with a perfect view of the Space Needle and Mount Rainier. But when it came to furnishing the place, she stuck to her belief in keeping everything to a minimum. Sparse would assure that no one mistook their work for anything but what it was.

The Artemis Foundation located missing children. Period.

Since they were funded by private donations, Skye Cree intended to make sure every dollar went back into the foundation for just that purpose. Not only would she see to it personally, she would have it no other way.

Unlocking the door to suite three-hundred, Skye stepped into a barebones operation. Looking around, she knew the furnishings didn't exactly jibe with the ritzy address. Even though Josh had done his best to talk her into ordering modern, sleek desks and accessories, Skye had refused to give in. On this one thing she wouldn't budge on principle alone.

That's why, at present, a six-foot-long folding table she'd found at a big-box hardware store doubled as a desk. She'd picked up a used but still comfy, ergonomic mesh chair on Craigslist for thirty bucks. Josh provided a credenza from one of the vacant offices upstairs to hold all of the files she'd put together over the years on abducted and still-missing children.

On the wall behind her workspace, a huge map hung pinpointing each and every child abduction that had taken place within a seventy-five-mile radius of Seattle. Some dated all the way back to 1970. Pictures of each child were tacked to the paper as a reminder.

While Josh might have pushed her face-first into this foundation business, Skye had to concede that over the summer she'd settled into the role as director. Even though she still didn't spend a whole lot of time here, she had to admit it was a better place to organize than the cramped four walls of her crappy apartment. Here she could set up her MacBook and devote her time and energy to hunting down Seattle's missing children along with the predators who had snatched them.

She'd even come to terms with making the commute into downtown three or four times a week, even dealing with the headaches of finding an available parking place in the packed garage. While Josh had offered her an assigned spot with her name stenciled on it, she had passed on that perk outright. No doubt she'd been tempted. But it didn't seem right for her to take up someone else's space when she didn't always make the drive in, as many of his employees did five days a week. So, once again, she'd opted out.

When the desk phone rang, she dumped her bag down onto the fake walnut-grain tabletop and all but fell over the metal to answer it. "Artemis Foundation."

"Hello, my gorgeous Skye. What are you wearing?" the voice on the other end greeted her.

Breathless, that familiar voice had her bursting out a laugh. "Josh." It still made her heart race a little each and every time she heard that sexy way he said her name. She thought of his silver-colored eyes, his black mane of hair that only recently had grown long enough that he had to tie it back in a stubby ponytail. Despite the crime scene she'd visited earlier, a smile formed on her lips.

"How'd it go with cranky pants?" Josh asked.

A giggle snaked out. "Harry wants to make up."

"Good, I knew he'd come around if you gave him enough time."

"Josh, he needs help dealing with a serial killer. I sorta agreed both of us would help him on this case—as consultants. At the moment, he has nothing but DNA matching five crime scenes. So far, no hits in CODIS."

"Interesting. And you didn't puke at the crime scene?" Josh mused.

"I was a consummate professional."

"Good job. What impressions did you get about the guy so far?"

Skye gave him a blow-by-blow of Sylvia Waterston's crime scene, of what she knew firsthand, of what she'd sensed about the killer.

"Okay. Sure, we'll give it a shot. But you never answered my question. What are you wearing?"

Another laugh escaped. After months together, Skye had yet to perfect the art of flirting. Even with Josh it didn't come easy for her. She'd lived too many painful years—between thirteen and eighteen shy and reticent after her kidnapping ordeal—before she'd decided to leave that part of herself in the dust for good. Josh had made that transition possible.

So she gave the flirting thing her best shot. "I'll tell you what I'm wearing. But you have to go first, share a few deets." She should've known better than to try to one-up Josh Ander, who always seemed primed to take it to the next level.

"There's this thong. You could come up here and take it off. I'd let you."

Once again, that had her breaking out in laughter. "You could come down here."

"If only I could ditch all these pesky marketing people and software engineers who want to make my life more difficult."

"The gamers want updates. They made *Hidden Cities of Mars* a greater success than *Mines*."

"That they did. And I'm grateful, not saying I'm not. That's one of the reasons I'm stuck here today. It seems we have a few bugs to work out if we intend to make our deadline, which we always do even if it involves cracking the whip over my very dedicated staff and making them put in overtime. But you and I could go to lunch around one if we make it quick."

"Josh, I'd love to, but I promised Harry I'd put together some data for him."

"What kind of data?"

"This guy likes to spend an inordinate amount of time with his victims. Hours in fact."

"So Harry needs to contact a profiler at the FBI. That's what they do."

"He's done that already. But I suggested he might look into other serial sexual homicides, the facts and figures, specifically what's called need-driven behavior. I'm pretty sure it's this guy's signature, some kind of fantasy he's playing out each time."

"So we've got a cat burglar rapist who kills and spends an inordinate amount of time with his victims. He's not a quick, in-and-out kind of guy. Sick puppy."

"Harry gave me copies of the case files."

Josh didn't like the sound of that. "I want you to tell me now if you're up to looking at those kinds of photos, Skye," Josh asked.

She grinned into the phone. His concern always touched her. "I was at the real deal this morning, Josh. I'm pretty sure I can browse through and study a dozen or so photographs of the other crime scenes."

It was Josh's turn to laugh. "My warrior goddess. I should've known. Sometimes I forget she's made of sterner stuff. How about we go over all this when I get home tonight. How's that? Before you head out on your nightly rounds."

"Good. Because I'll need some time to come up with all the data."

When they disconnected, Skye went into the little kitchenette area the suite provided to brew a pot of coffee. Even though it was almost eleven o'clock, she didn't feel as though she'd had enough wake-up juice. After waiting on the ancient Mr. Coffee she'd brought from home to gurgle and perk, Skye fixed herself a cup and settled in at her laptop for research.

There were a number of decent Internet sites that provided a glimpse into deviant and ritualistic sexual homicide. And the fact that she knew all the words to put into the searches to get optimum results was a pretty sad mindset. But you couldn't track predators if you didn't keep up on the stats and the particulars of their crimes.

And Skye Cree made sure she never missed an update.

Chapter Three

Once Skye left the downtown area, she headed to the gym to put in some serious time in the weight room. As she'd discovered over the years, it was the best place to work out her frustrations. As busy as she'd been this summer with getting the foundation up and going, she needed to remember that staying in shape meant staying at the top of her game. Josh might not need the reps in routine as much as she did these days to stay in shape. Being ten percent wolf might mean he could miss a run on the treadmill once in a while. But she couldn't. Sitting behind a desk for hours and hours didn't mean she should get soft and sloppy now.

But that was hardly the reason she felt like punching something right this minute.

In her computer searches she'd discovered two murders in Portland, Oregon that fit the pattern of their serial killer down to the letter. The fact he'd used a knife on those victims had weighted the scale. And it seemed the Portland women had nothing in common except they were attractive and lived alone. The homicides had been committed months apart and went back years earlier. Both remained unsolved and relegated to Portland's cold case files.

Skye knew in her heart the two crimes were related to Seattle's. But proving it was the challenge. She wasn't sure her investigative skills were up to the task. But as Harry had already pointed out, the cops were already at the "grasping at straws" stage. She couldn't very well make the case any worse even if her visions had been greatly weakened since Kiya, the wolf, had abandoned her, gone over to the other side, or rather to Josh's side.

As she circled the block for the third time, trying to find a parking place on the street, she decided she was doing her damnedest to handle the fact she'd lost her spirit guide. Since Kiya, the wolf, took the leap into Josh and saved him from certain death, Skye's path, her destiny had changed.

Kiya now belonged more to Josh, was stronger in him, than she had ever been in her. And there wasn't a whole lot she could do about losing something inside her that she'd had her whole life. She couldn't pitch a fit about it and have Kiya pop back to return to the way things had been before. So she'd have to suck it up and learn to live without that essence inside.

When she spotted a place to park, she pulled her Subaru to a stop, snagged her gym bag out of the back, and started footing it the two blocks in the opposite direction.

As soon as she reached a set of stairs that led below street level, she hustled down the steps to a brown door with white letters that read, "Private Entrance Keep Out."

She chuckled at the sign knowing full well Travis had his "privacy issues." Slipping her key in the lock, she entered what could only be described as a basement-type locker room. Like her office space, Travis Nakota's personal gym was pretty much barebones in its simplicity. The musty smell here was as familiar to her as the breakfast special at Country Kitchen, another place that belonged to Travis and one where she'd once spent her share of time flipping burgers.

But now, looking around the workout room, she noted the high beamed ceiling sported its share of water stains from decades back. Faded green, well-worn indoor/outdoor AstroTurf covered a concrete floor. In certain spots duct tape did its best to hold down mismatched seams that wanted to turn up at the ends.

The plain workout area sported a fancy treadmill that could be used in bad weather, a decent weight bench, a state-of-the-art elliptical, and the not-so-fancy punch bag Travis was now jabbing.

From across the room, Skye heard the thudding of a fist hitting leather in repeated quick blows. She spotted Travis going toe-to-toe with the old-fashioned speedbag. Even though he wore a sweatband around his head, sweat trickled down his cinnamon face. His long black ponytail trailed down his back and bounced with each punch to the bag.

The fifty-year-old Native American man, who stood about five-feet-ten, glanced over at Skye. "'Bout time you got around to working out," Travis grumbled. "Gettin' lazy lately. All that time spent in your fancy downtown office is taking away from your training time. Taking away training time leaves you vulnerable when you go out at night."

Even though his voice held a certain amount of disapproval, Skye saw him wink in her direction. Because she knew her dad's oldest and dearest friend could be a pain in the butt on the best of days, she didn't allow his mocking tone to get a reaction. The man was her oldest and dearest friend, particularly when she'd moved back to Seattle after leaving Yakima behind at eighteen. Since then, Travis had been her rock.

He'd given her a job as a fry cook at his Country Kitchen diner until the day a lawyer by the name of Doug Jenkins walked through the door. Doug had been her parents' attorney. Without her knowing about it, Doug had taken the small amount of money her parents had left her and invested it so that Skye could live off the inheritance for several years without having to go to work for anyone else. That is, if she didn't develop extravagant spending habits.

Skye would be forever grateful to Doug Jenkins and his investment expertise for giving her the opportunity to work on her own.

If only the courts at the time had seen fit to send her to live with Travis instead of packing her off to her aunt and uncle life would've been so much better. Who knew if that one decision by the judge would have changed Skye's path in life? Certainly she could have benefited from the guidance of someone like Travis. Travis's influence could've provided some much-needed insight into a lot of things, mainly in the spirit guide department. In that, she could have used an instruction manual. Travis could have played that role for her. As it was, getting shipped off to Yakima, which to thirteen-year-old Skye, had amounted to Siberia, she'd experienced major problems with the transition.

Trying to handle the deaths of her parents was traumatic on its own. But having to adhere to a fanatical religious regimen was culture shock. About that same time, she'd had to accept Kiya, her spirit guide, as an integral part of her life. Having so much thrown at her at once had been damned near emotionally impossible. Add in the normal teen angst at the time, along with everything else, sometimes Skye wondered how she'd survived those years at all.

"Well, I'm here now," Skye finally sniped back at Travis in the same derisive tone. "Looks like you're working off a mad. What happened?"

"Always were perceptive."

She tilted her head to study him. "Come clean. What's up?"

"My rumor mill has been working overtime. Little birdies told me Harry wants to drag you into this serial killer case. I don't like it."

Skye let out a sigh. How was it Travis always seemed to know things before she ever got around to telling him the news?

She puffed out a breath and pointed a finger at him. "You're overreacting. Again. It's a consultant job and the money will go to the foundation."

"And pit you against one of Seattle's most dangerous individuals. I don't think it's a good idea, Skye. Josh might be better backup now than he was before. But you get in over your head with this serial killer business and you could easily be in deep shit. Both of you could be."

"Why is it you never have any faith in my abilities to catch the bad guys? Why is that? Why is it you automatically think I can't take care of myself when you're the one who trained me?"

The accusation had him stopping in mid-punch. "I have every belief in your abilities. It's this psycho I'm worried about."

"What exactly do you know, Travis? According to Harry, the general public doesn't even know about this guy yet." She kept studying Travis's face then narrowed her eyes. "You have someone on the inside, don't you? Why have you never mentioned this to me before?"

She watched as Travis stalled for time, watched him pull off his gloves, and go over to the mini-fridge to grab a bottle of water. Growing impatient, Skye snapped, "How long have you been keeping tabs on things without coming clean with me about it?"

Travis held up a hand. "Do you think I liked knowing you walked the streets at night in some of Seattle's roughest neighborhoods looking for that damned pervert Whitfield? Seven years, Skye. You've been at this for seven years. All the while I worried myself sick about you. Even with Kiya at your side, there were nights I couldn't sleep knowing you were out there alone. If I could have, I would've hired an army to make sure you were safe."

"So you've been keeping tabs on me all this time? Who do you have on the inside, Travis?"

A "deer caught in the headlights" look came into the man's eyes. "It isn't what you think."

"Then it shouldn't be a problem leveling with me now."

"It's Drummond, okay? Satisfied now?"

"You and Harry?" Skye blinked in amazement, truly stunned at the revelation. But then she considered the past few years or so and realized now that the two men had avoided being in the same room with each other. Had that been deliberate just to throw her off? She opened her mouth to say something and couldn't. For several long seconds, she stood there staring at the man she'd trusted. "I don't believe this. All this time spent training me and you had absolutely no faith that I could take care of myself. What did you two do? Have me followed?"

"Of course not. Now you're being ridiculous. What with Kiya, you would have picked up on that in a heartbeat. As for Drummond, I knew you didn't want him discovering how you were finding and rescuing the girls. Do you think I'd betray that trust?"

"I don't know what to believe. So how exactly did this work with Harry?"

"We just kept in touch by either phone or text, a few emails now and then, made sure you were okay. It's not that big a deal."

"Except for it being on the sly this whole time, right? You've always had a thing about privacy, always been secretive. But there are times like this, I don't think I know you at all, Travis."

⸎ ⸎ ⸎ ⸎

Still steaming from what Travis had admitted, a couple of hours later, she pulled her Subaru into the resident parking garage located under Josh's loft. She came to a stop next to the space where he usually parked his Fusion. As she gathered up her laptop, gym bag, and cell phone, she had to admit she still wasn't completely comfortable at the fashionable address.

She wasn't sure she'd ever get used to the snooty lobby decorated in its French provincial furniture, or the expensive bric-a-brac that sat under the fancy crown molding. She couldn't believe she shared space and a bed with a guy who owned such upscale digs.

As she made her way to the elevator, she passed a gold-plated commemorative plaque reminding her, once again, that the structure was built in 1909 and had historic significance.

She shook her head. Maybe this was one more indication she was so out of her element.

Once the elevator reached street level, she popped across the lobby to another elevator that would take her up to the penthouse suite on the eighth floor. She slid her card key into the slot to get it moving. Even though she and Josh had talked about getting a place in the country, a place of their own, they had yet to contact a realtor to look for one.

There were reasons for that, she supposed, other than her dragging her feet. Josh had been trying to catch up with his duties at Ander All Games while Skye had the foundation to get up and running. So far the busy summer had been to blame. There'd been no time for Sunday drives in the country looking at houses with realtors. At least that's the excuse she'd used.

Once the elevator door slid open, she walked into the airy loft. The one thing she couldn't complain about was how much light the place got. This place made her studio look like a hole down in a dungeon. If she ever decided to move in here for real, her plants would more than likely thrive from all the sunshine.

A wall of windows took up the west side of the living room with a high-rise view of the harbor. It was a spectacular place to sit and watch a sunset. The opposite wall held what she termed Josh's private stash of electronic gadgets and equipment. It included a state-of-the-art stereo system and one of the biggest flat-screen TVs she'd ever plopped down in front of on movie night.

Skye looked over at the Aubusson rug, just one of several scattered over the hardwood flooring, and realized once again, why she might feel out of place here. It wasn't simply the masculine décor, Josh's brown leather sofa, or the matching plush, cushiony side chair, it was pretty much the entire place.

She threw her stuff down on the hall table so she could sort through the stack of mail she'd picked up from her own apartment. Going back and forth between addresses had its downsides. One of them was remembering to deal with the never-ending postal drivel that always seemed to clog up her box. After discarding all the advertisements in the wastebasket, her eyes zeroed in on a plain white envelope, hand-addressed to The Artemis Foundation but using Skye's home address, which not everyone knew.

She ripped into the paper and unfolded the letter inside.

Skye breathed a sigh of relief when she recognized the familiar writing. Erin Prescott, one of the girls she'd rescued from a brutal kidnapper and rapist, had written her an update of sorts along with another three-page thank-you.

A grin spread across her face at the news. Erin, it seems, was improving, attending her therapy sessions regularly. The teen was doing so well that she would start a new school in the fall as a junior. There would be no long-drawn-out trial to endure, no testifying to the intimate details of her attack and capture, since the sexual predator, Brandon Hiller, had copped a plea deal. Hiller had already been sent back to Clallam Bay where he was serving a life sentence with no possibility of parole.

But as Skye read Erin's words of hope and praise, tears welled up in her eyes and ran down her cheeks. She swiped at her face with her fingers.

Didn't Travis and Harry understand that kids like Erin were the reason she had to go out every night? Didn't the reward of saving one child outweigh the dangers and the risks she might encounter out on the streets?

Feeling a sense of pride, Skye sauntered off to the kitchen to put on the roast she'd picked up at the marketplace. She decided there was no better time to open up a new bottle of Chardonnay than tonight at dinner to celebrate Erin's successful road to recovery.

Walking through the swinging door to the huge gourmet kitchen brought a smile to her lips. While the rest of Josh's impressive loft might intimidate her, she felt completely at home in this room. She couldn't help it. She appreciated each of the shiny stainless steel appliances so much more than Josh did. Much like the living area, this room got tons of natural light thanks to an overhead skylight. Not only was it larger than her entire studio apartment, she thought she might be in love with all the rich, oaken cabinets.

She set her bag down on the sleek marble countertop and started putting away the groceries in the walk-in pantry. Craving a cup of coffee, she took out beans and poured them into the grinder. As soon as she got the state-of-the-art espresso machine going, she turned on the oven to pre-heat. This, she had to admit was where she felt the most relaxed and content, a domestic scene she relished. Whether it was here or in her apartment she realized cooking, preparing a meal, gave her a degree of pleasure. And lately making dinner for the man she loved was what made her the happiest.

Josh tossed his keys in the catch-all bowl on the entryway table and sniffed the air. Skye had to be cooking up her now infamous pot roast with the little red potatoes and baby carrots. He wasn't much of a veggie eater these days. But he had to admit there were some meals that just begged a full range of the four food groups. Skye's slow-roasted brisket qualified. He hoped she'd baked some of her yeast rolls to go with the gravy.

Once he pushed open the kitchen door, however, the desire for food headed south. Literally. He sucked in a breath as his own hunger ramped up at the sight. There she stood at the kitchen counter wearing a navy tank top, a pair of low-riding, hip-hugging white shorts, her butt wiggling in rhythm to the sound of Dave Grohl's voice as he remembered Aurora.

Josh cocked his head to study the way her ponytail swayed to the beat, the way her bare feet kept time to the music.

By the time Skye heard footsteps and heels coming from behind her as they crossed over on the slate flooring, she realized she wasn't alone. Startled, she pivoted, led with an elbow and stopped just in time when she noticed who it was. The arm that had swooped out relaxed in an instant. She blew out a breath. "You know better than to sneak up on me like that. Is it too much to ask for a, 'hey honey, I'm home' from you so I won't belt you next time?"

Josh grinned in response. "Like you could hear me or anything else over the Chili Peppers." He reached over to turn the dial down a notch on her docking station. The music shifted to Mozart and a soft piano concerto.

Skye studied the man who looked exactly like what he was. A man who'd had a run of good luck with code and 3-D graphics. A few strands of loose black hair draped down his forehead while the longer length fell to his shoulders. His piercing gray eyes, almost silver in color, held just a hint of both mischief and haughty. "I wasn't expecting you home so soon."

"Meeting broke up early. Besides, since we didn't get a chance to have lunch together, I figure taking off a half hour early, who's gonna mind? I own the store." He nipped her neatly around the waist and lifted her up off the floor. In one deft move, he plopped her butt back down on the counter to face him. "So you think you can take me, huh?"

"I used to be able to," she groused as she looped her arms around his neck.

"Then I guess you'd better show me whatcha got," Josh said in challenge as he settled in between her legs. Nibbling at one corner of her mouth then the other, his hands came around to the front of the tank top. His long fingers slid neatly under the fabric to finger a ripe nipple.

The need to mate gnawed at the fringes. As his mouth covered hers, he picked her up and together they eased down to the kitchen floor.

While they moved, they began to undress each other. She unbuttoned his shirt, ripped it back and off. But as he turned, she caught sight of the tattoo Josh now sported on his left shoulder. A grin spread across her face. A silver wolf with blue eyes matched the one she had on the right side of her upper back.

When he saw her mouth curve up, her dimples take shape, he simply tugged up her tee, pulled it over her head. "What are you grinning at? I've been waiting for this all day. I bet I can give you something to smile about."

"I love you. I'm entitled to smile before I show you."

"Mmm, I love to see your smile. You don't do it often enough." Josh rolled to his back, leaving Skye to straddle him. While hands tore at the rest of their clothes, while they shifted to remove shorts and pants, they couldn't get at each other fast enough. Fierce took over reason. Lips and tongue skimmed lightly along each other's skin.

He brought her head down, kissed the corners of her mouth gently before moving on to nip at an earlobe. He feasted along her neck, moved to flick his tongue back and forth over rose-tipped, pebbled points. Lifting her body farther up to his mouth, he went after her belly and then lingered downward.

Moist. Hot. The orgasm rocked through her.

She responded by taking hold of his head, dragging her fingers through his mass of long hair, untangling the strands as she went. Thrilled at the way he explored every fold, every tender part of flesh, she wanted him.

"Now," Skye breathed out. "Inside me, now!" With that, she reached down to make that happen.

Bodies slicked. They found an easy pace for mating, strong and fast, hard and mellow. While the sonata soared, joy and delight flitted in and out. An explosion of dazzling colors brought them both up and over the peak of velvet greens then fell, blissfully into silky blues.

They glided along, diving into deep water, each riding the wave through the swell. Clinging to each other, they faded into the peaceful afterglow. While that pleasure took hold it was enough to lead them to the brink of what they'd never known before, the oneness, unique only to them.

Still coupled, breathing hard, they stayed locked together on the floor. Josh leaned up to Skye's ear and whispered, "I love you. Marry me, Skye."

But as he watched her eyes go big right before she rolled off him to start gathering up her shorts and top—without giving him an answer—his temper flared. He watched as she took a step backward figuratively, away from him. She wasn't exactly jumping with joy at the prospect of becoming his bride. Instead of sniping at her about it though, he grabbed his shirt and pants in a snit and started to storm out of the kitchen.

"Josh…" Skye finally managed.

But her comeback died a quick death when Josh's cell phone sang out. The ringing broke what was now awkward silence between them.

Josh stared at the phone he'd set down on the marble countertop. He was reluctant to talk to anyone right at this moment. Would she ever completely trust and commit to him? He was beginning to wonder. While he pondered that question, he snatched up his cell and saw the caller was Brad Jones, the detective working on Annabelle's homicide case. What lousy timing, Josh thought as he gave Skye a go-to-hell look, and hit the screen to accept the call.

"Yeah," Josh said into the receiver, clearly not in a good frame of mind.

"I'm glad I caught you, Mr. Ander," Brad began. "I wanted to let you know the district attorney was notified this afternoon that the judge ordered Michelle Reardon to undergo further evaluation."

"Goddamn it!" Josh railed into the phone. "So Michelle kills Annabelle and gets a pass to a psychiatric ward? That isn't right."

"I knew you'd be upset, that's why I wanted you to hear it from me," Brad detailed. "It seems Michele has been putting on quite a crazy act in her cell."

"Like what kind of act?"

"Talking to herself mostly while she rocks back and forth. Then she pulls her own hair out, so much of it that they had to cut it off. You wouldn't recognize the woman you once knew."

"Believe me, I wish I'd never laid eyes on her. But I told all of you that Michelle was a clever con artist. There's not a thing wrong with her mental state except she's a superb manipulator. She played Annabelle. She played me. Did you even bother to delve into her past, to see if she's ever done this kind of thing before? Michele knew exactly what she was doing when she filled that syringe with succinylcholine. She had to know since she used to work as a nurse. And now…"

"Calm down, Mr. Ander. As of this afternoon Reardon's being shipped off to the Laurel Lake Facility in Kirkland where she'll be under lock and key for at least three months. There isn't a thing I can do about it. The judge has already made his ruling. They'll evaluate her to see if she's sane enough to stand trial."

"She's sane enough now," Josh pointed out, clearly agitated by the turn of events. "And now she's simply scheming to pull a stint in a mental hospital instead of prison."

"For what it's worth, I happen to agree with you."

"And then what? What happens after this evaluation period?"

"After the ninety days are up, the judge will go over the recommendations by the staff psychiatrists, make another ruling. Let's hope the doctors will come to the same conclusion that we have: that Michelle Reardon murdered your wife in cold blood so she could make her move on you. That after planning it for months, Michelle used her considerable knowledge of lethal drugs to kill Annabelle Ander, and she should be held accountable for her actions."

Josh rubbed at his forehead where a headache had already kicked in. "Yeah, that all sounds fine and good but I guess now all we have is the hope that Michelle doesn't get away with it."

Chapter Four

For the rest of the evening the tension between Josh and Skye grew worse with each ticking of the clock. By nine that night, when it was time for Skye to make her rounds, the two of them were pretty much ready to part company for a few hours.

They hadn't said a word to each other since they finished dinner. So when he heard the sound of the elevator door clanging shut, he grimaced.

Would things between them ever be normal? How many nights had he heard that ding and hoped like hell the woman he loved would be okay going out at night into Seattle's mean streets without him?

Since the transformation he might be ten percent wolf but that meant ninety percent of him still required sleep to function. Tonight, he wasn't sure he'd ever get used to Skye leaving the house every night without him. And right this moment, he wasn't even certain he had a right to worry about her. Did she even want him to?

Hell, who was he kidding? He'd never stop stressing about her during those hours between nine at night and three or four in the morning. He could never quite settle until she crawled into bed beside him after her "rounds" were done, after she'd exhausted the notion that there were kids out there she could find and rescue.

It helped somewhat knowing that Kiya, the silver wolf they now shared, accompanied Skye into the streets. It was true the wolf protected her, was with her every step Skye took down alleys and dark unlit walkways.

But just because Josh was connected to Skye's spirit guide now, didn't mean he wouldn't prefer to be out there with both of them. While woman and wolf patrolled, searched, and hunted, he hadn't yet figured out a way to run his company during normal business hours and put in another six at night with Skye.

So he bided his time on his own at night—while she went out with her wolf in search of—whatever it was Skye needed to hunt. Be it predator or a child in trouble, he knew she felt compelled to go out. Period. But understanding and knowing Skye had to go out every night didn't solve their problems. Not by a longshot.

Josh understood the evil out there. He did. Since he'd seen it firsthand in his own dark, disturbing dreams, he *knew* what it smelled like, what it looked like, what it felt like. But there were nights when all he managed to do was torture himself with the anxiety of knowing she was out there, while at the same time he'd get a minimum amount of shuteye to function during the day. He wasn't sure he could keep doing this night after night.

And did he have to keep working on her every single day to get her to trust and commit to a long-term relationship with him? Did he want to *work* that hard at getting her to talk about it? Marriage. The woman couldn't even bring herself to say the word.

Frustrated, disgruntled about the whole thing, he had to get his mind to focus on something else. Opening his laptop, he logged on to try to get a little work done. He wrote and sent a few emails, but after forty-five minutes of effort, he just couldn't concentrate. So he logged off, snapped the lid closed harder than he meant to do.

One glance at the clock got him even edgier. Goddamn it, why hadn't he gone with her? Something was off. It felt…wrong for Skye to be alone right now.

He reached for his phone, slid the arrow over to unlock. He thumbed over to favorites while moving to the elevator. With his hand he banged on the button four times in rapid succession. The door couldn't open quickly enough. But when it did, he hopped into the car.

Why wasn't she picking up?

Because something was wrong. He could feel it in his bones.

To hell with this reasoning, he needed to get to Skye. And he couldn't move fast enough.

After leaving the loft, it didn't take long for Skye's senses to fill with the familiar sounds and smells of the night. As she drifted over to Fifth Avenue and Jackson near Union Station, she caught the unmistakable aroma of fried shrimp coming from Lute's Seafood Shanty on the corner.

She heard a foghorn somewhere out in the harbor, the sound she'd heard a thousand times before. Glancing to her right, she noticed the hazy blue fog swirl up out of the ground and up into the misty night. Skye pursed her lips at the thick smoke. It always amazed her to watch Kiya take shape.

The vapor turned bluer, thicker. The energy blast to her system was like a shot of adrenalin. The boost of inner strength ran through her veins. Kiya's eyes appeared first, a deep violet like her own. The body came next, silver in color. Sleek and elegant, Kiya flicked back her ears in greeting.

Skye had a moment to enjoy the meeting of mind and spirit as the wolf nipped at her booted feet. But then Kiya let out a low guttural growl in warning. Out of the corner of her eye, Skye caught movement. Suddenly she was surrounded by a group of five street thugs. Each hard-edged teen looked as if he was looking for something to do and had just hit pay dirt.

"What the hell you doin' out here this time of night, bitch—alone? You in the wrong neighborhood. Mine."

Skye drew in a ragged breath, sized up each male of various size and age. In her estimation, none was older than twenty. They did, however, look tough and determined. It was hard to distinguish their eyes clearly in the darkness. But she knew jittery pupils when she saw them and recognized an addict chasing a meth high. Three clutched knives in their fists that they waved in the air to make sure she saw they were armed.

Why was it always a knife? Skye wondered.

"Nice night for a walk," she finally answered, pulling her nightstick from under the black jacket she wore.

"Whaddya plan on doin' with that thing? That ain't gonna do you no good here, bitch. Are you too stupid to see we got switchblades? Besides, you can't take all of us."

"Wanna bet," Skye countered, about the same time Kiya bared her teeth in a menacing snarl. While the wolf's corporeal form got their attention and seemed to mesmerize the bunch, Skye took the time to assess each one holding a weapon. She was pretty sure she could disarm at least two. The third one might be a problem. But what she intended to do with five she didn't know.

"That's some dog you got there," the tallest one pointed out. "Won't do you no good though. In case you haven't noticed, you're outnumbered."

"And surrounded. You on our turf now," one added.

"Not the first time," Skye admitted, thinking hard about how she could stall until she'd formed a mental plan. "You guys must be new hereabouts 'cause I've never seen you before tonight. You're not sporting any tattoos I recognize."

"What do you know 'bout it anyway?"

"I know you're from out of town." She tilted her head to study the bigger, more imposing one, the one she'd already judged would give her the most trouble in hand-to-hand. "By the looks of the blue fashion statement and the SUR tattoos, I'd say you're branching out from eastern

Washington, looking over the sights here in Seattle, seeing what you can score before heading back to Spokane."

She must've hit a nerve because the big one tossed out, "You're a mouthy bitch, know that?"

"I'm a lot of things. Mouthy just happens to be one of them. Don't tell me you like your women meek and mild."

"Give us your money and we might let you live," the bold guy sneered.

"Go away now and I might let *you* live," Skye boasted, beginning to feel that edginess creep in just before a fight.

That valiant statement brought a round of laughter from the youngest follower, the one who looked to be about fifteen. As if contagious, the hilarity spread to the rest of the bunch.

Skye didn't wait another minute. She took advantage of their merriment and struck out, whacking her nightstick into the largest man. Pivoting, she whipped out a leg, knocking the second-in-command into one of his buddies. Righting herself, Skye shoved her metal baton into the leader's belly, watched him double over. She brought her leg up and into his chin. The force sent him reeling backward. He went down, but to her dismay he didn't drop the knife.

Skye didn't have time to worry about it as Kiya leaped, became airborne. The wolf attacked the one closest to Skye, sank her teeth into his forearm and wouldn't let go.

As another man advanced, she caught Josh's form as he appeared out of the mist. But she didn't have time to do anything but ram an elbow into her attacker's gut. Skye dodged a blow, did a flip backward. As soon as she landed, she backhanded the youngest one, connecting a leg kick to his jaw. The force knocked him to his knees.

Skye glanced over, saw the mouthy one doing his best to gain his feet. She went over, sent a booted foot to his head, finishing him off. He dropped like a rock to the cement.

Meanwhile, Josh waded in with fists and punches of his own. "Not so tough now huh, punk?" Josh muttered as he shoved one man into a utility pole head first. The other, he gave a series of kicks to the hands and face. The knife the teen had clutched in his fist flew through the air. Josh heard the clatter of the blade as it hit the concrete. Josh began to pummel the teenager, now unarmed, who stood about his height. But after taking several blows, the youth fell back, cowered in the street and started yelling, "No. Stop. Don't hurt me. I give up."

Josh turned his head long enough to see Skye finishing off the guy hugging the wooden post. Josh zeroed in on the one doing the most begging. He picked him up by his blue tee. Staring long and hard into the teen's brown eyes, Josh said in a conversational tone, "Tell me something. How many people do you think you've mugged in the last year? Beaten to a bloody pulp? How many people have you left on the streets to bleed to death?"

The guy swallowed hard before answering. "I…I…don't know."

"Wrong answer," Josh stated as he pinged him into a parked car, knocking him out. Josh spun toward Skye, noted she'd taken care of her three.

"That isn't fair. You got a hat trick while I only got to play with two."

"Actually Kiya took care of one. So the score is really two to two. How come it took you so long to get here anyway? I thought the mind meld was supposed to work. It didn't exactly go down the way we thought, now did it? I didn't think you'd ever show up. What the hell took you so long?"

"If you'll take a breath, I'll tell you," Josh said, grinning wildly at her in the dark. "I had my head up my ass, my mind on something else. It won't happen again because I'm not letting you do this alone anymore."

Skye narrowed her eyes. "Letting me? I had this."

"You most certainly did not." Prepared to argue his point more fully, he pointed out, "You could've handled three, maybe four, unarmed. But three of these bastards had knives, Skye. And five? No way could you take down five. I'm not watching you walk out the door anymore and into this kind of combat on a nightly basis."

"Damn it, Josh. We've been all over this. I know you're upset with me, upset because I didn't answer you before when Brad Jones called."

Josh held up a hand. "This isn't the time or the place for a discussion about our relationship. So don't confuse the two, as it seems we have several things we need to deal with in order to wade through."

"Agreed."

"Good. Because right now it's about you not doing this alone—"

"Don't start this crap now! Especially after Travis and I went another round about this very thing just this afternoon."

"I'm not Travis," Josh stated flatly. "Whatever you and Travis discussed doesn't enter into play here, not tonight, not right now when we're standing in the middle of the street after we just took care of a bunch of meth heads."

Skye huffed out a breath. "We need to call the cops and get this scum off Seattle's streets before we go toe-to-toe. Again…tonight." Skye glanced around at the bodies littering the road. "I'm pressing charges."

Josh took out his cell phone, dialed nine-one-one himself. "Damn straight you're pressing charges. We both are. But there's no need to argue with me about this. I mean it this time, Skye."

While Josh relayed the information to a dispatcher, Skye waited for her opening. When he disconnected the call, she pounced. "I wasn't alone here, Josh. Kiya took corporeal form tonight just as Travis told us she would. These idiots heard her growl. It distracted them long enough to give me an advantage. Both of us charged and it worked." Skye glanced over at Kiya, still holding onto the man's arm with her teeth. At Skye's command, the wolf finally relinquished the thug's arm. When the man slumped to the pavement, Kiya trotted over to rub up against Skye's legs.

"See? We had this," Skye said again.

As Josh laid a hand on Kiya's head, he reasoned, "Not good enough."

"Says you."

"That's right. And I'm tired of sitting at home while the woman I love does this alone. Even with Kiya here, there are times, like tonight, you'll be at a disadvantage."

While they stood in the middle of the street debating the issue, the sound of sirens grew closer.

"*Might*," Skye emphasized in disgust. "Why make a big deal out of something that might happen once every month or so? There's no need for you to give up sleep and do this with me. Do you want your company going into the toilet without you sharp every day?"

Just as stubborn, Josh said, "I'm not willing to bet the law of averages will not eventually catch up with you, Skye. And I've decided my company will be just fine if I don't drag in to the office until ten or so in the morning."

Their difference of opinion came to a halt when three cop cars pulled to a stop. Six of Seattle's finest popped out of their older model, light blue cruisers.

"Is either of you armed?" one of the cops wanted to know as he got out of his car.

"Do we look armed?" Josh retorted. He threw out an arm in the direction of the gang sprawled out in various locations on the street. "Those are your bad guys—a gang of thugs from Spokane who thought they'd attack a woman walking down the street alone."

"Hey, I recognize you two. Josh Ander and Skye Cree, right?" another cop said as he approached the pair. "You're the woman who finds all those missing girls, right?"

"No missing girls here tonight," Skye pointed out. "But we were accosted by these drug dealers without provocation."

While the cops started picking up bodies and slapping handcuffs on wrists, Josh and Skye went over their statements. The senior officer wanted all the particulars about the newly-minted Artemis Foundation, which Skye and Josh were happy to provide.

It took almost an hour of details and relating what had happened before the uniforms let them go. Afterwards, they picked up their tiff in progress, deciding it was best to argue over a late-night stack of pancakes.

They walked to a retro eatery with dated décor in a section near downtown that saw plenty of Seattle's nightlife. Musicians, third-shift medical personnel, or any other night owl awake at two or three in the morning could feed a craving at Country Kitchen.

The place was like stepping back into another era. It wasn't fancy but you could order breakfast anytime of the day or night or get a chicken fried steak with gravy at four in the morning. Diners could opt to sit at the counter on one side and watch the fry cook or sit in one of the booths with a view of the foot traffic on the street.

Even though Travis had owned the place for more than twenty years, he'd never changed the color scheme. It was still blue-green or as Velma called it, "tacky turquoise."

As soon as Josh and Skye took a seat in one of the booths, Velma appeared with a coffee pot in one hand and dirty dishes in another.

"You kids eating or drinking?" Velma asked.

"Eating," Skye replied. "Pecan pancakes with a glass of orange juice for me."

"Blueberry for me and a side of bacon, but I'll drink milk."

When Velma left to put in the order, Skye grumbled, "We don't have to be joined at the hip twenty-four-seven, Josh."

"Is that what you think? Just because I'm pointing out you were outmanned tonight and you needed backup other than Kiya."

"We took care of it."

"*After* I showed up."

Skye huffed out, "You don't intend to let this go, do you? You're determined to jeopardize what you've worked for by stubbornly refusing to let me take care of myself. I'm perfectly capable of doing that while you continue to get a decent night's sleep."

"Me? Stubborn? Since you wrote the book, right back atcha. I know you're more than capable of defending yourself. Did I say otherwise? Why are you making such an issue out of this? I own the damn company. I'll go in later in the morning. Issue solved. I don't know why I didn't do it sooner. Probably because on some level I knew I'd meet with this kind of resistance. But prolonging this won't change the fact that tonight you were in real danger with those assholes."

"Okay, okay. Maybe I overreacted."

"Maybe?" He dazzled her with a smile and reached his hand across the table to hers just as Velma rattled their plates down on the table. "Besides, if I go out with you at night, we can make this part of the regular routine."

"Eating late-night flapjacks?" Skye shook her head. "And probably gain five pounds before the end of the month."

"Not the way you train," Josh said.

"Okay, I admit I'll relish having a partner. But you have to promise me two things."

Clearly skeptical of what she wanted, he put down his fork and picked up his milk. "What?"

"If things start falling apart at work, you have to level with me and take care of business first."

That didn't sound so bad. "Okay. Not a problem. And the other?"

"You won't talk my ear off while we're walking down some dark alleyway at two in the morning doing our damnedest to be discreet."

Josh laughed. "I'll try to contain myself. How's that?"

She reached her hand across the table to shake his. "Then I guess we have ourselves a deal."

They dug into their food.

They had no way of knowing that less than seven miles away from where they ate, a serial killer was just hitting his stride…yet again.

Chapter Five

The temperature had dropped to sixty-seven degrees as the clock ticked toward one a.m. What had started out as gray and overcast was now clear enough that a beam of moonlight radiated around him like a halo.

The wind picked up making the leaves dance on the cool August breeze. The lone figure watched as a string of fat clouds hung low in the sky and drifted overhead soft as cotton.

Standing across the street from a three-bedroom townhouse in downtown Ballard, he stopped stargazing and refocused on his purpose. It had taken almost two weeks for twenty-nine-year-old Frank De Palo, Jr. to stake the place out. What with three women living inside, with three distinct schedules, it had taken some creativity on his part to make his visits count.

Frankie, as his mother had been fond of calling her only son, had already spent enough time scouring the stylish residence to make him feel as though he knew the occupants—intimately.

He was about to know at least one of them a good deal more.

Tracy Lewis, a twenty-four-year-old Seattle native, manned the phones as a receptionist at a chiropractor's office not five blocks from this spot. Tracy's longtime roomie, Erica Bentley, was a twenty-nine-year-old flight attendant who worked for Alaska Airlines and flew the Minneapolis—St. Paul route. But it was the third female,

Julie Freeman, the newest arrival in town who had first caught his attention. He'd been perusing the neighborhood when he caught sight of Julie getting out of her car. With such long legs and flowing brown hair, Julie was a looker. It saddened him to learn she didn't exactly have a stellar job history or the smarts to do any type of work other than customer service rep for the local cable company.

Even now, Julie was alone outside, soaking in the steamy hot tub located off the back patio. He could surprise her now. But of course, he would not. One didn't rush things no matter how he was tempted. She might start screaming out in the open or worse, break away and he'd lose control. No, best if he waited for her to crawl out of the water and head back inside the house before he made his presence known.

It was more of a challenge that way, to wait for her to feel safe and secure, to wait until she'd settled under the covers. He liked the idea of surprising Julie once she'd tucked herself in between the sheets, just as she dropped off into a deep slumber. In his experience, it made for a better shock, made for more abject fear and confusion in the victims. Not only that, it gave him more of an adrenaline rush, more of an advantage.

But tonight he envisioned going a different direction. It was time to shake things up. That is, if he could put the brakes on long enough for Tracy to come in from her date, it would work. Although the woman was taking her sweet time about getting home on a Thursday night, he thought now. He couldn't very well stand in the same spot for this long without drawing attention to himself. One never knew when a nosy neighbor might panic and decide to call the cops.

He let his mind drift back to Tracy. The black-haired beauty more than likely had stayed over with Kyle, the new boyfriend of three weeks. After considering how late it had gotten, he wasn't sure it was worth the trouble to wait for Tracy to come home. Bearing in mind what he knew about Tracy, the slut would probably not crawl through the door until morning.

Since that feeling had already started to wash over him, he knew he was getting itchy. That urge to dominate, to control every part of the *act* was beginning to snap at the outer banks and take hold as it usually did. He wasn't sure how much longer he could keep the urge at bay.

That initial fear he always saw in the eyes of his victims kept creeping into his brain. He recognized it for what it was. The pure joy of the hunt, to subdue, to conquer, to watch the last breath go out of their bodies as they slowly took the final gulp of air they would ever take.

Now, he desperately wanted two at the same time in the same place. He hadn't done two since… It had been a *very* long time.

That probably meant he was out of practice on that score. He hashed that out and began to do his mental checklist of the townhome's layout. He hoped to Christ he wasn't getting it confused with the one four streets over on Sedgwick Way, the one with the petite little redhead. At some point, he intended to get around to her. That thought had him glancing across to the similar design and shape of the townhouse itself. It struck him then. Both addresses had a festive front door decoration with the same shade of trim. Both had a white mailbox.

He gone through so many homes he couldn't keep them all straight. Without his notebook handy, which he used to jot down specific details, he would have to wing it tonight.

How could he have been in such a hurry that he'd gone off without bringing what he considered his bible along with him? Why did he go to such great lengths to keep painstaking facts and figures about his victims if he went spacey and left it behind? How could he maintain the source of all his hard effort if he didn't keep the book with him at all times?

For several minutes, he fretted over it and wished he had his notes. But wishing didn't do him any good at the moment. He'd have to remedy that next time. Bitching about it now didn't help while he stood in the dark on a street corner.

How is it he remembered how much money each woman had in her individual checking and savings accounts but not whether he had the correct house? Maybe he was losing his touch. It wasn't like him to lose focus. He considered that and thought about calling it a night.

He tried to get his mind back on track by going over each woman's stats, each bedroom, the placement of the furniture, the insides of their closets, their personal belongings. Keeping to the finite details helped the process once he got inside.

But then the difference in locations suddenly came to him, like a fog lifted. The redhead's townhome on Sedgwick Way didn't have a hot tub. Confident he had the right address now, he forced his attention back to his target.

Of the three roomies, Julie was the one overdrawn at the bank. He considered that fact for a moment longer and decided he was probably doing poor Julie a favor by putting an end to the financial struggle she'd been having for the past six months.

He would take care of her monetary woes tonight—along with a few other things he considered essential. He certainly had that urge to take it up a notch. The timing seemed right. The stars had lined up just so. But the idea of harmony converging and him being a part of that made him chuckle. He was more into delivering chaos bordering on hell than anything harmonic. Besides, the same old thing became boring after so many years.

When Tracy's bright yellow bug pulled into the driveway, a grin spread across his face. Oh yes. When opportunity presented itself a man would have to be an idiot not to kick in the door. Tonight, he would give the media a little something special to put on the front page of their newspapers.

As always, he had the option of adding a different spice to the punch. It would make for an interesting night.

There was no doubt about it. Julie Freeman's life had taken a turn for the better. For the first time in months, she could almost see the light at the end of a dark tunnel. Okay, so maybe she was still having a few money problems. But she was employed now. She'd been trying to catch up on her bills. And she couldn't believe her luck in the roommate department. She'd really hit the jackpot when she found Erica and Tracy. It wasn't just the hot tub either, although who in their right mind would turn down a nice soak on a rare starlit summer evening like tonight? Certainly Julie Freeman recognized a good thing. Maybe it was all those years she'd struggled to catch a break back in her native Los Angeles that had her appreciating things now.

No more worries. Things were definitely looking up.

With her eyes closed, Julie slid farther down into the bubbling froth of the heated water. She let the stress of the day fade away. Unwinding, she moved her shoulders up and down and let her head fall back on the cement lip of the pool.

After she'd finally made the decision to relocate from the crowded, smog-infested confines of her hometown to the much friendlier city of Seattle, she managed to nail down a customer service job. It wasn't much but it had taken her almost nine tough months to find anything that paid more than minimum wage.

Since last January there was no denying she'd had a tough time of it. But after all that, she'd found a position that at least paid her enough to cover the bills. Finding an affordable place to live had been an equally challenging ordeal. For the first three months in Seattle, she'd lived out of her car. But now she had two kickass roommates she'd found on Craigslist.

Erica wasn't even around all that much and when she was here in town, she spent much of her time with her long-time boyfriend. Same with Tracy, only Tracy went through men pretty fast. Sometimes it was like a revolving door and Julie had a difficult time keeping up with all of the men Tracy brought around. For the past few weeks it had been Kyle, a guy who couldn't string two sentences together without talking about himself.

At the rustle of leaves in the alleyway, Julie's eyes popped open. She brought her head up to scan the darkness beyond the pool lights. Except for the soft sway of the row of tall evergreens surrounding the backyard, she saw nothing out of the ordinary.

She settled back down in the water. It was silly to be this jumpy. But lately, no matter what she did, Julie couldn't seem to shake the feeling that someone was watching her. For the past couple of weeks she had the nagging suspicion someone followed along behind her wherever she went. Just the other day while she picked out vegetables at the marketplace, she felt a man standing way too close. And she knew how crazy that sounded. But when she'd gotten home, she even thought someone had been inside her bedroom. Her earrings were out of place. Each pair had been lined up in a different but neatly arranged way. Not the messy, unorganized place on the nightstand where she'd left them, but an almost too tidy lineup. Which was ridiculous she thought now, even silly since she'd only been living in Seattle a short time, not long enough to make that many acquaintances. Except for the people she worked with, no one even knew where she lived.

At the sound of a car engine, Julie tilted her head to listen, once again, on alert. But the noise sounded like Tracy's VW bug pulling to a stop in the driveway. Julie relaxed again, letting the bubbles and the foam relax her body.

A few minutes later, Julie heard the sliding glass door open and Tracy joined her outside. She popped her head up to see Tracy carrying two glasses of white wine, one in each hand.

Julie watched as Tracy handed a goblet out to her and leaned over the steamy tub. "Here you go. Thought you might need a nightcap."

"Thanks. Aren't you getting in?"

"Nope, I'm having this glass of wine and heading off to bed. Tonight, I plan to get my eight hours of beauty sleep. I don't have to be at work on Fridays until ten o'clock. Besides, I've decided Kyle is a major bore. I'm sending him a text in the morning and dumping his ass."

Julie grinned. "What gave it away?"

"He spent the entire evening tonight talking about how *he* wanted to move to Alaska. *Alaska*, Julie. I'm not moving to Alaska."

"I should think not. You've only known the guy three weeks."

"Well. Yeah. But I just spent the entire evening with a freaking windbag who wants to live in a cabin in the woods. That's his life's desire. Can you imagine me living in some shack in the woods?"

Julie snickered and shook her head. "That's a deal breaker all right. Who do you have lined up?" Julie knew Tracy and knew her roommate would always have a backup. Tracy had to have a guy waiting in the wings or at least somewhere on her radar to even consider breaking up with a man this close to Friday night and the weekend.

"Oh Alaska is a deal breaker all right," Tracy sang back in agreement while the two women tapped their glasses in complete unity. "Besides, there's this hot-looking UPS guy who keeps asking me out. I've decided to let him."

When Tracy began to shimmy out of her jeans, Julie pointed out, "I thought you weren't coming in."

She shrugged. "I've decided life is too short. I can always sleep. I'm gonna soak for a while and then swim a couple of laps in the pool. Then I'm texting that hunky UPS man and asking him out for happy hour tomorrow night."

By this time Frank had walked to the alleyway and positioned himself where he could watch Julie and Tracy in the backyard spa. But the adrenaline was already beginning to race through him. It took another twenty minutes before the two women finally decided to crawl out of the water to go inside.

When they moved to the sliding glass door, Frank took a pair of gloves from his back pocket and slapped them on. He undid the latch on the gate to move in closer all the while keeping his eyes on the back door. He crept closer, so close that he could pick up bits and pieces of their ongoing convo.

Tracy came back outside to pick up her jeans which she'd left draped on the chair. That made her the last one inside. Frank listened for the lock to flick into place. The women were so deep in conversation that Tracy hadn't bothered to flip the catch on the sliding glass door.

Frank shook his head, grinning. Some nights it wasn't even a challenge. It didn't appear Julie or Tracy had caught the evening news. Nor did either of the women seem concerned about Seattle's latest serial killer.

He had to wait another fifteen minutes before he saw the lights go out in Julie's bedroom. She would be first, he decided. It took another ten minutes for Tracy's bedroom to go dark.

From that point, Frank inched open the unlocked patio door and walked into blackness. Since his eyes had already adjusted to the dark while in a holding pattern outside, he set his bag down on the floor, unzipped it. He removed the penlight dangling from his neck and stuffed it down inside the bag. He took off his running shoes and socks first. His shirt came off next, then his jeans. Once he'd stripped down to skin, he reached for his larger flashlight. Searching his bag, he gathered up the pre-cut nylon ropes he'd brought, pulled out his mask and grabbed the seven-inch knife.

With the nine-millimeter Smith & Wesson he'd stolen last winter, he had his hands full. But not for long. He slipped the fabric of the mask over his head, adjusted the eyeholes so he could see, and headed down the hall to the bedrooms.

He reached Julie's room first and turned the knob. Once he saw her begin to stir, he rushed over to the side of the bed to cover her mouth with his hand.

"Hello, Julie. Shhh, now don't worry," he whispered in her ear. "I won't hurt you as long as you do what I say, okay? Nod if you understand me."

Julie blinked at the brown eyes behind the mask. Realization dawned that he was naked and that meant he was here for only one thing.

Julie nodded.

He crawled on top of the bed so he could roll Julie over onto her stomach. He put the nine-mil down while he began to bind her hands and feet with the nylon rope. Once that was done, he went to the dresser, took a pair of her panties out, balled them up, and stuffed them into her mouth.

"Stay right there, sweetheart. I'll be back in a flash. Don't you move now, hear?"

He picked up the pistol from the bed and went next door to Tracy's room knowing Julie would do exactly what he told her to do.

When he stepped into Tracy's personal space he found her snoring softly. As he tried to straddle her to tie her hands, though, it proved to be more difficult. Tracy's arm came up swinging. The punch she threw at him barely missed his nose. It pissed him off. He flipped her over on her stomach, jerked her hair and pulled backward. "Listen to me, bitch. You do that again and I'll make you pay. Do you understand?" Frank yelled as he tugged harder on her hair, making her head bob up and down in response.

"Get off me you stupid jerk!" Tracy screamed. With that, she came out of her daze doing her best to buck and fight back with her entire body.

Fuck this, Frank decided. He turned her over onto her back—picked up the gun and used it to bash her in the face—hard. Blood sprayed his hands, which infuriated him. When Tracy fell back, he grappled with her hands, secured them as tightly as he could. When she kicked out with her legs, he whacked her across one knee, then the other, hard enough that he heard bone crack.

He took another length of rope, wrapped it around her throat. With everything he had, he pulled tighter until she stopped struggling. He flipped her to her stomach. Unbridled rage had him entering her from the rear.

He'd told the bitch she would pay.

And Frank De Palo always kept his word.

Vivid images came to Josh in sleep. Deep red for all the blood. The black and brown gore was almost too much to bear. He saw tissue and flesh separating from bone as the man kept up a brutal attack with precision blows to the face and skull.

It didn't matter because even in sleep, Josh knew the woman was already dead. She'd been strangled by a piece of white nylon cord the killer had brought with him. Then to be on the safe side, he'd used the gun.

A voice inside his head kept repeating the same phrase over and over again. So much that Josh's head pounded with a steady roar. Josh could make out the violence just beginning to ramp up in another room.

Through the fog of sleep Josh could see the deadly brown eyes of a madman—make out the rage in them as fury pumped through each slash of the knife—as easily as gasoline flowed through a hose. Because of that it didn't take long for the other bedroom to become just as bloody as the first, just as bad as the one he'd witnessed as if he was right there.

Josh could almost feel each blow as the defenseless, tied-up woman lay beaten to a pulp. He'd switched weapons. Again. From somewhere the killer had picked up a softball bat. The aluminum had done its damage. Her skull appeared crushed while her assailant kept up the brutal pace shattering bone after bone throughout her body.

Even in slumber, Josh shuddered. He could smell the iron as the woman's blood spilled and spattered the walls. He recognized the odor of death, the wrath of a truly evil man.

The scene was so intense that Kiya had to leap into his line of vision as a warning, much like she had done months earlier when she showed him his current path. That was after he'd gone through the cleansing ritual at The Painted Crow. In his mind he went back to that night when the wolf had showed him the faces and smells of evil.

But Kiya had missed the mark.

This was so much worse than Josh had seen that night. Because what he'd seen then in his vision hadn't seemed real. But with so much carnage now, so much blood to deal with, so many broken bones...

"The bones...the bones will tell," mumbled Josh, over and over again as he slept.

Skye watched Josh's fitful movements, let them play out until he settled. She curled into him, wrapped her arms as best she could around his body. For some time he lay there shaking, trembling. Powerful dreams, she knew, could do that—and more—if you let them.

Every now and again, the nightmares from when she was twelve still wanted to creep in and take hold. Even though that feeling of helplessness had lessened, she could relate to Josh's torment.

She would try to walk him through it tomorrow. But as she tried to close her eyes, she couldn't help but wonder what his words meant. Questions started humming through her head as sleep eluded her.

How could bones tell a gamer anything, even if he was ten percent wolf? Were he and Kiya onto some scent that only they could detect? And more importantly, why had she been excluded from the hunt? After everything she'd done, after everything she'd endured, why had the bonding between Kiya and Josh been stronger than it ever had been with her?

Because for her, over the last couple of weeks, her visions had completely dried up. Instead, Josh was now the one who seemed troubled by images he couldn't stop from coming. She wasn't sure how she felt about that. For the first time since she was thirteen, there were no voices inside her head keeping her up nights, no vivid colors bombarding her brain.

After all, Kiya was *her* spirit guide. So why had Skye suddenly been left out of it all? On some level, it hurt to be left out. On another, she could sleep without fears of disturbing images coming to her at all hours. That had to be the major bonus.

Maybe it was this shared life she now had with Josh. Maybe it was someone looking out for her. There were a hundred maybes, she decided as she tried to close her eyes and blank her mind, let sleep overtake her thoughts.

But no matter what spin she put on all of it, it still bothered her. So much that she wasn't sure how long she could handle the feeling of being left out.

The ringing phone beside the bed pulled Josh out of images he couldn't shake. Even as he rolled to his side to grab for the noisy device, he knew who was on the other end and why they were calling.

Skye stirred beside him and grumbled, "It's only seven-forty."

Josh wasn't quite coherent when he fumbled the pickup and snapped, "Hello."

"How soon can you and Skye get to Ballard?"

Josh blinked at Harry Drummond's all-business-like voice. He sucked in a breath, ran a hand through his disheveled hair. "Give me the address."

He heard Harry rattle off a location he already knew was in Ballard. It didn't surprise him when Harry added the warning, "And if I were you, I wouldn't eat breakfast first."

Josh had known it wasn't all a dream. But hearing Harry's warning had him turning to Skye. "Harry has a double murder. Two women this time, same house."

More awake now, she pushed her hair from her face. "You tossed and turned all night, Josh. Does that have anything to do with the fact we're crawling out of bed to go to another crime scene?"

"I'll tell you about it in the car. Let's not waste time. With rush-hour traffic, we need to move."

By the time Josh and Skye reached Ballard it was almost nine o'clock. They had no trouble picking out the right house because cop cars lined the curbs. And Harry waited for them at the curb alongside a string of yellow crime scene tape.

"I'm telling you right now, both of you are going to want to prepare yourself for what's inside that house. In all my years in homicide this is the worst thing I've ever seen. This time, there are two victims."

Skye and Josh traded glances. On the ride over, Josh had already given her a vivid replay of the night before.

"What he did to Tracy Lewis—" Harry stopped talking, tried to regain his composure. He glanced up at Josh and for the first time noticed the sickened look on the other man's face. "If you're that green now, you won't last five minutes in there," Harry admonished.

Skye took hold of Harry's arm. "I think it's a little too late for that."

Harry didn't ask what she meant. Instead he studied Josh's face again, this time longer, buying all three of them some time. But to Skye, it seemed as if Harry had already decided there was something else going on here which was a good thing.

"Why do I get this feeling that Josh here has already somehow seen the carnage firsthand?" Harry asked.

But Skye simply shook her head.

"Well, let's give this a try then. Follow me." Harry grabbed two pairs of latex gloves from a crime scene investigator and handed them off. "Just because you have those on, doesn't mean you can touch anything. In fact, I'd prefer you didn't."

Josh removed his sunglasses before turning to Skye. "Will you be okay in here?"

"Don't worry about me. I did this before, remember?"

Josh had done his best to prepare her on the drive here for what she'd likely see. But stepping into the house, his sense of readiness plunged. He wasn't sure he could follow through. He already *knew* what was down that hallway and wished like hell that Skye did not have to witness it.

As they moved through the doorway, the unmistakable smell of death hung in the fetid air.

While Harry directed them to the first bedroom where Julie's body lay on the bed, Skye trailed behind. But Josh hung back even farther. Finally she walked into the room behind Harry. This time, the killer had not left an orderly murder scene behind.

Julie Freeman's space had been violated much as her body had. Bruises were already starting to form along the throat and around her breasts just as they had with Sylvia Waterston.

But the battering and wounds were far worse this time around, Skye decided. The rage more pronounced. "Who found the bodies?" Skye wanted to know.

"Tracy's boyfriend, a man by the name of Kyle Mattingly. Tracy spent the early part of last night with him and left her cell phone behind at his apartment. On his way into work this morning, he swung by here to drop it off. He found the front door unlocked, walked inside…to this. If it hadn't been for him wanting to return the phone, we probably wouldn't have known about this until Saturday. That's when the other roommate was due back from out of town. She's a flight attendant."

"Good thing she was gone. Otherwise this could've been a three-for-three deal," Skye suggested, as she took in the bloody mass on the bed that passed for Julie Freeman. "So unlike the Waterston crime scene," Skye muttered. "Julie must've really pissed him off."

Harry cleared his throat. "You think this is bad? Tracy is worse and there isn't much left of the face that's recognizable."

Skye shook her head, met Harry's eyes, and then turned to Josh who hadn't said a word at this point. "You okay?" she asked.

Josh shook his head. "I might need a minute before going on."

Skye patted his shoulder. "Take all the time you need." Just one of the things she loved about the guy. Even with everything that had happened, even with all the changes his body and mind had gone through since last spring, since the transformation into part wolf, the man still had a tender heart. The same as he'd had the night she saved his ass in an alleyway. It truly amazed her that Josh Ander could have gone through so much in so short a time and managed to keep his own sense of being, even a sense of humor.

But not today.

She left Josh standing in the hallway while she followed Harry into the other bedroom, the other crime scene. Skye wasn't prepared for the amount of blood or the violence here.

If Julie's bedroom had been in disarray, Tracy Lewis's bedroom had been trashed. The killer had taken a knife and shredded the bedding along with every stitch of clothing in Tracy's closet only to leave the tattered remains all over the room.

"Your impressions?" Harry asked Skye.

About that time, Josh appeared in the doorway. But he stood where he was without actually setting foot inside the room. With a heightened sense of smell, courtesy of Kiya, Josh used that to replay what had taken place here only hours earlier. In his mind's eye, he retraced the steps of the killer, watching the crime play out in progress. When he tried to speak, he found his voice a little scratchy. But he did his best to concentrate and get through this.

"He goes into Julie's bedroom first. Julie's willing to oblige him, do whatever he says, whatever he wants. Julie wants to live more than anything and believes she will. That is, until he leaves her and goes into Tracy's room where it goes badly from the start—because Tracy fights back. Julie overhears what's happening. All the while he's in the other bedroom, Julie hears Tracy struggle, hears everything he does to her, the grunts, the sounds of a scuffle. It gets bad. And when the killer takes out his gun..." Josh swallowed hard and turned to look at Skye before he added, "He hits Tracy, over and over again, bashing her head in. After he has her subdued, he rapes Tracy. After the sexual assault, he places the gun between Tracy's legs and pulls the trigger."

As if from the end of a tunnel, Josh heard Skye let out a gasp.

But it was Harry who had questions. "How do you know that?" Even as the words flew out of Harry's mouth though, just as quickly, he held up a hand. "On second thought, I promised Skye. I don't care because it's right on the money. We think that's exactly what the killer did."

"I'm not sure what good it will do knowing this but—"

"Don't hold anything back. I want to hear everything you think you know. That's why you're standing in the middle of a crime scene," Harry said with some emphasis.

"Okay. The killer undresses, takes off his clothes as soon as he gets inside the house before he ever goes down the hall after either victim. He has surprise on his side. And he's confident, swaggering even, doesn't appear outwardly nervous. Neither woman heard him enter. He subdued Julie first, tied her wrists and ankles before going next door to Tracy's bedroom where he tried to do the exact same thing."

"But Tracy struggled, fought back," Skye repeated. "She was no match for a man though. What was she?" Skye glanced at what was left of Tracy's body on the bed as she tried to gauge the woman's height in life. "Maybe five-three?"

Harry nodded. "According to her driver's license, that's about right."

"Go on, Josh," Skye urged, knowing he needed to get it all out. "Tell us everything you see."

"When Tracy started swinging, it pissed him off. He beat her face to a pulp, broke her nose, raped her, stabbed her, shot her. I think what he did to Tracy your FBI experts would call overkill."

"Julie must've heard the shot," Skye added.

Josh shook his head as if coming back to himself. "No. The gun had a silencer. By the time the killer got back to Julie though, the woman was terrified. She'd had at least thirty minutes to consider her fate. She knew she was going to die. During that time another hour probably went by. He played with Julie. He taunted her. He took his time like you said he did with the Waterston woman. But then, he had to take his time before he raped Julie. He waited around at least an hour, maybe a couple before he was able to perform again. He caused both women a great deal of pain before they died. Both women suffered…terribly."

A little stunned at the details, Skye finally asked, "Josh, you see *all* that?"

"Yeah," was all Josh could say.

But Skye prodded, even with Harry standing there curiously watching them both. "You see the fine points enough to make out the scene in your head. Wait. You said something in your sleep last night. Something about the bones will talk to you. No, wait, that isn't right. The bones will tell. That's what you kept saying, over and over again."

"The bones will tell, Skye. That phrase keeps bouncing around in my head. I don't know what it means. Yet. The bones will always tell," Josh repeated.

Skye furrowed her brow, doing her best to follow his line of thinking. "Okay. So exactly what are they telling you right now? You see what he did here. They're telling you that much now. So give us all of it."

"The man's orderly, a bit of an obsessive-compulsive guy. He does the same thing again and again at every crime scene unless he gets distracted or overly pissed off like he did here. Then he loses it. If he gets out of his rhythm, he gets frustrated, easily sidetracked. He loses patience." Josh snapped his fingers. "Just like that, he'll go ballistic."

"And spends a lot of time with his victims," Harry tossed in. "Skye was right about that. The coroner surmised that he brought the Waterston woman into the bathtub. Probably slit her throat there before taking the time to carry her back in the bedroom where he posed her on the floor."

"How do you know that?" Skye asked.

"The crime scene techs found a substantial amount of blood in the drain."

Skye paced so she could think. "So he isn't here just for the rape, even if the woman cooperates, he's here to kill his victim no matter what she says or does. He doesn't plan on leaving a woman alive. The degree of violence changes from scene to scene depending on how pissed off he gets at the victim during the time he's here. Have I got that right?"

"That's it exactly," Josh said in agreement. "By targeting vulnerable women, comfortable in their homes, by controlling them on every level that's everything to him, he sees it as a coup because the control makes him feel superior."

"Ah," Skye said. "So he likely won't move on to prostitutes or drug addicts?"

"No. Those women he considers beneath him, considers them the dregs of society and too easy to grab. They offer no challenge. And I've been thinking about this. It also might mean…it's just a hunch really…"

"You might as well say it," Harry grumbled. "I've known cops who solved cases with less."

"Okay, I think he's probably from a good family, maybe people considered to be pillars of the community, wherever that turns out to be. He's patient. He doesn't mind waiting for these women living with partners to leave them alone so he can seize his opportunity."

"Like Sylvia Waterston."

"It's a challenge for him to come into these houses, having the freedom to move around whenever he wants while they're away. He'd been here before the attack. It's likely what he does. He's proud of his scouting abilities."

"Could he be military?" Skye questioned.

"Military?" Josh considered that. "No, I don't think so. Just my gut feeling. But it doesn't really matter to him if his target has a roommate or is in a relationship. Obviously. He waits for that perfect opportunity. Then does what he does."

"So maybe he's striking out at this little piece of suburbia the only way he knows how, hitting them where they live, where they should be the safest. He isn't snatching them off the streets. That's for sure."

"Wait a minute," Harry said, interrupting their byplay. "How is it you see all that but can't tell me who did this? What he looks like? That's bullshit."

"He wears a mask over his face," Josh explained matter-of-factly.

Skye's eyebrows went up. She exchanged a look with Harry. "You forgot to mention that, Josh."

"Sorry, but there's a lot hitting me here all at once, I'm a little overwhelmed. I can tell you how tall he is though. A little under six feet. I'd say about five-eleven in his bare feet. I can tell you he has stone-cold brown eyes. He's physically fit, toned abs, muscular legs. He probably likes to think of himself as an athlete. But I'd say that lame description fits at least half the men within a fifty-mile radius of Seattle."

"And then some," Harry mumbled in disappointment.

"Sorry, Harry. I know you wanted more," Josh admitted.

"Yeah, but you're not a magician. You've given me more than I had when I got to Ballard this morning. That counts for something. I'm gonna do everything I can to get this sick bastard."

"That's good. Because Skye and I plan on doing the same," Josh said by way of a reminder.

Chapter Six

For Josh and Skye, downtime was almost nonexistent. But when they were able to relax, they excluded the world in order to spend time alone with each other. They turned off cell phones to watch a movie. They did the same with their laptops, making a pact to not check emails or go near social media. There were times like tonight when all they did was stretch out on the couch in the living room at the loft and talk.

With Josh's head, resting on Skye's lap, they tried to sort out the changes taking place in him. It had taken him a couple of days to get back to his old self again. During that time, Skye did her best to walk him through how best to handle the images which were becoming a nightly ordeal.

"Why do these visions only come to me at night? Why don't they hit me while I'm sitting at my desk in broad daylight staring out at the Space Needle? Why don't they point me to the sick bastard?" Josh wondered, clearly frustrated.

"Hmm, how do I explain this to a smart, sci-fi geek like you so you'll be able to grasp the big picture? Let's see. First, the brain is most susceptible to a vision when you don't have your shields up. That would occur at night when the subconscious is prone to suggestions during sleep, the dream-like state. Second, if he ever takes off that damned mask, you've got him in your sights."

"Shields up? I like that. My sci-fi influence is obviously rubbing off on you, admit it?"

"What I admit is that all your tossing and turning is keeping me awake at night," she teased.

"Sorry. But I don't see how you handled this at thirteen, Skye. Some of these images are disturbing and I'm a grown man. For a child...I can only imagine. I just don't see how you kept from going crazy."

"I'm the reason you're having these dreams, Josh."

Josh let out a loud sigh. "Come on. Not this again. We've rehashed this no less than a hundred times. I am what I am now. Do you hear me complaining? No. Want to know why? Because I'm happier than I've ever been before in my life." He picked up her hand. "That's because of you. You seem to forget that if you hadn't come along in the alley to save me that night, I might not even be here. If we hadn't crossed paths I might be dead right now long before Kiya ever brought me back from the other side."

"Don't do that."

"Do what?"

"Try to make it sound like it was meant to be or something."

"Why? I believe you and I were meant to be. I'm sorry you don't." Bitterness clawed its way into his reason, began to inch up to full anger.

"I didn't mean it like that."

All at once he sat upright, looked over at her, long and hard. "You won't even talk about our future together. It clearly makes you uncomfortable when I even broach the subject. You can't even bring yourself to use the word 'married' where we're concerned."

"Josh, I can't even have children."

He continued staring at her with those silver eyes of his, until she finally added, "Don't deny it. You wanted children. You said so—with Annabelle."

"Okay, I did—once upon a time—with Annabelle. But Annabelle's gone. I'm not fixated on having children, Skye."

"That's because *you* can have children," she snapped in a huff. "There's nothing wrong with *you*."

Josh tried for patience, rubbed his forehead where a headache wanted to join the growing resentment. "And there's not a thing wrong with you. You're perfect in every way." When he saw her scoff at that, he went another direction. "Did you ever get a second opinion about that diagnosis from another doctor? You had to be very young when they told you that."

She shook her head.

"We could always adopt."

"You'd do that?"

He sighed and took hold of her chin. "I'm pretty sure before we head to an adoption agency and sit down with social workers, you'd have to marry me first, which up to this point, I can't even get you to agree to discuss. Do you love me, Skye?"

"Of course I do."

"Then that's the next logical progression for people who love each other. They commit to be together, usually marking that commitment with something known as a ceremony, either formal with a member of the clergy performing the ritual or something more casual with a judge in attendance to make it official in the eyes of either God or the state."

She rolled her eyes. "Smartass. I know what it entails, Josh."

"Then maybe you just don't want to mark that rite of passage with me."

"Don't be ridiculous. If not you, then who? I love you, Josh. But marriage? With me? What if, at some point, you *do* want your own child? It wouldn't be with me."

"If we adopt, the child would be *ours*. Period." But even as he studied her face, those words didn't dent her stubbornness on the subject. "I don't get you. Your parents were married for how long? They loved each other, correct?"

"They adored each other."

"Then you have a model to pattern." Getting more irritated with her by the minute, he stood up, walked to the bank of windows on the west side of the loft. Staring out at the night sky, he stuck his hands in his pockets before he turned back to her. "We love each other. We're living together. We get along well. Explain this to me so I can understand it. Because your unwillingness to tell me is starting to piss me off. Twice now I've gone into a jewelry store to buy a ring only to walk out without it. Mainly because of this wedge you keep putting up between us right here." With his hands now free, he waved at the imaginary wall in front of him.

"We've only known each other a few months."

Josh bristled at the words. "So that's it? We haven't known each other long enough? Okay. But you won't even discuss a wedding down the road. You're dragging your feet about the future, Skye. For God's sake, we can almost read each other's thoughts. What more do you want?"

Without answering him, she pushed her hair back from her face and got up to go into the kitchen.

But Josh yelled at her back "We aren't done with this yet." Just as obstinate, he followed her through the swinging door. "What the hell else is bothering you?" When she remained quiet, he grumbled, "Why do I keep begging someone to marry me who obviously doesn't want to?"

"That isn't true."

"Then what the hell is going on with you?" he shouted.

"There's no need to raise your voice to me."

"Skye, this is bugging me. *You're* bugging me." At the first sign of waterworks, he closed his eyes to keep them from affecting the equation, putting him at a disadvantage. But when Skye's tears became sobs, he couldn't stand it any longer. He closed the distance, wrapping her up. "What *is* wrong? Tell me."

"I'm not comfortable here, okay?" Skye finally admitted.

"I told you we'd get rid of the damned loft and get a house in the country where you can spread out if you want, grow stuff."

"It isn't that simple."

"Oh, I can see that. Nothing ever is with you," Josh grumbled.

"You couldn't possibly be in love with me. You only think you are."

"What?" He set her back, snagged her chin so he could look into her watery eyes. "Where is this coming from?"

"I'm not lovable. You keep telling me that you love me and I keep saying the words back to you, but I don't fit into your world here, Josh. This is all like Cinderella or something. My parents were middle class. I spent five years in Yakima with people who treated me like I was worthless—"

He narrowed his eyes. "That's bullshit and you know it. Is this some sort of mood swing—or something else? I thought you were past those zealots in Yakima. They aren't worth your time. They certainly aren't worth calling them family. No, there's something else in play here, Skye. Level with me."

"I'm losing Kiya," Skye stated flatly. "I've lost my spirit guide—to you." When she recognized the hurt on his face, she quickly added, "It's okay. I felt it happening several months back. I'm not the same. You aren't the same. You and I are connected through Kiya. But Kiya is more yours now than mine. And something else is bothering me. If everything could change in one leap, one transformation like it has, this whole thing between us might not last. It might not even be real. There might be something else at play."

"You're kidding? Like what exactly? Where are you getting this stuff? That's ridiculous." But when he realized she was serious, he thought for a minute. "You mean you think what we feel for each other is due to some kind of outside force because of the merge between human and wolf? That's bullshit."

"How can you be so sure?"

"For one thing I know what's in my heart for you, my very human heart. But I see now your losing your spirit guide is at the bottom of this. Let me get this straight, you aren't able to see victims the way you could before—at all? As in a blank screen."

"Pretty much. I get a weak image every now and again. But it's not the same as it was. Besides, I told you Kiya's spirit is stronger in you than it ever was in me."

Josh let her go so he could pace, back and forth, back and forth. "As much as I hate to admit this, Nakota might've been right. Having Kiya's blood coursing through my veins has strengthened me, but weakened your wolf instincts. Where you had Kiya all these years, in the process of saving my life we've affected your path, apparently sapped what used to be so strong in you to virtually nothing." He frowned, scrubbed at the stubble on his chin. "Over the past few months Kiya and me bonding has somehow managed to change your destiny." He took out his cell phone. "Which means we need to get Nakota's input on this. He'll know what to do to get your spirit guide back on track."

"You think so?"

"Hey, don't give up now. We'll fix this. We have to get you back on the course you were meant to walk. Otherwise this lack of sight will affect everything around you. Like how you feel about me. I had no idea you were questioning what you felt."

"I love you, Josh. I just feel different without Kiya."

"Understandable. It explains a few things."

"You mean that?"

"If I'm inviting Travis Nakota to have dinner here, I'm pretty sure I mean it," Josh admitted with a grin and a wink as he punched in a number on his cell phone that he'd added to speed dial.

Chapter Seven

There were times when dealing with "family" could be a pain. Sitting down to dinner and spending an evening with Travis Nakota wasn't exactly high on Josh's wish list. But the man was as close to family as Skye had. That alone was enough to force him to be nice to Travis for the sake of the woman he loved. And now they needed the man's help again, this time to figure out why Skye had lost her "power of sight" along with the spirit guide she'd had all her life. It wasn't something Josh could ignore.

And he didn't want to. It was obviously weighing Skye down enough to trouble her. They'd already waited months for the transformation to level out. It hadn't. It was time to try to get answers. Travis might be the key.

Plus, it gave Skye a good excuse to make use of his gourmet kitchen to the max. She'd been busting her ass all day preparing appetizers, a four-course meal, and some kind of creamy custard for dessert she refused to let him sample.

The aromas coming from the oven were distracting him from doing any work at home on a Sunday. When the buzzer sounded, letting him know a guest was in the lobby downstairs, Josh got up from his desk chair to answer.

"How long do I have to stand down here?" Travis grumbled.

Josh sighed, not looking forward to facing several hours of the infamous Nakota chip. But he pressed the buzzer to allow him access. "Come on up."

Josh met the gruff man at the elevator. He almost didn't recognize him. His hair was down instead of gathered back into his usual ponytail. Neatly dressed in a pair of dark jeans and a white dress shirt, Travis held a fistful of pink roses.

Josh stuck out his hand in greeting. "Aw, for me? You really shouldn't have." Josh could tell Travis had a hard time holding back a grin. That was a start, he supposed. Cocking his head toward the buds that had yet to fully open, Josh went on to offer, "Want me to take those?"

Travis clasped Josh's outstretched hand and the two men eyed each other with lingering mutual mistrust hanging in the air. Things weren't about to change overnight between the two men. But when Skye appeared an unspoken pact had them heading to neutral corners for the next several hours.

All smiles now, Josh watched as Travis morphed into a gentle father figure. As Travis reached out to hug Skye though, images blasted at Josh's brain. He caught several rapid-fire glimpses from the past. A ghost-like image flickered for a moment. Then, like a sudden flare out of nowhere, images raced toward Josh even harder, faster. They were so strong, packed such a punch, he thought he might lose his balance. Like a camera lens going off with a flash device to capture the best light, the series of pictures became as crystal clear to him as though he were flipping through a photo album.

Josh had seen shots of Jodi Cree, Skye's mother. Now he saw the woman again. But he wasn't quite prepared to witness the affection between Travis Nakota, the man standing two feet away from him, and what was happening with Skye's mother. Somewhere in the montage, Jodi Cree and Travis had been talking about the birth of their child, *their* child's future.

Dumbfounded, Josh tried to reel in his emotions. He needed to sit down.

It was tough to mask what he was feeling toward the man now. On automatic, Josh followed Skye and Travis into the kitchen. But what he'd seen remained with him. And when he took the time to replay the last five months, a ton of things clicked into place.

First and foremost, Travis's role of overprotective father figure became clear because that's what he was, Skye's father, her *biological* father. Now, as Josh thought back to the way Travis had acted from the first moment he laid eyes on the man, all Travis's resentment made sense.

Travis Nakota was Skye's real father. Josh couldn't shake that one fact.

How the hell had she missed that flashing neon sign? And why hadn't Kiya clued her in to her heritage years earlier? Could that be one reason why Skye's destiny seemed to be changing?

All through dinner the questions kept Josh from tasting the food. Which was a damned shame since Skye had outdone herself with the meal. Even the normally sedate Travis went on and on about the way Skye had grilled the salmon to perfection.

Even when the talk turned to the killer who kept Seattle's women gripped in fear, Josh couldn't engage. He listened to the back and forth as if he were standing at one end of a tunnel. He felt like he'd been transported to soupy fog and struggled to see anything beyond several inches in front of him.

The awkwardness Josh felt didn't abate by the time Skye served a delicious cappuccino crème brûlée for dessert and poured coffee.

Any other time, Josh would've enjoyed the French custard, but now he couldn't even taste it. He glanced at the woman sitting across from him, easily chatting with the man who'd fathered her. What the hell would she do when she found out?

Josh didn't even want to consider the possibilities. He stared over at Travis, who was relating his latest horse acquisition as if nothing was amiss.

When it came to cleanup duty, Josh and Travis went through the motions together, making small talk, or trying to. From horses to the Native American paintings done by Ty Moon, the topics stayed light and safe. In fact, Josh found himself postponing the inevitable. Retiring to the living room for a more detailed discussion about what was happening to Skye's abilities suddenly became something he very much wanted to put off.

But after loading the last spoon and fork in the dishwasher, Skye tugged him into exactly that. It was, after all, the reason Travis was there in the first place.

While Travis and Skye got comfortable on the sofa, Josh could not. The shock of it all still hadn't worn off. Ten percent of him paced like a caged wolf in front of the bank of windows, uncomfortable in his own surroundings, in his own home.

The minute Skye excused herself to go to the bathroom, Josh turned to confront Travis.

"What the hell's wrong with you?" Travis barked. "You've been rude since I walked in here. You haven't said two words all evening."

"Me?" Josh tossed back, jingling the change in his pants pocket. He leaned forward and said in a low voice, "Do you ever intend to tell Skye the truth about her parentage?"

Josh thought he saw Travis go pale or as close to it as he'd probably ever see.

"What exactly do you think you know?" Travis snarled.

Josh raised an eyebrow in challenge. "You think it's invisible, that I don't pick up on the secret you're keeping? I guess you really don't understand the transformation in me yet or those wolf tendencies I now possess in spades. You should know though. You're the one who warned me what it involved. If you don't come clean with Skye soon—"

"You'll do what?" Travis pointed a finger at Josh's chest. "Do not threaten me."

"The woman I love has no idea of her true father. Don't you think she deserves to know? How long do you intend to deny her the fact that her father is alive and standing right in front of me?"

"Do you think I like living this lie? Do you think I haven't wanted to confess before now?" Travis ran a hand through his loose hair in frustration before folding into the nearest chair. "I've been tempted to tell her no less than a dozen times since she came to live in Seattle at eighteen. Hell, I even drove down to Yakima once, the day before her sixteenth birthday, determined I'd come clean to her then and there. But once I got to the crazy aunt and uncle's house, I couldn't even get out of my damned truck to make the walk up to the front door. My knees were shaking, my palms were sweating."

Josh blinked in surprise. The man standing in front of him didn't look like he'd scare so easily—which told Josh a lot. All he had to do was look at the nerves emanating off the horse breeder and it had Josh feeling a measure of sympathy. But that didn't do a thing to help Skye. "Why? Why keep this? It's obvious, you and Skye's mother—"

Travis stood up and thrust out a pointed finger in Josh's direction again, this time more fierce. He raised his voice. "You don't know a damned thing about it."

"That's right and neither does Skye."

"It isn't what you think. Oh hell. Don't you see? I made a promise to Daniel and Jodi I'd take this lie to my grave. But now…you're right, of course. Skye needs to know."

"Know what?" Skye said from across the room. "What do I need to know? What did you promise Mom and Dad?"

Travis let out an audible sigh that filled the loft. "Sit down, Skye. I might as well get this over with and tell it one time. I don't want to have to go through it twice."

Chapter Eight

"Go through what twice? What are you guys talking about?"

Travis sent Josh a pleading look. "I don't know where to start."

"Sometimes the beginning works," Josh prompted.

Travis sent a lethal look in Josh's direction while Skye took turns glancing back and forth at both men. She began to get a funny feeling in the pit of her stomach to go with the fish she'd had for supper. Her spirit guide might be a recent memory, but she still possessed instincts that told her Travis was holding something back. When she saw Travis rub his sweating palms on the thighs of his jeans that little voice became a scream.

"You know how much I loved your parents, right?"

"Of course," Skye uttered.

"Daniel Cree and I grew up together on the reservation. We lived eight houses from each other, went to the same school, played together, took our first drink at the same watering hole when we were still underage. Daniel was like the brother I never had and—"

"And my mother like a sister," Skye stated.

Travis rubbed the back of his neck, clearly uncomfortable. "Not exactly. You see, we all met when we were very young, just eighteen. By today's standards that's incredibly immature. But even as young as we were, right away, Jodi and Daniel just clicked. They started talking about marriage like a runaway freight train. The next step was thinking about having kids. But after years of trying, they got frustrated. Jodi insisted they both get checked out. The doctor said Jodi was fine. Daniel, on the other hand, found out he was sterile. When your father was around twelve, Daniel suffered a severe case of the mumps. As it turns out, he was never going to be a father in the usual way."

"No," Skye murmured as the revelation built to what he was getting at. She would not sway or sit. Instincts forced her spine straight as steel as if preparing for battle.

"If you'll just let me explain for two minutes," Travis pleaded.

But Skye was across the room in three strides. Her lean body vibrated with so much anger that her hands shook. "Please do not tell me that you and my mother had an affair."

"I loved your mother, Skye," Travis acknowledged.

"What are you saying, exactly? You and my mother? I don't believe it."

"I loved your mother," Travis repeated. "I went up to her first that day we all met. That one summer afternoon when Daniel and I were in town messing around at the Dairy Queen getting ourselves a burger and a Coke. Jodi had been visiting relatives in our little neck of the woods." Travis rubbed his chin. "Seems to me now that I think back about it, it might've been Ginny and Bob she was staying with at the time. But Jodi had grown up in Seattle. Hell that was a different world to Daniel and me back then, two Native teens fresh off the reservation, wet behind the ears in every way. We recognized Jodi as an out-of-towner, a white girl at that, with these huge blue-violet eyes. You have her eyes, Skye." He cleared his throat, reluctant to go on, but knowing he had no choice.

"You see, Jodi was stuck in this little bitty town for three months for the summer where she didn't know a single soul. Daniel and I were out to change that when I went over to where she was sitting in a booth by herself and struck up a conversation with her. But as soon as she got a load of Daniel, it seems Jodi only had eyes for him. From the first time they set eyes on each other, it was the two of them as a couple. I never stood a chance."

"So let's have it."

"Years later, when we all ended up living here in Seattle, when the two of them came to me for help, it was as a last resort."

"Help? You mean to give them a baby? That's what you're building up to, isn't it? Why would you agree to that, Travis? Because you had a thing for my mother?"

"There's no need for that tone, Skye Melody Cree. For your information, at first, I told them both no, a resounding hell no. In fact it turned into many times. A couple of years went by. Daniel and Jodi kept pressuring me, reassuring me they were both fine with it. They were persistent, Skye."

The reality of what he'd confessed was still sinking in when Skye put the accusation on the table. "You didn't go to a clinic." It wasn't a question.

When Travis turned away, refused to even look at her, Skye had her answer. She grabbed his arm to get his attention. "At least face me, Travis. Or what am I supposed to call you now, *daddy*? I don't think so. For starters, how about I try coward?"

At the insult, Skye noted a tic in his facial muscle. But she didn't care. "I want to hear you say it, all of it. The words, Travis, say the words. Now!"

"I am your father! Is that what you want me to say? Daniel Cree couldn't have children so I did what he couldn't. Is that clear enough for you?" Travis shouted in a clipped angry tone.

Skye sucked in a breath. "Crystal. I don't know which is more deplorable. The fact that you slept with my mother under the guise of getting her knocked up so you could fulfill some teen crush you had on her. Or the fact that you stood by and did nothing while I went to live with those despicable people in Yakima. All you had to do was tell the court the truth. The truth, Travis. Was that too much to ask back then when I was thirteen years old? But you did nothing. I spent five years in hell with Ginny and Bob while I could've been right here in Seattle living life as your daughter. What a spineless, gutless thing to do!" With that, Skye stormed to the elevator. When it opened, she stepped inside and was gone.

Travis dropped down into the nearest chair with his head in his hands, defeated.

When Josh started to speak, Travis held up his hand to stop him. "Is this what you wanted?"

"No. But I knew she'd be angry. She's messed up right now, Travis. She's been having a difficult time since the transformation, since Kiya's spirit has weakened. Give her some time."

"Time? I don't think she'll ever forgive me."

Josh said nothing else. There were no words of reassurance that came to mind. Because he wasn't exactly sure she would forgive or trust anyone—ever again.

The aftershocks from Travis's disclosure made for an interesting four days.

The repercussions were neither pretty nor dull.

Skye's temper in the form of rockets-in-the-air fireworks went off regularly and with precision. The Fourth of July seemed tame compared to Skye Melody Cree in rage-mode. Since Travis had unburdened his secret, her dark side had bubbled to the surface where it had remained unleashed.

She didn't walk anywhere. She clomped. Her voice seemed to take on a high-pitched squeal if Josh even hinted bringing up the name, Travis Nakota.

But on the fifth day, Josh had had enough. "How much longer do you intend to make Travis suffer?"

"This is none of your business, Josh. Stay out of it."

"To hell it isn't. I'm the one who encouraged him to level with you, got angry at him because of it. Had I known you were going to act like such a thirteen-year-old drama queen—"

Skye whirled to face Josh. "How dare you say that to me! He stayed mum on the sidelines and watched during the most heartbreaking time of my life. For God's sakes, I lost my parents. Or rather the man who I thought all this time was my father. But what does Travis do back then? The son of a bitch stands beside me at the double funeral and never once claimed me as his daughter. He stood by while the court sent me to Siberia a.k.a. Yakima. He let me go live with those religious fanatics all the while knowing the truth. At the time, all the man had to do was step forward and come clean to the judge, say something like, 'This happens to be my *only* child, my *only* daughter. Don't believe me? I can prove it through a DNA test. She should be allowed to come live with *me*.' Does he do that? Hell no! Not Travis Nakota. He keeps his mouth shut while I spend five fucking years having to bow and scrape to Ginny and Bob, listen to them tell me what a horrific person I was for letting Whitfield rape me."

Horrified Josh let that sink in before he said, "I know you're angry, Skye. Okay, you're livid. You have a right to that. But he's your father and there isn't anything you can do about it."

"Angry doesn't cover what I am, Josh. Not by a longshot. For five years, I felt like I was going nuts, crazy. Don't you understand? At some point, I started believing Ginny and Bob."

"I'm sorry, baby." He took her chin, lifted it up so he could stare into her eyes. "You're right, Travis should've stepped up. But he's your father, your blood."

"Which means squat to him. If it meant anything at all, he would've said something when it counted. And I might point out that just because a man can be a sperm donor in the sack to a woman desperate to have a child, it does not make him father material. I will now and forever think of Daniel Cree as my *father*, not some churlish horse breeder who waited a quarter of a century to come clean."

"But we could use Travis's insight right now into how to get your ability to come back," Josh pointed out.

"Screw my ability. I don't want Travis Nakota's help with anything. I'll work this out myself just like I have everything else in my life. Kiya and I will connect again. I feel it down to my bones. You'll see. Everything will be just fine without Travis Nakota."

And that had pretty much ended any further discussion.

That's why two days later, Josh wasn't the least bit surprised when Travis called him wanting to talk.

These days inside Ander All Games, security had to be a top priority. A company didn't create the latest in video games without making sure the competition couldn't get wind of the next product update. Visitors to the building and the company that occupied the top floor had to get clearance before boarding the elevator.

When the guest showed up to see the president of the company, the guard on duty notified Josh by way of a phone call to his secretary, Kendra Dunning. Kendra, in turn let Josh know the visitor was imminent.

So Josh waited in the doorway of his corner office and watched as Travis Nakota got off the elevator. Josh had to give it to Travis. The man was prompt. Travis had said ten o'clock and it was now nine-fifty-nine. But as Travis got closer, Josh noted the crow's feet around the eyes he'd missed on the man's face just a week earlier. "Travis, are you okay?" Josh asked the minute the two shook hands.

"Not really," Travis replied as he settled into a chair across from Josh's desk and got comfortable. "How's it going with you?"

"You have one stubborn and very pissed-off daughter. She's been slamming doors and stomping around for a week now."

"She won't return my calls, hasn't been to the gym either. I even tried emailing her. Do you think she'll ever forgive me?"

"Give her time. That's my best advice. Let her cool down. She will, I think, it'll just take…I don't know how long it'll take. I've never seen her so angry before. But I need to ask you something, for my own edification. I'd like to know why you didn't step forward after her parents died. Why *did* you allow her to go live with people you knew were not quite all there? Even you admit that Jodi had told you on any number of occasions what they were like."

Travis blew out a heavy breath. "Did you ever make a promise to someone you loved?"

"Of course, I was married for two years. Look, I'm sorry, Travis. But that won't cut it with me. At the time Skye got shipped off, Jodi and Daniel were dead and buried. Your daughter, however, didn't have to endure five years in Yakima, ostracized at a time when she would've greatly benefited from having her real father around to guide her through it all."

"Oh God," Travis said as he scrubbed both hands over his face. "She'll never get past this."

"Never is a long time."

"How long then?"

Josh smiled. "Travis, you're the one who told me there's no playbook here, no rules to check or look up. For something like this, I don't know. There are other things going on with her though. That night we never got to the reason we asked you to dinner."

"I wondered about that. Like what?"

Josh went into a detailed account of how Skye had lost her connection with Kiya and the fact it wasn't sitting well with her.

"Ah, I was afraid this would happen. When Kiya the wolf made the leap, she knew the risks, knew what was at stake. Kiya's joining to you is detaching from Skye."

"What do we do about it?"

Travis shook his head. "Honestly, I'm not sure there's anything we can do. But without Kiya she's vulnerable on her nightly rounds."

"Since last week, she hasn't been going out alone for that reason. I've gone with her."

"How do you do that and get up the next day, come here alert enough to work?"

"I won't lie, it isn't easy. But since she got into some trouble with a gang, I'm not letting her deal with the street alone anymore. Besides, now that I think back to that night, it was Kiya that alerted me something was wrong. I thought it came from Skye. Turns out, the bat signal came from the wolf."

"Interesting. Kiya's getting stronger in you while diminishing in Skye. I'll do some research. See if I can come up with something to bring Kiya back to Skye. There has to be a solution, we just have to look for it. In the meantime, the elders of the tribal council wanted her to know they are inducting her into our Warrior Society. I planned on telling her the night she got so upset. The ceremony is the first week of October."

"An all-male tribal council is letting a woman into their midst."

"It's about time, don't you think?"

"I do, but then I'm not Nez Perce. What exactly does this entail? There has to be a lot of history at stake here."

"Very much so. The Warrior Society started out as dissenters, those who did not want their leaders making peace with the white man. They were considerable in number back then who never wanted to give up the land that belonged to their forefathers. So they left their homes to strike out on their own to try to find allies and rally them to their cause. There was a battle near Snake Creek." Travis shook his head. "They went down to defeat that day. Eventually the elders chose to sing about their exploits. However, the U.S. government had another name for it entirely. Anyway, in the end, the warriors lost their ancestral home and were shipped off to the Midwest. As the years progressed though, like any people, we still celebrate our soldiers. Skye is one of those who bring honor to us as a tribe. In October, they'll commemorate her successes. She'll have to make a speech."

"She won't like that," Josh pointed out. "In fact, knowing Skye, she'll do everything to back out of going, especially if it means she'll get attention."

Travis smiled. "I know that. But this is where you'll have to use your considerable powers of persuasion. It's a great honor and she should not turn it down or think of some reason not to show up. The Warrior Society is looking to the future. They must. Times have changed. This is the twenty-first century. Skye has done some amazing things here in Seattle. It's time the council recognized that."

"No one deserves it more." Then Josh realized what he wasn't saying. "You did this. You got the council to let her in?"

"She's made headlines lately. At the time, every member of the society sang her praises. I simply took advantage of the timing and reminded them that she's contributed more in a positive way than anyone has in a long time. To be recognized by your own is a great honor. Don't let her say no."

Josh laughed. "How exactly am I supposed to get her there short of kidnapping and delivering her against her will?" Josh wanted to know. "I'm open to suggestions."

"You'll think of something. Besides, you don't have to worry about me showing up and spoiling it for her. I won't. I've already bowed out of the ceremony."

"You shouldn't do that, Travis. You deserve to be there to see it happen."

"I'd love nothing better than to see her accept her rightful place on the council, but she's made it clear she doesn't want anything to do with me. I won't go against her wishes."

"A lot could change in two weeks," Josh said wanting to offer some kind of assurance. But when he glanced down at the time on his watch, it occurred to him there was another more immediate issue. "You might want to consider heading out. Skye's due here in about twenty minutes. We're meeting here to brainstorm on how to catch this sick bastard who's been terrorizing women."

"I don't like Drummond dragging her into this."

"I'm with you there. But someone has to catch this guy. It might as well be your daughter."

"*My daughter*. I like the sound of saying that out loud. But look where that got me. And why does it have to be Skye who catches this asshole?" He rubbed at his temple as if his head were pounding. "I don't believe this is really happening. It's difficult to believe she's this angry with me. I mean, I know she has a right to be. But still she should know how much...that girl means everything to me."

"I know she does. I saw that from the first time you and I met. But right now, if Skye catches sight of you, believe me, you'll know this is real, in a big way."

"She does have a temper, doesn't she?" Travis pointed out, grinning.

"Oh. Yeah. And then some."

Chapter Nine

Personal problems aside, Josh and Skye were committed to catching a coldblooded killer. Their guy had been idle for eight days. Eight days in which the FBI profiler referred to it as his probable "cooling off" period. Skye had another name for it. More than likely the man had gotten called out of town for some reason, or had, God forbid, moved on elsewhere.

Even without the strong influence of Kiya, Skye still relied on her instincts. She'd been doing that for more years than she could count. Because of that one fact, she didn't think the guy had left Seattle for good. Which meant he had some type of activity that took him out of town. Like that of a long-haul truck driver maybe.

But it didn't take long for Skye to nix that idea. Not this guy, Skye determined. He hit too frequently between his victims for a long-haul trucker to have time to make his trip cross-country and back again. She moved on to other options. Did he travel for business? Did he have some type of interest that took him on the road?

As she walked past Kendra's desk to get to Josh's office, she realized the guy could be right here in the building and they'd never even know it. He could be anybody.

But then, Josh's office door flew open and Todd Graham came out playing with a handheld game console. Skye grinned at his boyish enthusiasm.

"Whatcha got there, Todd? You get a new toy for Christmas?" Skye teased.

"As a matter of fact, it feels like Christmas morning before Labor Day. Look at this game we've scheduled for next spring." Like the proud designer he was, Todd went through all the bells and whistles for Skye's benefit.

"Nice graphics. When do I get to play?"

"You stop by my office after your visit with the big guy here and I'll see to it you get a beta copy. How does that sound?"

Before she could answer, Josh appeared in the doorway. "Don't distract my partner, Skye. He's a sucker for a beautiful face."

"Flattery will get you a kiss," Skye said as she leaned in, brushed her lips lightly to Josh's. "I'm here for the strategy session—and nothing more. I brought some files we should go through. I just left Harry and the FBI team. They're concerned that our guy's moved on."

"Left Seattle? He hasn't," Josh assured her, as he closed his office door. "I've spent some time surfing the Internet though. We have the general public here buying guns at an alarming rate. We have women signing up for self-defense classes in record numbers. There's panic setting in. And that's just the first couple of days after the headlines hit the papers all over the state. Then there's the buzz that's gone viral about what he's doing to his victims. They read that stuff and it sends women into frenzy."

"You can't blame them, Josh. Every female within a hundred miles of where we're standing is scared to go to sleep. They read what he did to these women, either real or imagined, and they go to bed with the lights on and a gun under their pillow."

"I'm not saying different. They should be cautious, take all the safeguards available to them. Because they'll more than likely need everything they can get to gain some peace of mind until he's caught. This guy won't stop until he's off the streets."

"How can you be so sure these are his only kills? I still say he was in Portland five years ago before here." She picked up a file, took out a photograph, and slapped it on the table. "Bianca Valencia, single, lived alone in a townhouse, no roommates. She was found with her throat slit by a next door neighbor who hadn't seen her for three days. Notes say Bianca was vivacious, a frequent visitor to the gym in her neighborhood." Skye dug out another file, another picture. "This one is Lisa Towson. Strangled, but had knife wounds through both breasts. If you look up the addresses of these two women, the murders are four streets apart, same neighborhood with identical floor plans. Lisa liked to workout. See a pattern here?"

Josh studied Skye's face. "You've done your research." He picked up a snapshot of Lisa, one of Bianca. "What are the odds that two beautiful women living four streets from each other would end up murdered? And I never suggested that Seattle was his first and only hunting ground. Mainly because his methods indicate his trail goes back several years. No doubt, he's perfected his craft and will continue to get better at it. But let me ask you something. If he started out in Portland with Bianca and Lisa, how is it when Harry put this guy's DNA from Seattle into CODIS he didn't get a hit there?"

Skye frowned and grabbed the files, started thumbing through them. "That's a very good question and one I hadn't considered." Scanning the info she'd compiled from the Internet, she was stunned. "There's no indication he raped these women according to the articles online. I'd have to have the police reports from Portland to know that for certain though."

"Remember when Harry told us different jurisdictions don't always share info, even some go so far as to refuse outright to divulge stats on their homicide cases?"

"I do. But the cops down in Portland would still put the DNA into CODIS if they had it," Skye insisted. "Right?"

"If they had DNA? Sure."

"You think they don't."

"There has to be a reason his DNA isn't in CODIS before Seattle. He either didn't rape his first victims or didn't leave enough for analysis. But there's a third possibility."

"They didn't submit the DNA they had," Skye determined.

"That's why I have an idea. I've decided to do something about the lack of cohesive info."

Skye shot him a dimpled smile. "Really? Why does that not surprise me? You're really getting into this investigating thing, aren't you?"

"I guess I am. I put together a team, one dedicated to cracking into various police department databases. For starters, a six-state area, including Vancouver, British Columbia."

Skye shot him a surprised look. "You think he'd go as far north as Canada to find victims?"

"Why not? It's less than three hours from here, Skye. When you think about it, if he's desperate to fly under the radar, he might end up there trolling for vulnerable women, upscale neighborhoods."

"What exactly are you suggesting this team do?"

"They start by looking for similar homicides, especially any up and down the West Coast. You've already found those two in Portland. I bet there are more. After they scour police departments from Vancouver to San Diego, they branch out from there to surrounding states, Idaho, Nevada, Arizona, see what they can find there."

Impressed, she all but shouted, "That's brilliant! Illegal but a great way to see for ourselves what kinds of cases are out there and use the info to our advantage. If you should get caught though—"

Josh sent Skye a questioning stare and shook his head. "Oh ye of little faith. We won't get caught."

"Who exactly is *we*?"

"The less you know…"

"Oh no you don't. We're in this together, all the way up to our necks."

"I have several programmers, three to be exact, Leo, Winston, and Reggie. They contract with Ander All Games on a regular basis. We use them when we're on overload and down to crunch time. None of them like holding regular nine-to-five jobs which makes them, shall we say, ideal and flexible in the assignments they take on. But trust me, all three are exceptional at what they do."

"Can they be trusted?"

"I trust them with our upgrades four times a year, Skye."

"If you'd show me, I'd be happy to help these guys out. I'm a fast learner, remember?"

He stepped to her and whispered in her ear, "Don't I know it. More like insatiable."

She jabbed him playfully in the ribs with her index finger. "I'm fairly certain insatiable refers to you, Mr. Ander."

"Who me?" he asked all innocent. "Ever do it in an empty office?" Josh asked, wiggling his brows up and down. He noted the flustered look flash in her eyes. Even with her cinnamon skin, he could tell her cheeks pinkened. He reveled that he could still make her blush when it came to the mere suggestion of sex. He took her chin, looked into those violet eyes. "Skye?"

"What?"

"I love you."

"I love you, too. But sometimes you exasperate me."

"I know. That's the bonus. Well, that and incredibly hot sex."

Skye glanced back at the closed door, turned the lock. "I think today I'll call your bluff, Mr. Ander."

Patting her fanny before lifting her up off the floor so their eyes were level, he whispered, "That's my girl. And I think today I'll see your raise and go all in."

Frank's skills and success as a killer were due largely to the hours and hours of meticulous preparation he put into his craft. "Death night" as he referred to the actual event, didn't just happen. Cautious planning, surveillance that would make any Navy SEAL proud along with a dedicated work ethic and a mission-oriented mindset were what separated Frank from all the rest. It wasn't ego. He knew he was, in fact, better at killing than others who'd been caught. He didn't intend to get caught.

When he wasn't spending time training at the gym, his thorough stakeout of victims made up his daylight hours. Frank neither counted on luck nor gave a thought to chance. Everything he did had to be strategized down to the last detail. He didn't do anything without devising the best plan and calculating all his options.

The cops were convinced he'd gone into a cooling off period or worse, moved on. They didn't have a clue. Frank De Palo didn't cool off and he didn't quit.

He scoured the paper every day for updates, always looking out for any little tidbits that hinted what the cops might be organizing because of him. He knew Seattle's women were panicking. But that didn't mean he couldn't maintain the same level of kills.

From the Internet, Frank had already learned the identity of the consultants law enforcement had added to their task force in hopes of catching him. One of his adversaries was a tall, gorgeous Native American female, known statewide as Skye Cree.

To Frank, her name conjured up images of a female warrior. This one happened to be physically fit with a toned body even some of the fighters he knew would envy. If he'd chosen a competitor to go up against himself, he couldn't have done better. Knowing your opponent was always a plus. Knowing his foe was a woman *and* an athletic one at that gave him extra incentive.

Articles on the Internet confirmed that Skye was a kick-ass urban warrior. Seattle was her hunting ground. Her prey, sexual deviants.

Frank hoped that was true. But time would tell.

Because at some point, Frank intended to find out the woman's secrets, her strengths, her weaknesses. Everyone had them. He would get to know her intimately, even her thought process. And by doing so, he would determine many aspects about the many sides to Skye Cree. He would make his assessment using the skills he'd honed with each of his victims. He'd find out just how good she was at martial arts. He'd learn her habits, her routines. In other words, he would invade her inner sanctum, her refuge. He would violate the place where she felt safest.

Getting inside her home would tell him everything he needed to know about his very beautiful and somewhat legendary adversary, Skye Cree.

Chapter Ten

Summer came to a close with a cloudburst and a twenty-degree drop in temperature. The mild sunny days gave way to drizzle and the chilly nights of fall.

Zoe entered eighth grade and was, for the first time, actually enjoying school. With some legal maneuvering and clever words, Doug Jenkins had been able to persuade a family court judge to sign papers making sure Lena Bowers officially became the teen's foster mother. Zoe's real mother had bypassed showing up for the hearing.

Annabelle's little brother, Tate Brock, quit school before beginning his junior year at UDub. Over the summer, Tate had taken on source code while still trying to get the hang of 3D graphics. But when the guy had come knocking at Josh's door for a job, Josh hadn't had the heart to turn Tate away. So Josh had found a position for Tate in testing. It wasn't much in the way of salary but for a college-aged kid with roommates, it would allow Tate to pay his rent.

When Josh's mother called out of the blue and requested he come home to Laurelhurst for a Saturday night dinner, he had to explain he'd be bringing his…what was Skye anyway? Certainly he should introduce his girlfriend to his family. But he would love to tell his mom that he'd met the woman he intended to make his wife. It was a little hard to do that when the potential wife-to-be kept dodging the issue as cleverly as a politician.

And it didn't get any better when Josh told Skye about the invitation that night over steak fajitas. Hearing the news, he thought she might choke on her mouthful of red peppers and rice.

"You want me to meet your family?" Clearly agitated at the idea of that, Skye tried to think of a reason not to make the trip with him.

Her demeanor didn't go unnoticed by Josh.

"But…we'd probably have to leave around nine or so—"

"So we can go out on our rounds," Josh finished. "I didn't forget. It won't hurt this one time to leave an hour later." He picked up his glass of white wine, doing his best not to get irritated with her. "It's time for you to meet my family, Skye."

"I know it is. But…what if they don't like me?"

"That isn't possible."

"Sure it is. I bet they'll ask a ton of questions about…questions…I don't want to answer. They'll recognize my name."

"They won't ask questions."

Her brow creased. "Did you tell them not to?"

He sipped his wine then set down his glass with all the patience of a man in love. "Skye, I accepted the invitation, made small talk with my mother, asked about the health of my dad and then wanted to say, 'oh by the way, I'm bringing the woman I'm in love with,' but I didn't say that because of this prickly-pear reaction I'm getting right this minute."

Across the table, Josh heard the sigh long before she finally said, "You're right. I'm being ridiculous. Of course, we'll have dinner with your parents."

Phyllis and Douglas Ander's stately Tudor-style house in the section of Seattle known as Laurelhurst—the neighborhood once home to Bill Gates—came with its own private jetty on Lake Washington and a stunning view of the Cascades to the east.

Skye gawked when Josh pulled his Fusion up to a set of iron gates and watched as he punched in a code allowing them entry onto a circular driveway.

They drove around a manicured front yard ringed by soaring evergreens, neatly trimmed hedges and a water fountain lit up like a tower hugging the Seattle skyline.

"You might've mentioned you came from money."

"This? It represents *their* money, Skye. I had to make mine on my own. And I did. So relax, will you?"

She did her best as she threw open the door and crawled out of the Ford. Smoothing out the vanilla and mint-green dress she'd worn with the kick of lace and tulle overlay, she asked, "How do I look? Do I look like I'm sweating? Because I think my deodorant gave out about halfway here."

Josh stared at the strapless outfit with its belted waist and flared skirt, the silk wrap she'd draped around her shoulders. It wasn't the clothes but her cinnamon skin and exotic violet eyes that took his breath away. But knowing she needed a boost to her confidence, he gave it all he had. "Beautiful. Gorgeous. Stunning." And just to make sure she didn't panic, he added, "You really rock those spring colors. It's not the image of the warrior I wanted on my game packages, but I could always stop the presses and get marketing to go another route. Do you want me to go on?" Before she could answer, he nipped her around the waist. His mouth fused to hers in a heated swap of lips and tongues.

They were still going at each other when the door flew open. They popped apart as Phyllis Ander stood on the other side of a tiled floor, a curved staircase at her back. A fifty-something woman with stylish, short-cropped, graying hair, she stared at them with hazel eyes, looking intrigued. "Did it ever occur to my handsome son to call once in a while to let me know he was still alive and kicking?"

"Hi Mom," Josh said easily as he cocked his head and leaned in to give her a kiss on the cheek. "Mom, I'd like you to meet Skye Cree." He tugged Skye forward as they stepped inside the entryway. "Skye, my mother, Phyllis Ander."

"It's nice to meet you, Mrs. Ander," Skye managed to breathe out as she stuck out a hand in greeting and got a hug instead.

"Now none of that. You call me Phyllis. Everyone does. You are as lovely as your name. Why don't I take your wrap? Unless of course, you're cold."

"I am a little chilly," Skye told her as she nervously bunched the shawl around her middle. Just then, an older version of Josh appeared beside his wife. He had his son's same black hair but graying at the temples, and the same silver eyes.

"And this is Doug, Josh's father," Phyllis pointed out.

"Nice of you to finally drop by and see your parents," Doug Ander told his son with a slap on the back before he put his arms around him for a bear hug. Doug lifted a few strands of Josh's long locks and said, "You really need a haircut."

"Not gonna happen," Josh returned evenly with a grin.

"It's so very nice to meet both of you," Skye repeated, glancing around to take in the arched passageways, the gleaming wide-planked floors, and the vaulted ceilings.

Phyllis put an arm around her son's waist on one side and Skye's on the other, neatly ushering them both into a den tastefully decorated in what Skye termed modern with classic black-and-white lines.

A cozy fire burned in the massive stone fireplace that took up an entire wall. Floor-to-ceiling glass windows at the end of the room offered up a tropical terrace with a shimmering lighted pool beyond.

"Sit down and get comfortable. What are you drinking, Skye? Josh, you will play bartender while Doug and I get to know Skye here."

"Chardonnay's fine," Skye answered, sending Josh an I-told-you-so look. But Josh simply smiled back at her.

"I'll take the same," Phyllis echoed.

"Dad, what can I get you?" Josh asked.

"Whiskey. Neat," Doug replied with a grin. "There's a reason Skye's still wearing her wrap. There's a nip in the air tonight."

While Josh dutifully went over to a built-in, well-stocked bar, Phyllis settled in and leaned over, patted Skye on the knee. "Okay, I'm going to get nosy right off the bat. How long have you and my son known each other? And before you answer, realize that this is only so I can yell at Joshua for not bringing you around before tonight."

"Uh, since last spring. I met him last spring."

Phyllis shook her head and turned to Doug. "Didn't I tell you so?" the woman sighed. "Well, it's a pleasure to finally meet the famous Skye Cree. You're doing such marvelous work with The Artemis Foundation."

"And now that you're no longer a secret from us, we'll be making regular contributions to your cause," Doug added.

Skye's mouth dropped open slightly. Nervously she flicked her tongue around to wet her lips. So they had recognized the name, if not the face.

When Josh returned with two white wines, his mother gave him a mocking glare. "Joshua Sebastian Ander, I'm very disappointed in you."

"Wouldn't be the first time," Josh sang out as he went back to pour the other drinks.

"At least Skye finally explains the reason you've ignored your family over the entire summer. It's abominable behavior and you know it."

Doug chuckled at his wife. "But what a reason for staying away," Doug imparted as he raised his glass to Skye in salute. "Here's to you for getting our Josh back on track. We're indebted to you for that."

At the man's words, Skye felt a measure of guilt and sympathy for the Anders. She would love to have told them they were lucky to have Josh here at all tonight to be able to pour drinks and sit down to a nice meal. But that would require a replay of what had happened to their son last spring with Kiya merging wolf instincts into him to assure his survival.

Skye knew she couldn't take credit for getting Josh "back on track" at all. Sure, she'd fallen in love with the guy. But if his parents knew the truth about their activity from last spring, she doubted Doug and Phyllis Ander would be toasting her at all.

In fact, she was sure they would consider escorting her to the gates of the estate with a stern warning to get out and stay out and keep away from their son for good.

As she sat there listening to the banter between the son in question and his parents, it occurred to her she'd have trouble staying away from Josh Ander if they ever decided to issue an edict like that.

He wanted to marry her. Why was she dragging her feet about that?

But one glance around the room had her wondering what kind of base the two of them could ever build for a marriage. Skye had never considered the belief that opposites attract. She'd never had a reason to before. But now, did she really know Josh Ander, the man she slept beside every night? After all, she hadn't even known he came from this kind of money.

When a maid interrupted her train of thought with the pronouncement about dinner, Skye got to her feet on automatic, followed them into a dining room with a crystal chandelier over the huge mahogany table.

At the time she made that statement about Cinderella it had been nothing more than a bit of a drama moment on her part. But now she realized that's how she felt sitting down to dinner with the Anders.

Over salad, prime rib, and asparagus tips, the talk turned to Orcas Island and the cabin there that had been in the family since the 1930s.

"Josh tells us you two spent the Fourth of July over there? How did you like the place, Skye?" Doug wanted to know.

"It's beautiful. The second time we spent there was much better than the first though. Over the Fourth we got to bike around the area, take the nature trails into the hills and explore. Josh even took me out on the water."

"So you've been over there twice," Phyllis asked eyeing Josh's face.

Realizing she'd said way too much, Skye attempted to tap dance around the truth. "Well, the first time we went—"

"We spent most of the time indoors as I recall, never left the cabin," Josh admitted without the slightest hint of embarrassment. "We didn't take advantage of all the area had to offer until the holiday, which meant everywhere we went was jam-packed with sightseers."

"That's true. The shops in Olga were very crowded. And the roads...the roads were clogged so Josh suggested we...we motored over there in the boat."

Taking pity on a nervous Skye, Josh reached to pick up her hand, placed a kiss on the palm.

Delighted with her son's reaction, Phyllis went on, "Isn't that the cutest little hamlet for artists? What did you buy?"

Skye smiled. "We bought a gorgeous giclée print by James Hardman depicting a trail and the forest in soft pinks and blues."

"We have his *Mandolin Player* framed in one of the guest rooms. It's a shame you two can't stay the night. But Josh tells us you have to get back."

"Yes, I'm sorry about that," Skye said and meant it. She sent a sideways glance in the direction of Josh, and added, "I suppose we could stay longer. There's no real hurry."

But Doug surprised her. "You should do whatever you have to do. Your work is essential. No other private citizen

I know can do what you seem to be able to do with such a success rate. We understand that."

On the way back to the loft, Skye had to admit she adored the Anders. "Your dad is a hoot. I see where you get your sense of humor."

"He's fond of you, too."

"Did he say that?"

"Skye, in case you didn't notice, my parents are so grateful I have a woman like you in my life, they can hardly see straight."

"It's hard to follow in the footsteps of Annabelle. Your mother took down your wedding photos and showed them off tonight while you and your dad were outside on the terrace. You both looked so happy in those pictures. It's sad that Michelle Reardon took away that happiness from you."

Josh ground his teeth, a little annoyed with his mother for doing that. He tried to downplay the anger and sadness that wanted to creep in. "Yeah, well, that's why I want to be there when Michelle's ninety-day evaluation is up. I'm already working on my statement that goes to the judge. Hopefully it'll make an impact." He reached for Skye's hand. "But my mother shouldn't have shared the album with you, Skye."

"Why not? That's a part of who you are, were. Both of your parents told me enough times tonight that they were happy we were together so I know Phyllis didn't do it out of malice or because she thought it would upset me. It occurred to me she might've been hinting at a repeat performance for you."

Josh sent her a wide grin. "I could get onboard with having another advocate in my corner about that."

"She wants grandchildren."

"She said that?"

"She was angling at it, very cleverly I might add. She wasn't too subtle about making her wishes known."

Josh ran a hand through his hair and breathed a huge sigh. "One thing about my mother, she's never been shy about letting me know right upfront what she expects."

Chapter Eleven

Ten days went by and Seattle's serial killer was still out there somewhere. But during all that time he hadn't surfaced.

It might have been because the police had ramped up their efforts and increased their manpower. Members of the task force put in massive amounts of overtime, spent twenty-four-seven on call. They followed up on tips that came in via phone, ran down leads the old-fashioned way on foot. Extra patrols were set up particularly in the neighborhoods where petty burglaries or break-ins had occurred before a murder.

But they turned up nothing.

That's why husbands and boyfriends did more to keep a vigilant eye on the women in their lives. They purchased extra guns and ammo to have on hand just in case. Single women moved in with sisters, brothers, cousins or anyone else who would offer them a bed. Those women who chose to stay put bought weapons of all kinds, added locks for their doors and had security systems installed.

During this dormant period, Josh's vivid dreams came to an abrupt halt. Since Skye's hadn't returned either, business went on as usual. Skye still went out every night on her patrols and Josh went with her.

But the woman still refused to have anything to do with Travis Nakota.

Toward the end of September, the North American Gamers Association, NAGA, put pressure on Josh to appear at their fall convention in Denver as their keynote speaker. For two months, he'd been putting them off. Kendra had given him hell about it, pestering him to give her the go-ahead to make his travel arrangements. While he'd neatly resisted his secretary's repeated requests, when Skye learned about the invitation, she was a lot tougher to dissuade.

Because he had no desire to go out of town and leave Skye to deal with things alone, Josh had spent a week trying to convince Todd Graham to make the trip in his place—which, of course had turned out to be a waste of time. Even though Todd was an unlikely candidate to make an appearance outside the company, Josh had given it his best shot. When that hadn't worked out, he had spent an additional week attempting to persuade Skye to come with him out of town as a change of pace. But when reality set in and he realized he had surrounded himself with very stubborn people, Josh eventually gave Kendra the go-ahead to finalize the necessary travel itinerary.

"There's no need to worry," Skye assured Josh as she helped him fold the last of his things into his suitcase. "I handled myself just fine without you for seven years, I'm certain I can handle going out for three nights in a row alone. Stop worrying about me."

His hand tightened over hers. "Please be careful. I know the dreams have stopped for me, but that doesn't mean he isn't out there waiting somewhere, watching for the right opportunity to strike. You and I both know that. It could be while you're walking the streets down some dark alley."

"I'll be careful, Josh. But it doesn't mean I'll stop what I've been doing all this time. Because I also know there are other kinds of predators out there who have to be dealt with. The world doesn't revolve around our serial killer, no matter how much he wants us to believe that. Deviants come in many shapes and sizes. They don't stop. They don't give up."

"That's right and neither will our serial killer. That's why I'm worried."

"Josh, we talked about this. Worrying isn't gonna cut it. You can't run your company and hold my hand twenty-four-seven. Now go to Denver and enjoy the time you have there. Get some work done. And stay away from the groupies."

Josh's forehead creased with worry lines. "Why are you not getting this, Skye? My heart is here with you, not at some convention giving a damned speech."

"I know. But there are two sides to Josh Ander now. Maybe there's always been two. Josh the business owner. And Josh the superhero with wolf tendencies still has to relax once in a while. You started out as a gamer. Now go game."

"Just be careful out there. Listen to Kiya. Don't take any chances. Promise me."

"Yes, I promise I'll be extra careful. Now go and try to have fun. The cab's already waiting for you downstairs. Come on, I'll walk you out."

"I'll miss you."

"And I will miss you," Skye said as they hopped on the elevator. "A lot. Who's gonna nag at me about stuff?"

"There is that. Stay here at the loft while I'm out of town. Security's better here."

"I already told you I would," Skye agreed as she rolled her eyes.

"This guy will be gunning for you, Skye. He's that crazy."

"You and I both know if he wants to find me, he will. I'm not that difficult to track down."

"That's it," Josh said as he punched the stop button for the elevator. "I'm not going. I'm cancelling the trip."

"Josh Ander, you have no confidence in me, do you?"

"I have every confidence in you. It's the sexual deviants who keep me from getting a solid eight hours sleep anymore."

Skye reached around him, pressed the button to get the elevator moving again. "Then know this. I am perfectly capable of handling this guy if he decides to come around and hasn't already left Seattle for greener pastures."

Their back-and-forth banter continued until Josh crawled into the taxi and it sped away.

As Skye stood watching the car disappear around the corner and Josh with it, she had to wonder if he had a point.

She'd gone up against sexual predators who preyed on little girls before. Even though they were violent in nature, this might be the first time she'd have to go head-to-head with a guy bent on brutalizing his victims just for the fun of it. Which made her wonder exactly when the guy's serial killer instincts had kicked in? How many years had he been at this?

She refused to admit to Josh or anyone else for that matter, that the guy they were after unnerved her. Considerably. But then she wouldn't be human if a monster like that didn't get to her. Even after Josh left, she wasn't surprised he called twice from the cab. In fact, she bided her time. When he phoned again from the airport, their conversation took on a gentler tone and lasted forty-five minutes before he had to board the plane.

But there was unease on both sides.

Skye wondered if he suspected she'd held back. If what she was sensing was a premonition, then she'd keep it to herself. There was no need for Josh to miss out on his convention. That's why she hadn't mentioned anything to the stressed-out man for that very reason. Telling him would only make him worry more and she didn't think that was possible. Besides, she needed to do this herself. They weren't joined at the hip. So she had kept her mouth shut and had blocked her thoughts, making sure he couldn't pick up on anything.

For the remainder of that morning, she logged onto her computer, determined to search for sex offenders using the program Josh had built for her. The application allowed her to access several different databases that would spit out a commonality list. Things like the sex offender registry could cross-check with state employment records, the motor vehicle department, and tax record databases across the Seattle area.

After several hours, she hit compile and watched as the program narrowed down a list of sex offenders. She hit print and watched as it spit out enough names and addresses to use as a starting point.

Crazy as it sounded, she would check them out on her rounds. If she ran across any of the houses that matched the one she'd seen in her dream, the one painted gray with red trim, then she'd have a starting place. At the very least, she'd have a neighborhood in which to look.

When she'd exhausted her resources and felt confident with the results, she donned her leather and black and sailed out the door with Kiya at her side to find a predator, the one who had been haunting her dreams for the past couple of nights.

She could only hope it wasn't too late to save the latest girl the man had been abusing over the last forty-eight hours. At least she thought it might be that recent. While her vision last night had been weak in its overall punch—certainly not like the ones she'd experienced so vividly for years—it had given her enough strong impressions of the house that she felt confident she could recognize it. But first, she had to put in some legwork. From there, she'd have to rely on Kiya, which of course, she would do.

Two hours and several blocks later, Kiya's instincts paid off. Skye and her wolf stood outside a wood and stone cottage that looked as ordinary as any grandmother's on the block. All it needed was the gingerbread trim and it could've jumped off the pages of a fairy tale.

But Skye was pretty sure there was nothing magical taking place under that roof. No, what was inside those four walls crossed into horrific. It didn't matter that the unusual color scheme made the place stand out from all the other houses on the street. That alone would cause anyone to take note.

Even in broad daylight, the slate-gray house with the red door and shutters and peeling paint job gave her the creeps. It could have been nothing more than the spit of rain that hit her face or the fact that the heavens overhead were turning darker and more threatening by the minute. The clouds indicated a storm churned and brewed out over Puget Sound. But that was nothing compared to the roiling in Skye's stomach.

She took out her iPhone along with the file she'd printed out. Once again, she logged into Josh's program to access it so she could get the ownership of the residence. The search results came back with the name, Perry York. She scanned the data. To her disappointment, York did not match any of the names on her registered sex offender list. She rechecked everything a second time and then a third. Still no Perry York came up anywhere. Damn. Maybe this guy had flown under the radar.

According to the public tax records database she'd accessed, Perry York was forty-five years old and worked second shift as a stocker at a big-box retail chain. He'd owned the house since his mother died six years earlier and left the property to him. At some point he'd taken out a second mortgage to pay for a new roof.

Skye studied the digital screen and then looked back up across the street to survey the layout of the small bungalow. Rocking back on her heels, she could tell the place had a basement by the windows at ground level. Every last fiber in her said this was the house from her dream. But she'd have to do her own reconnaissance to be certain of that. To get in there, she'd have to be patient and wait for the guy to leave. If the database was correct and he still had the job stocking shelves, he'd be leaving for work soon.

In the meantime, she logged out of one application and into vital statistics, checking to see if Mr. York had ever been married. When that didn't yield what she wanted, she tried Facebook. Sure enough his relationship status showed him as single.

Two hours ticked along and by the time the bright red front door flew open, her watch showed three o'clock. Skye eyed the man, around five-feet-eight, walk out and head to his dark green Dodge Ram pickup parked in the driveway.

During the time Skye had waited, she'd gotten fully drenched. Now, feeling like a drowned rat, she watched the truck disappear around the corner at the end of the block. Water dripped from her purple watch cap as she made her move around to the back of the house.

When she reached the back door, she took out the lock pick from the inside of her jacket. She squatted down, toyed with the tumblers. One at a time, each clicked into place until she could turn the handle.

Good thing there was no deadbolt, she thought, as the door creaked open. She stepped inside an older, dated kitchen. The room was neat as a pin, not a dirty dish sitting in the sink, or a mess left out on the counter.

But the late fall afternoon coupled with the cloudy skies had her straining her eyes just to see. Squinting into the area beyond the kitchen, she reached into the inside flap of her coat and removed her penlight so she wouldn't have to turn on the lights. The room was fairly dark anyway due to the old brown cabinets that needed refinishing and the ugly tan paint someone had slapped on the walls. The color combo didn't do anything to lighten the place up.

Skye moved farther into the interior of the small house. It didn't take her long to do a quick walk-through of the place to ensure she was alone. With each step, she shone the beam searching for the door leading down to the basement. Once she backtracked into the kitchen, she spotted what she'd missed earlier. A door at the end of the open space where the washer and dryer stood had to be the one that led down to the basement.

Hairs stood up on the back of her neck as she muttered to Kiya's form, "Unlike the back door this one's got a deadbolt lock installed on the outside. Not a good sign. Whatever or whoever is down there is locked in."

She flipped the lock back and sucked in a breath as she turned the knob. The smell of urine and feces hit her nose first with full force. She knew then for certain what she'd find at the end of those stairs. She hoped she wasn't too late.

But the odor had a memory popping into her head—that of another day last spring when she'd walked into a warehouse near the docks and found several young girls in holding cells waiting to be shipped out to South America. Their cells had reeked of the same foul mess.

Skye forced that image aside. With her penlight as a guide, she grabbed the old wooden railing and took each step in measured precision, stopping to listen for any sound as she went. Once she reached the last step, she took a chance and looked around for the light switch.

All of her instincts told her what she'd see, but she wasn't prepared for the reality of it. As tidy as the upstairs first floor had been, below ground level was chaos. A layer of filth and dank air had chills tingling up her spine. Skye stepped off the stairs into a river of sticky wetness. The bottom of her boots slipped on the cement floor.

Because of that she took careful steps to inch her way further into the abyss. That is, until she made the mistake of glancing up.

Revulsion hit her.

Perry York might've left to go to his shitty job but he'd left a naked girl chained to his basement wall. The teenager looked to be about fifteen. Her feet dangled about six inches from the floor. Her wrists were shackled with huge metal cuffs. The girl's body either twitched with involuntary spasms from the abuse she'd taken or shivered from the cold.

Fresh, deep purple bruises adorned her torso, her arms and legs. A rope burn around her neck told Skye all she needed to know about Perry York. In addition to everything else, the girl looked drugged and beaten down.

While Skye assessed just how long it would take to pick the lock on those manacles binding the girl's wrists, to her surprise, the girl opened her eyes and blinked in astonishment. The teenager immediately started whimpering.

Skye tried to settle her down. "My name's Skye. Don't worry. I'm getting you out of this hellhole. What's your name?"

"Kelly," the teen croaked out. "Donahue. There's security all over this place. He'll come back and when he does—"

"Should've known," Skye uttered. She moved to the girl. Knowing they might not have much time, Skye started working on getting Kelly's hands free. She dug out her lock kit again. Inserting the little metal rod into the hole, Skye waited for the tumblers to give. When they did, she reached around Kelly to hold her up while she slipped the girl's hands out of the restraints.

But at that moment, Kiya growled at the sound of the back door opening upstairs. Skye heard it too about the time she caught the footsteps overhead. "So he's come back," Skye acknowledged. "I knew it couldn't be this easy."

"He told me there was a silent alarm on all the doors and windows," Kelly whispered by way of explanation.

"Damn. Okay, stay here. This won't take long."

"No. Don't...don't leave me down here. You're my only hope," Kelly rasped out.

"Just for a minute. Don't worry, Kelly."

"No, he'll hurt you. He'll kill you," Kelly cried out.

Skye shook her head, lifted her finger up to her lips in a signal for Kelly to be quiet.

With that, Skye made her way back up the stairs. She didn't care if he heard the creaks on the wood or not. If he did hear them, he'd more than likely think that somehow Kelly had gotten loose. That Kelly had been the one to open the back door and set off the alarm. With any luck, the asshole would be expecting a weak, fragile teenager not a grown woman used to combat.

So as soon as Skye reached the space at the top of the landing, she listened for the jerk to move in front of the door, right where she wanted him. When she was certain she'd given him enough time to get in place on the other side, Skye threw all her weight into it as she burst through the doorway. The force knocked him against the wall.

Skye took that opportunity to advance, elbowing him in the gut. She pivoted, sent a series of karate kicks, first to his groin, and then took him the rest of the way down with one boot aimed at his head. The blow broke his nose.

As if dazed, Perry teetered then keeled over. He hit the floor with a thud. Skye took advantage of his condition to pat his clothes to make sure he carried no weapons. When she found him "clean," she reached inside her jacket, brought out her nightstick just in case.

About that time Skye realized Kelly had come up behind her. The teen stood clutching what looked like a two-by-four she'd picked up from somewhere in the cellar. Skye gaped as the girl brought back the lumber. With every ounce of strength remaining in her body, the teen started bashing Perry over the head with it.

If Skye hadn't rendered him unconscious using martial arts, the wood had done so now. The timber scored several gashes along his face and head, bringing with it a fair amount of blood. Skye could see stitches in Perry's immediate future.

For a minute, Skye simply stood by while Kelly exacted a measure of her own justice, hitting him again and again, one blow after another, anywhere on his body she could make contact.

But after several blows, Skye stepped in, stilled Kelly's arm in mid-strike. "Kelly, listen to me now. I know this piece of shit deserves it. But he's had enough. And even though I'd like nothing more than to let you finish him off, I gave my word to a friend that from now on I'd do my best to bring these bastards in alive. Do you understand what I'm saying?"

Kelly turned to look at Skye as if seeing her for the first time and nodded. With all her energy zapped, the fifteen-year-old collapsed in Skye's arms.

In his Denver hotel suite, Josh had just dug into his club sandwich and fries he'd ordered from room service when he hit the remote control to get the TV to come on. He had yet to completely unpack his clothes. But that hadn't stopped him from ordering supper. He munched on a crunchy pickle before taking a seat beside the window at the little table to eat.

Absently he picked up the remote control for the TV, started to arrow through channels to locate ESPN. One national news station caught his attention. At first he passed it by, until he caught something about Seattle. He hit the back button.

The words "developing news story" ran across the bottom of the screen. A familiar feeling tugged at his brain. Gut instinct, which had nothing to do with Kiya, had his jaw locking into place. Then he saw the name. The minute Skye Cree's image appeared, he felt his throat tighten.

Riveted now, he listened as the television anchor reminded the viewing audience how many teen girls the Seattle woman had saved over the years. From there, the on-air talent threw the story out to his reporter in the field, which happened to be the Seattle police station on Cherry Street.

The wind sailed out of Josh about the same time he recognized his own home turf.

He watched as the blonde journalist reminded everyone this was live feed—before she rehashed Skye Cree's entire history in case anyone in the viewing audience might've forgotten—or simply didn't know Skye's reputation for taking down sexual predators. The correspondent went back years to when Skye had been kidnapped at the age of twelve by a pedophile, reciting Skye's detailed survivor past.

Josh listened to the voice but all he could hear was the roaring in his ears as the woman went over the details of another escape Skye had miraculously pulled off. This time she'd rescued a girl by the name of Kelly Donahue from some sexual sadist's basement. A fight had ensued with the offender who had eventually been taken by ambulance to the hospital.

From fifteen hundred miles away all Josh wanted to know at that very moment was that Skye was okay. About that same time, in the background, he caught sight of her on camera as she tried to dodge the press outside the police station. Josh let out a gasp of air he didn't even know he'd been holding. So she was all right. That was the important thing. Wasn't it?

Because if she was fine, if she'd gotten out of that goddamned cellar unscathed, unhurt, right at that moment, he wanted to be the one to wring her stubborn neck himself. Fury took over aimed at Skye as he stared at the screen. She seemed to be walking without impairment in a hurried pace to get away from the reporters and the cameras.

"Damn it! I knew you were holding something back. I knew it," Josh yelled at the television. "We're a team now, when are you going to realize that?" he grumbled at about the same time his cell phone went off. The digital readout told him it was Travis.

"Where the hell are you? Why did you let her go into that house alone? I thought you cared about her," Travis barked into Josh's ear. "What were you thinking?"

"If you'll stop yelling at me long enough, I'll tell you," Josh snapped. "I'm in Denver attending some stupid gaming conference. She wasn't honest with me, Travis. She never told me what she planned to do. If she had, do you think I would've let her go in there without backup?

Now it all makes perfect sense. She let me get on that damned plane and afterward went straight out hunting this guy down before I'd even had time to get here."

No wonder he hadn't been able to reach her on her cell phone when he'd landed. She'd been giving her statement to the cops. "Have you seen her, talked to her? Do you know for a fact she's okay?"

"I've seen her on the tube but she still isn't talking to me, certainly not returning *my* calls. How about you? Have you talked to her?"

"She hasn't picked up all evening. But that's about to change," Josh assured him, as he turned the volume up on the TV. "Hang on a second, Travis. Harry's holding a press conference right this second and she's standing next to him at the podium while he takes questions from the reporters. Are you watching this?"

"I'm watching. It says the feed is live. I thought they said there was a fight. But Skye doesn't have a mark on her," Travis pointed out.

Josh chuckled. "No, she doesn't have a mark on her. But one thing you can count on. I'm sure the other guy looks a helluva lot worse."

Josh Ander and Travis Nakota were not the only men interested in Skye's whereabouts or movements. Frank De Palo had tailed her to the gray house with the red trim. She'd been so intent on her own target, the sexual predator known as Perry York, she'd never even sensed his presence nearby.

Perhaps she wasn't as clever or as talented as he'd first thought.

He'd be a fool not to recognize her considerable skills at hand-to-hand combat. Although when the cops dragged York outside, the man hadn't looked like much competition on that score.

And since Frank had waited across the street and watched her enter a man's home without key or invite, he wondered what she planned to do once she got inside. He stood by fascinated at the turn of events once the cops showed up. Along with the other curious neighbors, Frank had listened. He'd learned from the uniforms and their grumblings what exactly had transpired within that box of a house.

She had, after all, gone down into the man's personal torture chamber to rescue a girl. She'd taken down the man in question there in his own kitchen when he unexpectedly returned home. And doing it, she'd been alone without having the gamer in tow for backup.

An impressive feat to be sure, Frank decided and one that he could not dismiss. So while her intelligence was questionable at best, she might be a worthy opponent when he met up with her face to face.

And when he surprised her in her own space, when he stood over her in her own bed, he would make certain he'd get the most out of her. It was the only way he could assure she'd challenge him to the max.

Chapter Twelve

Even though Skye had tried to talk Josh out of leaving the convention early, assuring him she was just fine, he'd caught the next plane back to Seattle. He'd been pissed he couldn't get back to SeaTac until morning. And now, according to Josh's latest text message, his plane had pulled to the gate and was unloading.

That's why Skye sat behind the wheel of her Subaru parked at the curb outside the terminal, waiting for him to walk out.

She knew he'd be angry with her. But she hadn't considered the Ander wrath lasting for this long. She'd seen him upset before. But they'd never stayed mad at each other overnight. The amazing thing about their relationship so far had been that despite some major obstacles to overcome, they could talk most things out without wanting to walk away from each other. Until this instance, the marriage hot button had been the only thing dividing them. She had a feeling though, that Josh was waiting to explode up close and personal.

Last night she'd listened as he vented. His anger had gone on and on—over the phone. Over the past twelve hours she'd had time to think about the repercussions of going into York's home alone. After replaying the situation several times, she could understand why Josh was so furious. But she'd been on her own too long to change for anyone at the drop of a hat. And she realized now that probably wasn't fair to the person she loved.

When she spotted him exiting through the sliding glass doors with the suitcase in tow she'd helped him pack only yesterday, she honked the horn and waved.

He tossed his bag in the backseat and crawled into the front.

"Did you sleep okay last night?" Skye asked as she pulled out into traffic, not wasting any time trying for damage control. Noting the dark circles under his eyes, she already knew the answer to that. But knowing she had to make amends somehow, she went on, "Because it looks like you're still pissed and it kept you awake all night."

"Don't try to get on my good side right now, Skye. Okay? I'm still furious with you. And no, I didn't sleep well at all. Every time I closed my eyes, I must've replayed what I saw on the news no less than fifty times. With you here, and me in Denver, it might've been a good thing, after all, because I wanted to strangle you myself. At some point I thought I might even be having a heart attack."

"Now you're exaggerating."

Slanting her a withering glare from the passenger seat, he was slowly getting to a boil. "It turned out to be a nasty case of indigestion and the fact that I'm hooked up with the most stubborn hardhead I've ever known who refuses to give an inch. Since last night, I've had time to consider every 'what if' in the book. All you had to do was tell me what you suspected, share a little info and you know I would've hung around. I'd never have gone to Denver in the first place. But you didn't do that. Let's be clear here what's pissed me off. The fact that you deliberately held back you'd been plagued by dreams again. The fact that you were having dreams again is a big deal. But you went out of your way to make sure I got on that plane. If we're a team—" He stopped, shook his head. "Oh what's the point? We're not much of a team. Maybe you're right and this, what we have between us, just isn't meant to be." He rubbed at his temple, lack of sleep and jet lag beginning to catch up with him. "Anything could've gone wrong in

York's house and you might be dead right now. I don't even want to think about it."

"But it didn't go wrong," she pointed out. "And I'm still very much alive. And so is Kelly Donahue."

"Luck," Josh tossed back. "Don't throw the fifteen-year-old girl into the mix either. You know exactly why I'm upset. Don't sit there and deny it. If not for your deliberate deception, I'd have been right there to go in that house with you."

She tried for patience knowing she deserved some degree of hostility. But then she shifted gears. "Harry thinks this Perry York guy might be responsible for several other girls in the area who went missing since 2006, the year his mother died."

Josh cocked a brow. "And you think this helps your case? How? That you went up against *another* serial killer alone? Trust me, it doesn't."

"Speaking of which, I'm beginning to think our sicko has indeed moved on to another, more fertile, hunting ground." To her credit, she kept up the barrage and did her best to change the subject. "What do your dreams tell you?"

"You know it's been almost two weeks or more since I've seen anything. Don't try to placate me. Without fresh crime scenes, without new victims, it's as if the images are blocked to me now. And since we don't want new victims—"

"So no news is good news as far as the dreams go." She paused before adding, "I'm sorry I didn't share what was going on. You're absolutely right. I should've told you the dreams were back. But try to understand, this wasn't like in the past. I barely got a clear view."

"You expect me to buy that?"

"This partner thing is new to me. I'm still working on the kinks."

"Then try harder," Josh suggested as he leaned over the console to plant a kiss on her cheek. "All I'm asking,

Skye, is for you to show a little confidence in me. I'm your partner. Try acting like it."

She sucked in a breath. "You really know how to get to me."

"Yeah? Good to know. Then I need to get to you a lot more often."

After working a twelve-hour shift at the hospital the first thing thirty-eight-year-old nurse Betty Triplett noticed when she got to the door of her bedroom was that someone had been there.

Dresser drawers had been pulled out. Her panties and bras and various other lingerie were left dumped on the bed. Whoever had been there had carefully gone through the contents of her jewelry box. Earrings, necklaces, and bracelets were lined up neatly in an orderly fashion on the dresser, as if the person had wanted them arranged item by item in a particular way.

An eerie feeling crept up her spine. Betty went down the hallway to check on her teenage daughter Gina's bedroom. Even though she knew for a fact Gina had spent the day with her father at her grandmother's house, Betty still needed to make sure Gina wasn't in the house.

But in a teenager's room where disarray was the norm, here someone had taken the time to *tidy* up Gina's mess, not make one. He gone through Gina's things the same way he had Betty's.

Instinctively Betty reached for her cell phone to text her daughter. After sending the message, a frightening thought occurred to her. The intruder might still be in the house.

As fast as she could, Betty backtracked to the front door the way she'd come in. But as she darted past the kitchen, she saw the refrigerator door standing ajar. She took two steps and glanced at the back door leading to the yard. It too, stood open. It was as if someone had heard her come in through the front door and disappeared out the back in a hurry.

No way did Betty intend to stay in the house. Instead, she headed out to her car parked in the driveway to call nine-one-one.

About the time Betty reached her Buick, Gina returned the text, saying she was okay. Breathing a sigh of relief, Betty hit the numbers on her phone. At this point, even though she wasn't sure the prowler had taken anything of value, she still thought the cops needed to know—because someone had violated her home, her personal space.

With all the murders she'd heard about on the news, the ones occurring a few streets over, Betty wasn't taking any chances. She wanted a member of law enforcement to do a walk-thru with her. She wanted the violation logged into public record. She wanted them to document the fact that there had been some type of break-in. It might have nothing to do with the serial killer stalking Seattle women, but Betty wanted the cops to be the ones to make that determination. Even if it turned out to be nothing more than a teenager in the neighborhood, Betty wanted some assurance that her safe haven was still just that, if not for her sake, for her daughter's.

Frank was still standing down the street from Betty's house when a patrol car pulled up at the curb. It pissed him off. How dare she call the cops. After all, he hadn't taken anything. He'd show Betty. He'd come back. Even though she was too old, too chunky, and didn't fit his target range, he'd come back. He'd pay her another visit when Betty Triplett least expected it.

The woman didn't need to know he'd gone in there to check out her fifteen-year-old daughter. Of course, he hadn't known at the time the girl was so young. When he'd first spotted her at the mall she looked eighteen. So he'd followed her home. And now the cops were planted inside taking some kind of report—about him.

The whole thing had him considering changing whom he marked. Maybe it was time to go for the younger crowd and teach them something about life before they became bitter old hags like Betty. He'd use this period to reflect, to open up his mind to newer and better prospects. Maybe increase his surveillance to include a wider range. The drawback, and there was always a downside, is that the younger teens wouldn't provide much of a challenge. They were too submissive, too eager to please.

If he were getting bored now, it was his own fault. How did he feel about taking all the same risks but getting so little in return?

He could hardly rest on his laurels. He had to take it up a notch some way, somehow.

And he thought he knew just the place to start.

Chapter Thirteen

If it was true that their serial killer had moved on, then it meant they could both sit back and finally enjoy going out to the night's celebration when the Warrior Society would add one new member to its roster.

This evening Skye would take her place among the all-male leaders of her tribe in an event designed to showcase the woman who had taken centuries-old traditions and turned them upside down. A female warrior among an all-male cast was change in any society. In the Native culture it was the equivalent of shattering the glass ceiling.

As they got ready to attend the formal sit-down dinner that also promised a host of local celebrities, Josh stood at the mirror in the bedroom looping his black tie around his neck. But when he caught sight of Skye behind him coming out of the walk-in closet, he let the ends dangle as he turned to gape.

His eyes lit on the long legs, perused upward, beginning first with the five-inch Sergio Rossi open-toed mermaid pumps on her feet. The champagne dress set off her cinnamon skin and left little to the imagination. With the wrap-style top, the classic V-neckline, and the form-fitting pleats at the waist, it all came together to give her a red-carpet, sophisticated look.

Skye Cree might be a woman who routinely wore military-style boots on her nightly rounds but tonight's outfit showed she could rock an evening gown when the situation called for it.

She'd left her hair down to drape at her shoulders in that straight-angled cut he loved.

"Holy Christ, you look good enough to eat."

She tilted her head. "I'm pretty sure you did that already. About an hour ago as a matter of fact."

"So I did." With one finger he motioned for her to twirl around so he could get a look at her bare back. He laid a hand on his heart. "You take my breath away, Skye. You look amazing."

"It isn't too much, is it? I feel kinda silly. But Lena suggested I should go for classy. She and Zoe helped me pick it out at this store in the mall that specializes in evening wear. I picked this one out because the three-quarter sleeves were perfect so I wouldn't have to mess with a jacket or a wrap tonight."

That brought a laugh from him. "The sleeves? Oh yeah, the dress has sleeves. I see them now. Trust me, baby, no one will be looking at the sleeves."

She elbowed him in the ribs as she gathered up some of the skirt in her fist and lifted it off the floor. "There's more fabric here than I know what to do with. I hope I don't trip on the long gown."

"I've seen you wear a dress, Skye. You won't trip. By any chance are you nervous?"

"A little. Okay, a lot. But I have to make a speech. Everyone gets nervous when they have to get up in front of a lot of people. I don't like being the center of attention, especially when they're all staring at me. Why do you suppose they decided to let in a woman at this late date?"

He turned back to the mirror to finish the knot on his tie. "You're a smart woman. Think about this for a minute. Do you really think they did this without someone prodding them into it?" From his reflection he watched her eyes grow wide before her shoulders slumped.

"Travis. I should've known. With everything going on, I guess I wasn't thinking straight."

"It isn't too late to call him, Skye."

She thought about that for a minute and went another way. "There's a roomful of local people expecting me or I'd back out of this whole thing right now."

Josh recognized the tactic and knew which buttons would get her going. "No need to back out. All the press involved will be good for the foundation. What's good for the foundation helps every kid who has the misfortune to go missing."

"That's just it. I'm doing this *because* of the foundation. I don't need to actually belong to this warrior thing to make an impact. And I don't need Travis to put in an appearance," she finally snapped out with some heat. "Now let's get a move on. We don't want to be late."

As they boarded the elevator, a thought occurred to Josh. Just because Skye didn't want to speak to Travis didn't mean there wasn't a solution. Josh could and would act as a go-between. In his mind, it was bad enough for two longtime friends to be on the outs with each other, but when that "friend" had morphed into "family," it was a sad state. Not only that, but it left Josh squarely in the middle of the mess. And he didn't like it.

That's why as they headed toward the Belmont Hotel hosting the event, Josh decided to use his formidable powers of reasoning, the same he'd used to get banks to loan him seed money when they had to be convinced a game was a good return on their money. After all, he was a businessman who persuaded people to do things five days a week. With that thought at the forefront, he stepped his toe into icy water. "I know you still care about Travis, right?"

"Of course, I do. But…that's beside the point."

"No, not really. That *is* the point. It's the basic element of your tribe, its history, where you came from. I did my homework, remember? Family has always been a huge part of the Nez Perce. They care what happens to their own. How often will this event take place, Skye? Think about it. Once. Skye Cree won't be up there on that stage becoming a part of the elder council ever again after tonight. Do you really want Travis to miss out on this? Can you live with that if the answer is yes?"

He took his eyes off the road a split second to glance at her face, to see if his words had made any type of impact. He thought he knew Skye and the woman was big on doing the right thing. When he saw his opening, he offered, "How about this? I make the call. You don't even have to talk to the man. I'll take care of everything."

Skye chewed at her bottom lip. "It might be awkward. You know, seeing him there," she finally said while checking the digital clock on the car's dash. "And look at the time. He couldn't possibly get dressed and make it from Everett to the hotel."

Josh wouldn't want to bet against Travis Nakota making the trip in record time. Seeing the opening he wanted, Josh handed his cell phone to Skye. "Scroll through my contacts and hit the screen for me, will you?"

She sighed. "Just because *you* invite him does not mean I've forgiven him. Make sure you point that out. I don't want him to think that—"

"Skye?"

"What?"

"It's the right thing to do whether you've forgiven him or not."

"I know."

When she'd hit send, she handed it back to Josh, who took it and waited for Travis Nakota to pick up.

❧ ❧ ❧ ❧

In a ceremony that promised to last no more than two hours, it was a good thing it dragged in places. When the elders on the council took turns patting each other on the back for having the good sense to finally include a woman, it got bogged down with long-winded accolades.

After speech number five, Josh looked up from the dais to see Travis Nakota standing in the back. His bow tie hung loose, untied.

Josh grinned at the man in spite of the anxious woman fidgeting with her napkin in the seat next to him. He leaned over to Skye's ear and whispered, "Look at the people in the audience. Tonight they don't just adore you. That's respect you see in their eyes. You did that Skye. No need to be nervous. Besides, you look really hot in that dress."

About that time, the elder at the podium finished his intro. The minute Skye got to her feet, applause broke out across the packed event room from its two hundred or so invited guests. The clapping soon turned into a standing ovation.

A little self-conscious at the attention, she turned back once to glance at Josh. He gave her a quick wink, right before putting two fingers to his mouth and letting go with a loud whistle through his teeth. At that moment, no one could have been prouder of her than the man who planned to talk her into eventually marrying him.

Once she reached the microphone, Skye had to take a long, deep breath and exhale before she could speak.

"This is a great honor for me tonight. You've made me a member of a society that even history recognizes as strong, independent, and fierce. Even though up to this point, males have dominated within your ranks, I will not let my fellow warriors down. I pledge tonight that you will always be able to count on me. To defend those in our tribe, as well as those outside this realm who cannot take care of themselves, I will be there.

"Our forefathers sang about the hunters and the warriors of old. But tonight, we take those timeworn songs and make room for change as we move into a bold, new era. As I stand before you, I proudly claim my Nez Perce heritage, for I am both hunter and warrior. I will honor the rituals of my people and its customs. I will honor long-held traditions. But know this. I will also break them just as I have by your acceptance of me here tonight. I know that some were against letting me stand here among you as an equal. I want you to know there are no hard feelings in my heart for those individuals. It just means I'll have to try harder to show those who voted to keep me out that my war is against all those who prey on children, or the vulnerable, or the ones who cannot defend themselves. And that isn't going to change."

As the speech wore on, Frank De Palo sat at a table in the back with seven other local mini VIPs. He'd finagled an invitation through his Mixed Martial Arts promoter. The promoter happened to have connections with all the city council members. Because one in particular was a fan of the sport, Frank had found his way as a guest.

He watched as the beautiful woman took center stage. He listened as she articulated her thoughts and feelings about becoming a member of the Nez Perce Warrior Society.

He'd obviously underestimated her intellect.

Now, as he sat there hanging on her every word, he realized there were two sides to the woman who had saved Kelly Donahue. One was the savvy street fighter he'd seen at York's. The other was this stunning beauty capable of winning over an all-male club that usually had barred the opposite sex from participating in anything of value other than birthing babies. But with her clever acceptance speech, the smart woman had them eating out of the palm of her hand.

None of it went unnoticed by Frank.

He appreciated what he considered her manipulation factor. It had been his experience that every woman possessed that side in large quantities. But he had to give it to Skye Cree. She hid hers better than most. She would make an excellent opponent. Finally, someone worthy of his talents and skill set who he could go up against head-to-head—and defeat.

He knew she shared Josh Ander's bed, had for the last several months. But he also knew she kept her own little studio apartment where she'd lived for years before the gamer had ever appeared on the scene. It was a crappy rat hole, but he'd already made up his mind to get inside it tonight. He might even spend the night there, sleep in her bed.

Because Frank De Palo knew it was time to get back on the horse. He'd taken his supposed "cooling off" period as the experts wanted to call it. He'd relished seeing the media use those two words to describe what he knew to be false.

But now it was time to get back to work.

That's why after leaving the Belmont Hotel early, Frank had stopped at his place to change clothes and put on his all-black outfit.

A few minutes after midnight he made his way to Skye's fourth-floor walk-up where he picked the lock to get into the trashy little place.

As he swung the door open, he noticed the squeak first before ever setting foot inside. He took out his penlight to shine into the one-room interior. His eyes perused the four walls to make sure he was alone before striding to what appeared to be the bathroom. After checking that out, he located the light switch. He got his first look at the layout, the arrangement of the furniture.

He removed a small bottle of lubricant from the pocket of the hoodie he wore and went back over to the door. Placing a few drops of the oil on each of the three hinges, he tried the door until he was satisfied he'd taken care of the offending creak.

Since the walls of the dump were paper-thin and so was the flooring, he made sure to keep his footsteps light as he scanned the tiny five-hundred-square-foot studio. The only place to walk was a narrow slice of pathway that led from the front door and continued past a small loveseat and back to the full-size bed in the corner. A couple of homemade quilts reminded him people of Skye Cree's station in life set value on such outdated, ordinary accessories.

Checking out the rest of the shabby-chic furniture made him wince. Someone as beautiful as Skye Cree needed to spend her time in more elegant living conditions, not some hole-in-the-wall tenement.

Which made him wonder why she would insist on keeping this tiny flat when she had access to Ander's loft on a regular basis? A definite chink in her armor, Frank decided. Maybe she didn't plan on staying with the man for the long term. That might explain her reluctance to give up this miniature-sized crib in the bowery section of Seattle.

He made his way around the wall-to-wall furniture arrangement to the thin strip of kitchen. Colorful dishes took up one open shelf and another held what his mother had always called useless knick-knacks. When his eyes landed on her bookshelf he went over, picked up a copy of *Pride and Prejudice*. Why would a smart woman read such useless drivel? he wondered. Checking out the titles, he decided she didn't own a single book he'd consider adding to his to-be-read list.

When a dozen intricate stained-glass designs decorating the walls caught his eye, he thought back to whether or not he'd seen an artistic side to the warrior. He decided she didn't possess any particular tendencies toward creativity.

Although tonight she'd shown excellent taste in her evening attire: the classy dress had set off the woman's toned figure. He had to admit, in that gown she'd looked like a model, someone he would consider fucking. He hadn't even thought that possible because of the military get-up she usually wore. Now, her sense of flair had to enter into the equation.

He stared at all the plants she had lined up neatly in front of a sliding glass door. He wasn't sure that counted in the creativity column. But a second scan had him doing a mental calculation in his head. There had to be at least fifty containers holding a variety of herbs and other types of foliage. She did seem to have a green thumb when it came to growing things. Then he remembered a day last week when he'd followed her here. From street level he'd noticed the balcony full of greenery. If given the dirt and space the damn woman could probably grow her own forest full of flowers.

Okay, so her artistic side included a bit of gardening. He didn't like that. It reminded him too much of someone else.

About that time, Frank heard the whimsical tinkling of wind chimes coming from outside. It was then he realized this Martha Stewart side hovered at Skye's outer edges. He would exploit that as a weakness.

But as he continued to go through her things, it became obvious she did show a wide range of interests. He pulled out a spiral notebook buried under all the hardcover books, and then found another. Apparently his Skye Cree liked to jot down interesting side notes about people. As he flipped through the pages, he became fascinated with her meticulous details about the various sexual predators she'd tracked over the years. So she liked to keep notes on people just as he often did on his potential targets. An interesting similarity, he decided. Maybe they had more in common than he'd thought.

But for some reason Frank kept coming back to the only other space in the little rat-hole to store anything— under the old iron bed. He decided to see what had migrated underneath with the dust bunnies. Getting down on his knees, he scanned the area—and hit the mother lode. He slid out a laptop computer from its hiding place and realized he'd just found something that would keep him occupied for the rest of the night. The bonus would be getting inside the mind of another hunter.

And what a mind it was.

Tonight he would do without sleep as he made himself comfortable here. He'd soak up everything he could since he couldn't very well take the laptop. She would surely miss that and know someone had been here. That someone she would no doubt blame on him.

He pondered whether or not he really cared about her knowing. He decided to play it safe. So he pulled out his phone and snapped photos of her little sanctuary. He took screenshots of her notebooks and anything else he could think of that might come in handy for later. He even laid out each piece of her underwear and photographed that as well.

Over the next several hours, he fixed himself a plate with cheese he found in the fridge and some unopened sesame crackers in the cabinet. When he got thirsty, he drank from a carton of orange juice still in date. Meanwhile, he read through her journals. When that was done, he opened up the laptop. It took him less than fifteen minutes to crack her password and discover she seemed to be as obsessive-compulsive as he was in keeping notes and searching websites.

When bits of sun began to stream through the only source of light, the sliding glass door, he got up from the bed to stretch his back. Tidying the mess he'd made, he felt confident he could use everything he'd found to his advantage.

But first, he had to go back to doing what he did best. He'd pinpointed his next victim. Come nightfall, his evening was already booked.

Chapter Fourteen

No doubt the residents tucked inside the gated section of Seattle known as Brittany's Landing felt safe and secure. After all, the gate at the front of the complex was supposed to keep out the riff-raff. The eight-foot brick wall surrounding the little enclave didn't hurt either.

Designed to make sure the inhabitants didn't have to put up with annoying door-to-door salesmen—or the awkward face-to-face contact with people pushing their religious beliefs—or those on foot dropping off advertising flyers, in order to get past the gate, one had to enter a code into the keypad or press a handy remote for access.

Frank De Palo didn't have either. He didn't need them.

But he could have used a nice over-sized umbrella. By midnight the fine mist of early evening had turned into a heavy drizzle.

The rain made the barrier in the back of the neighborhood a slick mess. Slippery, but not impossible to climb and vault over. Frank stood there gauging its height. But since he'd been here before, it wasn't a big deal.

He threw his bag over first then dropped down on the other side into a row of bushes. Strolling along the sidewalk as if he belonged there, he moved in the shadows past a common area, a clubhouse with a sparkling swimming pool and a playground for the kids.

The neighborhood had everything the residents could want within easy reach of their front doors. Everything that is, except a guard out front or surveillance cameras to keep an eye on the perimeter.

After tonight, the real estate agents might want to reconsider the advertising campaign that living behind a gate kept anyone out. Truth was, if he wanted to get in, he found a way in, simple as that.

He made his way to the cross streets of Xavier and Allen as if he'd gone out for a breath of damp Seattle air. Because he already had mapped out his target, there was no need to scour the rows and rows of upscale homes.

As soon as he reached Kathy Monroe's two-story Mission Revival, or rather the house that belonged to her mother, he spotted the light burning bright in a downstairs window. He veered off in the direction of the side yard. He pushed the handle on the back gate, and kept to the fence line. Moving along the side of the brick structure, he hid in a row of bushes he could use as cover.

From the backyard, he noted Kathy had left her blinds open. The little brunette would be his youngest yet. Well…except for that other one. But she didn't count. She'd lived in another state—and was ancient history.

From his spot, he could see all the way into the kitchen and beyond into the open living area. He watched through the glass as Kathy, the just-turned-twenty-year-old, fidgeted with her cell phone.

Standing as still as one of the bronze statues in Ravenna Park, Frank lifted his head to peer into the house.

As always, he waited at the fringes—and for his opportunity.

‹♦ ‹♦ ‹♦ ‹♦

Still living at home, Kathy Monroe poured her third glass of Merlot and settled down to call her mom, Louise, who had flown out of SeaTac just that Sunday morning for an all-inclusive vacation to Hawaii. Maui to be exact. With the three-hour time difference between Seattle and the island, it was only a couple of minutes after nine o'clock there. Because it was still early, and because her mother had specifically left instructions for Kathy to call, she couldn't wait until morning to hear the details of her mother's first trip to paradise. Besides, her mother was her best friend. Kathy wouldn't think twice about pestering a friend on her first night in one of Kaanapali's best beachfront resorts. So why not bug her mom.

And even though Louise had only checked into the fancy hotel that afternoon, Kathy itched to get the low-down about the flight over, the accommodations, what the place had to offer. In other words, everything she was missing out on sitting back home alone in Seattle on a rainy night.

Kathy had wanted so badly to make the trip with her mother that she'd considered giving her notice at the design firm where she worked. But quitting didn't make any sense when she had a car payment due. She couldn't put Visa off either, even if her grump of a boss was a tyrant.

She could only hope her mother would give her updates while she was on the island and take plenty of pictures. She knew, of course, that photos weren't the same as experiencing all the pristine sandy beaches, the crystal clear water, and seeing the beauty of Maui firsthand. But it would have to do for the time being.

Just because Kathy worked as a lowly go-fer for a crabby boss known for his CD cover designs didn't mean she shouldn't get to take a vacation. Considering she'd only been employed there for the past ten months didn't make a difference to Kathy. She usually got the crap jobs no one else wanted to do anyway. She felt like her boss could've made an exception. He could've let her take a holiday two months before her anniversary date. But he hadn't done that.

With all the work she had piled up on her desk, Kathy didn't stand a chance of seeing anything tropical unless it was a pineapple in the produce section at Safeway.

When the call to her mother went to voicemail, Kathy sighed into the phone. She left a long message about how she wanted to hear each and every perk, all the amenities that came with the resort package Louise had booked.

Knowing her mother was more than likely out having a blast, sitting around a fire at the first-night, get-together luau with the rest of the group members, didn't help Kathy's mood any.

Draining her glass of wine and setting it in the sink, she decided it was time to head to bed. Kathy snatched up her cell phone just in case her mother decided to return the call whenever the luau ended.

With thoughts of hula dancers and bare-chested hunks flitting through her head, Kathy climbed the stairs to the second floor. She couldn't help but wonder if Louise, right at that moment, was sitting on a sandy beach sampling her first taste of poi. She knew her mother wouldn't dare pass up a nice Mai Tai either.

She headed into the bathroom to take off her makeup, the same makeup she'd painstakingly applied to drop off her mother twelve hours ago at the airport. Which was silly she thought now, she'd never even left the car.

As she lathered up her face she realized that in less than eight hours she'd have to put the stuff back on when she got up to go to work the next morning.

It was then Kathy decided life was too short to sit on the sidelines. She smoothed face cream onto her cheeks and forehead and realized she hated her job. She spent eight long hours every day working for a man she didn't like very much.

As she pulled back the covers on her bed, she came to a decision. If she ever got another chance to see Hawaii, she was ditching her asshole of a boss and taking the trip anyway.

Unfortunately for Kathy Monroe, Frank De Palo had other plans for the woman's future and a vacation didn't enter into them.

Like any good cat burglar, he waited until he saw the lights go out in Kathy's upstairs bedroom before he made his move.

Instead of walking back around to the front door and coming in that way, which he'd done on numerous occasions to other houses, Frank decided tonight he would use the roof. Maybe because the French doors on the second-floor balcony made a perfect entry point. Not only was it the darkest part of the backyard, but on one of his previous visits he'd fixed the lock there so it would easily stay open. That is, if no one else had tampered with it.

He pulled on a pair of gloves from his bag, then went over to pick up a deck chair from the back terrace that he thought would easily hold his weight. He carried the furniture over to the lowest roof point and positioned it so that he could reach the overhang.

He went back for his tool bag, grabbed the mask and stretched it over his head. He zipped the bag closed then hurled it up and over the railing where it landed with a slight thud on the concrete.

Hoisting himself up to the eaves, he grabbed the drainpipe, shimmied along the rim until he could throw his leg onto the roof. Balancing like an acrobat on the narrow ledge, he finished his climb the rest of the way across, edged his way around, no more than five feet, and dropped onto the balcony where his satchel already sat.

He checked the double doors and found the latch just as he'd left it. A simple piece of Scotch tape over the mechanism had prevented it from locking. He loved homeowners who didn't bother securing every door in their house before going to bed.

He picked up his bag, turned the handle and stepped into the master bedroom where Kathy's mother, Louise, normally slept. But since Frank had done his homework he knew Louise was three thousand miles away and that Kathy was alone.

The carpeted floor muffled his footsteps as he narrowed his eyes, scanning the already familiar surroundings. Since this would act as his staging area, he began to shed his clothes. He stripped down to skin. From the bag he took out his knife and this time, a Beretta.

He left the mother's bedroom and walked down the hall to Kathy's.

Kathy had left her door open. And she wasn't asleep yet.

Kathy thought she heard a scraping sound outside, and then a thud. She tried to get comfortable again. But when she heard the same noise again, she lifted her head to try to pick up where the bump-in-the-night came from. It sounded like someone walking on the roof—which was impossible. Kathy knew that. But then she heard what sounded like the floor creak, maybe down the hallway. Once again, she convinced herself she had to be imagining things. Her mother wasn't home so it had be the house settling. She rolled to her back.

And that's when she spotted him.

She blinked and tried to focus on something other than the dark figure looming in the doorway. Her eyes locked onto a man wearing a mask over his head. The knife he held in his fist glinted silver.

She panicked and grabbed for the phone on the nightstand.

But Kathy wasn't quick enough.

The man had already closed the distance. With his gloved hand, he brought the blade down, slicing a gash into Kathy's arm. Blood flowed from the wound which seemed to piss him off.

"Damn it! Look what you made me do!" Frank screamed as he yanked the charger from the outlet along with the cell phone and threw both up against the wall.

By this time, Kathy realized her attacker was naked—and fully erect. Even with what little light the bedroom offered, she noticed the deep brown of his eyes—and how empty they were.

She felt a muscular hand clamp down around her neck to drag her to the floor.

"You're lucky it isn't your hair," Frank hissed as he leaned over and then straddled her torso.

When she started to scream, he slapped her face. He put the cold blade of the knife under her chin and made sure she felt the skin prick and the trickle of blood it left.

"Try to fight me, and I'll slice your throat open right this minute. Nod if you understand?"

Terrified, Kathy nodded.

Kathy saw the knife move as he used it to cut the T-shirt she had worn to bed down the middle of her chest, exposing her breasts. He squeezed a nipple hard several times and then wrapped his fingers tighter around her neck. "You want to make me happy, right?"

Kathy's head bobbed up and down again. She could tell he got excited at that. But the pressure increased around her throat. She could barely breathe. She thought she might lose consciousness.

Right before that happened though, he loosened his grip. "Good. Now this is what I want you to do." In spite of the blood streaming down her arm and neck, he took her hand and brought it up against his lower belly, then slowly glided it down to his hard penis. He raised her head up slightly so she could put it in her mouth.

"But…but…my arm is bleeding. It hurts," Kathy protested.

"Huh, I didn't notice that. Stupid bitch," he snarled. "Of course, you're bleeding like a stuck pig. You made me cut you, didn't you? Do what I tell you. Put my dick in your mouth." When the young woman balked again, rage took over. "I thought you said you understood. Apparently you have a problem with basic instructions. Looks like you'll need a lesson in following directions."

And with that, Frank started carving.

Chapter Fifteen

By eleven o'clock, the rain had turned to a steady downpour and forced Josh and Skye to retreat back to the warmer, drier confines of the loft, making for an early night.

While they spent what was left of a quiet Sunday evening at home, the couple had no way of knowing what kind of grisly scene played out in another neighborhood a mere eight blocks away.

They'd taken their showers to wash the street off, fixed hot chocolate with little marshmallows, and were now stretched out in the king-sized bed with their laptops resting on their legs while ESPN rehashed the Seahawks game, quarter by quarter, on the flat-screen TV. Every so often Josh looked up from his computer screen to see the fifteen-yard touchdown pass completed in the second or the fumble at the goal line in the fourth.

"Nothing like football in the fall," Josh murmured as he finished his email to his marketing team and hit send.

"We've mined data from every source we can think of and we still don't know anything about this sick bastard," Skye groused as she took another sip from her mug.

While the announcer on TV went over the other late scores on the West coast, Josh shut down his computer.

And suddenly the temperature in the room dropped—noticeably. Like an Arctic wind whipping out of the frozen tundra, it nipped and bit.

"Did you feel that?" Josh asked.

In tune with the jolt and each other, their heads turned to stare.

"You mean that intense cold chill? Hard not to," Skye said. "Especially when it brings the temp in the room down a good ten degrees."

"Something just happened to cause the room to turn into a freezer section."

Instead of reaching for the covers, Skye bolted off the bed, snatching up her cell phone off the nightstand. "Death. Darkness. Another victim."

Understanding had him leaning across her side of the bed. "Do you really think Harry will believe you, Skye?"

"After pulling us into this thing, Harry had better. Did you get anything just now? Any bursts of energy, or flashes?"

Josh didn't have to ask what she meant. "Darkness, same as you. That's what hit me first. Second, a life ending. Next, a subdivision with a gate out front. A man peeping through an open window. He uses a chair to get up to the roof. The door's unlocked." Josh frowned. "She left her door unlocked. No, wait. He'd been there before and did something to it so it wouldn't close properly. I saw a knife, lots of blood. That's it. That's all I got. Not that much really. How about you?"

Disheartened, Skye pushed the button to disconnect the call before Harry ever had a chance to pick up. "This is crazy, Josh. What do I tell Harry? This guy could be anywhere, in any number of neighborhoods that have a gate. Your parents live behind one." She visibly shuddered at the thought of that. "It isn't Laurelhurst, is it?"

"No. That much I know. What did you see just now, Skye?"

She shook her head. "Nothing we don't already know. Darkness first, then a man standing in a house, carrying a knife, wearing a mask, and not a stitch of clothes on. I couldn't get a read on the neighborhood though, Josh. No landmarks. Nothing."

"See, this is exactly what's so frustrating. As we sit here watching Sports Center, our guy is out there torturing another victim."

Skye slumped back down on the bed. "He could be forty miles from here or forty blocks. He got undressed in that same room where he made his way into the house." She chewed on her lip, trying to think of what she wanted to say. "Josh, there has to be a reason he wears that mask all the time at every crime."

"To scare the bloody hell out of his victims and get them to cooperate." But Josh thought about that a minute longer before adding, "What are you thinking?"

"Could he be some type of local celebrity afraid of getting recognized?"

"Holy shit, wolf girl. You might be on to something. He's lean, fit, athletic. Local sports star maybe?"

"Maybe. Enough of a star that he thinks someone might see him without his mask and put two and two together."

"Talk about crazy but his general description *is* perfect for some type of athlete."

"Well, we know he doesn't play football."

"How do we know that?"

"You just watched highlights. The Seahawks were on the road."

"Good deduction, wolf girl."

"Stop calling me that! I could return the favor, you know, and call you wolf boy. How would you feel about that?"

"Come here and I'll show you."

"Is that all you think about?" she asked with a grin as she settled against his chest.

"Only when I'm awake," he replied, kissing her hair.

She angled her body, reached up, draping her arms on both his shoulders. Their eyes locked as she crawled over his legs and onto his lap. She grabbed the end of her top, jerked it up and over her head, letting his eyes go wide at her boldness. She took his hands, guided them to each breast. "I need you to touch me tonight, Josh. All of me."

Her hands snaked under his shirt where she ran her nails along his toned stomach. While working his boxers down and off, the breath whooshed out of her as he deftly reversed their positions.

Hunger roared up. Limbs tangled. Lips met. Tongues mated. Teeth nipped at soft flesh, grazed along tender skin.

His mouth settled at her breast. Suckling, long and hard, he lingered, drawing out the pleasure for both of them before moving down her body. Hovering over her, and then into her.

Warmth spread. The ripples made her shudder like rolling sprays of sea and foam. The spurt of climax burst forth powerful as lightning streaking across a thundery sky. Longing for more took root and bloomed as Josh drove, pumped, harder, faster. Glassy layers built, fast and hot, glory waiting at the edge.

Sinking, they plunged in free fall through the brilliant shine of shimmering gilded tide. The ebb and flow rushed them along melding heart and soul as one.

After a night tossing and turning, Josh wasn't surprised when the phone woke him at ten minutes after eight. Trying not to disturb Skye, he rolled to his left to reach the ringing cell. Squinting, he grappled with the device before sticking it to his ear. The guy on the other end didn't bother with preliminaries.

"Look, I hate to do this since it's a rainy Monday morning, but I need you guys out at Brittany's Landing A.S.A.P."

Josh recognized Harry's voice. "So that's where he hit. Skye and I wondered. That's only eight blocks from here. Let me guess. Single woman alone who lived in a gated community, felt safe and secure behind the walls. Our psycho had been there before and tampered with an upstairs balcony door to get in. He started the attack by slicing open her arm first…her right arm. It was another violent assault because he got pissed off that she wouldn't do what he wanted fast enough."

"How the hell do you know all that?" Harry barked.

"Let's just say, I had a restless night. Give me the address."

Forty-five minutes after Harry's call and sitting in traffic for a short eight blocks, they pulled up to a gated subdivision. The place was fairly typical of an area that hadn't needed a wall to keep people out when the homes were built decades earlier. But today, with all the police cars coming and going, the sliding gate between two stone pillars had been left open. After all, its presence hadn't prevented a serial killer from breaching the false sense of security.

They passed manicured lawns covered with autumn leaves and orderly flower beds bursting with fiery colors. While the tips of evergreens, heavy with rain dipped and swayed in the breeze, the dreary morning couldn't hide the fact that murder had taken place in the otherwise peaceful setting.

The address turned out to be what was commonly referred to in the region as a "Seattle box" also known up and down the West Coast as an "American Four Square." This one wasn't a typical "Prairie School" design but more in the vein of Spanish revival with its arched portico, red-tiled roof, and painted white stucco exterior.

"Hard to believe such horror occurred in such a cute little house," Skye noted, crawling out of the Fusion.

"Maybe that's why he picked it. Look around you," Josh pointed out. "This one is more ornate, sticks out from the rest because of its color and unique design, a tad more upscale than the others."

"You're right," Skye agreed, scanning the row of houses. "It does make a statement, attractive outside and trendy. He might consider the house *and* the gate something of a challenge."

"And the woman inside," Josh finished.

Harry met them at the curb, tossed two pairs of latex gloves at them. "Put these on. You know the drill. I appreciate you getting here so fast. Our victim is Kathy Monroe. Single but lives with her mother, Louise Monroe. Louise happened to be out of town on her first vacation since getting her daughter out of high school."

"High school? How old is Kathy?"

"Just twenty years old, Skye. Youngest one so far. We haven't even been able to get hold of the mother yet. Coroner's here, but I've held the crime scene techs at bay because I wanted you guys to take a look at the bedroom first."

Harry sent Josh a steely glance and said, "You may think you know what he did in there, but if you ask me, it's another one for the books. He went ballistic on the victim. Cut her face up, cut off a breast, mutilated the rest of the corpse."

Josh cringed. "The one on the left, the left breast, that is. I forgot to mention that when you called. I wasn't fully awake yet."

"What a homicidal freak," Skye uttered as they followed Harry into a rustic Saltillo entryway with bold tones in cinnabar and spattering flecks of blue and jade-green accents. Skye did her best to get her mind off what waited in another part of the house.

Harry went up a curved staircase with Mexican inlaid tiles dotting the steps. Just as she'd decided that maybe the iron sconces on the walls added a nice touch, they reached the second floor landing—and she caught the iron smell of blood and death. Without anything on her stomach, Skye almost gagged.

But all of a sudden Josh stopped outside one door to the right of where they walked. Skye peered inside, saw it was the master bedroom. She watched as Josh drifted farther into the interior until he stood at the French doors. Even with the dismal weather outside, a wash of pearly light snaked in, one slice stretching across the room causing an eerie glow.

"He came in through here. Before that he used a chair from the patio to climb up to the roof and swing over to this balcony."

"Why didn't he just use the front door?" Skye wondered aloud.

"He's an adrenaline junkie," Josh answered flatly.

"That plays into our local athlete theory," Skye pitched back.

"Local athlete?" Harry asked with a surge of disdain rolling through him at the prospect of that. He rubbed his aching temple. "That's all we need is to learn this bastard is in the public eye. You really think this guy might be well-known in the area?"

"Why else wear the mask?" Skye said. "If just one person recognizes him and you guys get any type of decent composite, he's toast. He knows it. So he protects his face."

"Maybe he has scars or tattoos on his face that stand out. That would be noticeable to a victim," Harry said hopefully.

"Or maybe he's a cop or a firefighter," Skye countered, shooting Harry a challenged stare. At the incredulous look Harry gave her, she added, "They're known adrenaline junkies, Harry. It's a fact. You have to keep an open mind here."

"Without a survivor to ID him, everything is speculation," Josh surmised. When Harry grumbled at that, Josh went on, "Whatever he is, by the time he walked in through these doors, he was already wearing the mask. So it figures that hiding his face is the first step once he decides to head inside. There has to be a reason he hides his face, Harry."

"At this point, I just don't want to consider that our guy's a cop, okay?" Harry fired back.

"I know you don't," Josh said in response. "But Skye's right. Keeping the door open to possibilities will maybe catch him in the net faster. Whoever he is he's physically fit."

Josh took a few steps over to the bed. "This is where he took off his clothes. Once he got undressed, he took out his knife and his gun from the black bag he carries. But it was the knife he took down the hall with him to use on the victim. He left the gun behind. Not his usual norm."

"He didn't use a gun here?" Skye asked, glancing over at Harry for confirmation. When she saw Harry bob his head, she asked Josh, "Any chance you see this guy at all *before* he puts on his mask, say when he's climbing up."

Josh shook his head. "It's too dark. It's always some damn thing that prevents me from seeing this guy's face. I'm sick of it," he groused as he realized he'd spoken out loud.

"Okay, you have most of it right," Harry admitted. "We found a sturdy teak chair under the lowest eave of the house that helped him get up onto the roof where he crawled along to the balcony. And once he finished with Kathy, the man pretty much strolled out the front door, leaving the chair right where he'd left it."

"He doesn't seem concerned about leaving his DNA behind."

"That and the fact he doesn't seem to care about taking the time to tidy up his crime scenes anymore either. Come on, I'll show you what I mean. You need to see this." Harry took a right out the door and continued down to another bedroom, this one smaller in size.

"The coroner started counting stab wounds but quit after reaching one hundred," Harry said as he stood back to let Josh and Skye get their first peek.

This time it was Skye who wasn't prepared for the viciousness of the attack. Her gloved hand flew to her mouth while she used the other one to steady herself on the doorframe.

Kathy's nude body lay on the floor to the left of the bed, her head bumped up against the nightstand, a bloody mass of tissue and bone. He'd done his best to pose her but since he'd obviously hacked his way down Kathy's torso in a fit of frenzy, there wasn't much left intact to prop up.

The blood splatter indicated overkill and would likely help some tech in the lab to provide the angle of impact. But Skye didn't think it would be necessary. Josh was right. If the madman had brought a gun here he had settled for the knife. He'd spent some time over the twenty-year-old in order to dice and chop.

Skye glanced at the walls. Cast-off might show his swing and movements, maybe even the depth of his rage. But again, Skye didn't need an expert to tell her the killer's wrath had caused him to lose control in this very spot. So much so that he had left telltale signs. One of which was Kathy's mutilated lower abdomen. Because he'd left her legs spread, Skye could make out the disfigured genital area.

"This guy is sick. He's either trying to make a statement or he's losing it flat out," Skye mumbled, as she bit back the urge to barf.

"Probably both," Harry agreed.

Skye had just started to back out to find a bathroom when she thought of something. "I don't understand. Why do this kind of carnage to the bodies of Tracy and Kathy, but not Julie and Sylvia? Even though he spent extra time with Sylvia and Julie our guy didn't go off on them, not like this, while Tracy and Kathy caught most of his blade work."

"It's all about how angry he happens to get during the assault. Julie and Sylvia probably did their best to give him what he wanted early on," Josh reasoned. "He rewarded them by not chopping them up."

"But the result is the same," Skye uttered in agreement, clearly fighting to keep down the one cup of coffee she'd had. "Even if they cooperate, he has no intention of letting them live."

Josh nodded. "He goes out to kill with a certain amount of surface rage anyway right on the fringe. But then if things don't happen to go exactly as he'd planned, he lets the fury loose for real. And if you ask me, it's getting worse."

"I was just thinking the same thing." Skye turned to study Josh. "An adrenaline junkie would want it to get worse, egg it on, wouldn't he?"

"In order to keep upping the ante each time, making sure he took it up a notch? Yeah, he would. He's losing patience with his targets a lot quicker than he did before. When he might have spent some time talking to them, maybe trying to calm them down in some way with reassuring words so they wouldn't panic, now he just starts cutting."

"And doesn't know when to stop," Skye finished.

Chapter Sixteen

By six o'clock in the evening, single mom Janie Holliman was about ready to drop. She'd already put in twelve hours on her feet, nine of which occurred at her busy hair stylist job—where she routinely had to deal with difficult customers—mostly walk-ins who weren't regular clients and liked to grumble.

If her day had only ended then and there when she had walked out of the salon, it might've been different. But after picking up her three-year-old son, David, from daycare, she'd noticed he was running a fever. His little chubby cheeks were beet red and he kept grabbing at his left ear. A sure sign an ear infection loomed. Another stop at the urgent care facility had confirmed her suspicions. Poor baby had to start a round of Amoxicillin which meant a second stop at the pharmacist to get his prescription filled.

Janie didn't reach her little bungalow in Olympic Hills until almost six-forty-five. She'd barely gotten dinner prepared, when her ex, and David's father, decided to change his visitation days for the upcoming weekend, which meant she'd spent twenty minutes on the phone with another irritable male.

But after finally getting her cranky toddler to go down for the night, Janie poured herself a glass of wine, a decent Chardonnay she'd tossed in the cart as an afterthought while she waited for the pharmacist to fill David's prescription at the drug store.

Sinking down on the sofa, she resisted the urge to sigh at getting to sit down. She pulled the afghan from off the back of the couch and wrapped it around herself, got comfortable. She clicked the remote past reruns of *The Golden Girls* and opted instead for an episode of *Friends*. But as the wine kicked in and the long day caught up with her, she noted the time on the cable box. It read ten-fifteen. As her lids began to flutter closed, right before sleep took hold for real, Janie's last thought was of her son. She hoped like hell the antibiotic she'd given her baby boy would work its magic and make him feel better by morning. Knowing full well his daycare wouldn't take him if he showed signs of being ill, she couldn't help but wonder how angry her boss would be when she had to call in sick tomorrow.

Exhaustion and the wine soon had her drifting off.

An hour and a half later a sound woke her from a deep sleep. Before her eyes could open, she thought she heard something outside the house. A stray cat or dog maybe?

Minutes passed as she fought the dregs of sleep and the inability to come fully awake. Ignoring the patter of footsteps coming from somewhere in the house, she thought she heard a dragging sound.

She groaned slightly and moved her head a little deciding she should probably get up to check on David. Had her three-year-old gotten up to pee or worse, to throw up? Or maybe he did feel better and he'd gotten up to play with his brand-new race-car set.

But about the same time Janie tried to toss off the throw and stand up, her eyes landed on the nude man no more than three feet away standing at the end of the couch.

Janie knew she was in trouble when she saw the mask that covered his entire face, even his neck. In the dim light, the God-awful cloth had an eerie sheen to it. Just as she opened her mouth to scream, a gloved hand clamped down over her mouth, his other hand closed tightly around her throat. Janie felt the strength in his fingers as he lifted her head off the cushion, keeping his grip squeezed so that she had a hard time swallowing, even breathing. The thought went through her mind he could easily snap her neck.

"Make a sound and I'll kill your son. Nod if you understand me," the man whispered.

Janie's head moved up and down as she sucked in his breath and smell, a sickening blend of cinnamon Tic Tacs and aftershave. The familiar scent of Paco Rabanne drifted to her nose. The strong fragrance had her looking up into his brown eyes. Vacant and cold, they simmered with anger and a lot of it.

She watched him reach down to the floor with one hand, retrieve several short strands of nylon rope.

While he looped the first cord around her wrists, her son ran into the room.

Three-year-old David yelled, "Mommy, mommy, who's dat man?"

The second Janie saw her attacker turn his head toward David, she bucked. Hard. With her entire body. The force was enough to jostle him off her. Janie clenched her hand into a fist and belted the asshole square in the side of his nose. She hit him so hard, blood squirted back onto her hand. When he rolled off her, holding both his hands up to his now broken nose, Janie didn't stop her momentum. Determined, she brought her foot up and kicked his crotch as hard as she could. Janie never waited for him to double over.

Scooting off the sofa, she scooped up David and bolted for the front door. Flipping the lock back, she threw it open and dashed outside. As soon as she reached the yard, she never stopped running. With her son clutched to her chest, she started screaming her head off—all the while making a mad dash across the lawn to Tara Cosgrove's house next door.

Janie didn't quit until she hit Tara's front porch where she bounded up the steps and began hitting the doorbell in rapid succession. When that did nothing, she started pounding on the door until she saw a light finally come on inside the house.

As soon as Tara's husband, Charlie, determined it was their neighbor Janie, he turned the lock to let her in. Janie pushed her way inside. As she rocketed past Charlie, only then did she allow herself to fall apart.

The single mom collapsed on the floor.

Officers Curtis Broward and his partner, Gary Pitts arrived on the scene seven and a half minutes after Charlie Cosgrove dialed nine-one-one. Charlie met them on the lawn. Pointing over to Janie's little cottage, he directed, "That's where it happened. She and her boy are in my living room scared to death."

After getting the story from Charlie, both cops did a cursory walk-thru of the little two-bedroom house, then checked the small backyard. It didn't take long for them to realize the perp had left the premises. After interviewing Janie Holliman and getting a vague description of a naked assailant wearing a mask over his face, approximately six feet in height, Officer Broward put out a BOLO for a prowler in the vicinity.

After discussing it with his partner, Officer Pitts decided to file the incident report as an attempted rape. Neither man thought to call anyone on the task force.

In sleep, Josh replayed the woman's escape with her little boy. As if rooting from the sidelines, he breathed a heavy sigh of relief the minute she got outside and ran across the lawn carrying her son. He might not know her name, but he knew what she looked like, knew the fear he'd seen in her green eyes.

Josh came awake, all the way awake. Throwing his legs over the side of the bed, he popped up, rubbed the back of his neck. "We have a survivor."

"What?" Skye muttered as she tried to come out of a deep slumber and sit up. "What did you see?"

"We have a survivor," Josh repeated. "And the first cops on the scene blew it. They didn't connect the rape attempt to our guy. But it was him."

Because he was shaking, Skye scooted over to him, put her arms around his neck. More awake now, she decided he needed to talk about it or he'd never get back to sleep. "What exactly happened?"

Josh went over what he'd seen, describing the guy taking off his clothes, how he'd entered through the little boy's room then crept past the child as he slept, and into the living room where the woman had been napping on the couch.

"You say the cops didn't suspect it was an attempt by the serial killer. You know this for a fact?"

"They didn't make the connection. Why wouldn't they make the connection, Skye? This case has been all over every news outlet in the state. If this is an example of police work, this is one reason we can't nail him. There's no coordinated effort."

"We'll change that. I'll get hold of Harry tomorrow."

"How many others are out there where the incidents didn't get linked to our guy?"

"This one won't fall through the cracks, Josh. We won't let it. Did you happen to catch where the attack took place?"

Josh frowned, scrubbed his hands over his face, thought for a minute. "I don't know. I'm not sure which neighborhood. But there has to be a way to check the logs of the patrol officers and find out which ones responded to a rape attempt on a woman where a little boy interrupted the attack. How many of those can there be in one night?"

Chapter Seventeen

Frank De Palo was beyond pissed.

How the hell was he supposed to explain his fucking broken nose to his trainer? Not only that, for the first time in ten years, he'd failed to control the situation.

He'd let the bitch get away from him.

Frank didn't take failure well. Never had. His fractured schnoz still hurt. The bitch had caught him right across the bridge when he'd been distracted by her kid. If he hadn't turned his head he'd have been able to take care of both woman and boy. Should've taken care of the damned kid beforehand, he thought now.

Frank popped three more Ibuprofen, even though he rarely took drugs of any kind, and gulped them down with half a bottle of water. He hoped like hell it eased the pain because he had a Goddamned match in less than two hours. What the hell would his opponent think when he walked into the arena with a bandage already stuck across his beak?

Just thinking about last night had Frank making a fist, ready to pelt the face of his next challenger he faced in the octagon, the place where he ruled.

For the past three years, he'd dominated the world of Mixed Martial Arts. Since pursuing his dream in MMA he'd discovered his calling. Without really knowing it, he'd been training for the sport most of his life. Originally a long-distance runner in high school, the sport gave him the one-on-one adrenaline of facing an opponent and beating the shit out of him with his superior skill. The game had turned out to be his means of escape. Even if that release valve didn't last very long, it had more than likely prevented him from getting arrested many times over the last thirty-six months.

Not only that, it encompassed all the disciplines he loved. Karate. Kickboxing. Jiu-jitsu. Judo. Muay thai. And of course, his first love, wrestling. Since he made varsity three straight years during high school, he'd been good enough to get a scholarship. Since first stepping into the octagon, he'd been able to maintain his welterweight status and the required minimum seven-percent body fat. Physically fit, in shape, he trained daily with Seattle's well-known fitness guru Mick Hyatt.

Mick hadn't really taught him anything he didn't already know. But appearances were everything, especially if you needed to hide a darker self. No one in their right mind would ever link Frank De Palo, the all-American athlete and MMA star, to his daily early-morning reconnaissance, or his B&E extracurricular activities, or Frank's personal favorite—outdoing Gary Ridgway, the local man dubbed the Green River killer—in body count.

While Ridgway had focused on many of society's throwaways, hookers and teenagers with problems at home, Frank aspired to achieve greater things with better more worthwhile victims. With his strict religious upbringing he refused to go near prostitutes. And teen girls didn't interest him much.

But snooty women who considered themselves independent and better than the common guy were a different story. Those types who thought they were so safe, tucked inside their upscale homes and snuggled in their beds where they were most vulnerable, presented a challenge to him. Getting to them, controlling them, and *having* them were the essence of the game.

As he took a second look at his broken nose in the mirror, he decided Janie Holliman hadn't been his first choice anyway.

Who wanted a woman who'd gone through childbirth? He should've passed up the bitch and left her to the sleazebags she'd hooked up with in the past. Obviously, she wasn't much of a woman in the sack if she couldn't live with the man who'd fathered her child.

From now on, he'd avoid single moms. They didn't really do anything for him anyway. They weren't worth his time and effort, too slutty. From now on, he reasoned, he'd stick with the hot single women he preferred.

"Harry, you have a survivor. You just don't know it. Check the log from last night. You had two patrol officers respond to an attempted rape by what they considered to be nothing more than a prowler in the neighborhood who got a little frisky. That prowler was our guy. And he got away."

"Goddamn it! I've told those beat cops to report anything like that to the task force. Which neighborhood, Skye?"

"That I can't tell you, Harry. Before you blow a gasket, I'm not holding back. I just don't know the answer. But the woman escaped his attack with a little boy in tow. How many times could something like that have taken place last night?"

"Good point. I'll go through the incident reports and get back to you."

"Let us know what you find out. Because Josh wants to talk to the survivor."

The wheels of bureaucratic red tape were slow. Wading through reports took another ten hours before Harry got back to them.

He had been able to confirm what Skye and Josh already knew. Janie Holliman had barely escaped from a serial killer with her life and probably that of her child. Over the phone Harry tracked Janie down at her mother's house and got the woman to agree to sit down with all of them to recall what had happened.

So the next day, Skye and Josh drove all the way out to Redmond because Janie refused to go back inside her little cottage in Olympic Hills.

Harry met them on the sidewalk in front of a two-story, Tudor-style house belonging to Janie's parents.

"It's probably a good thing she's staying with someone," Skye noted. "Just remember to go easy on her, guys. The woman's been through a life-changing event."

Josh and Harry exchanged glances before turning to Skye. "I'm a little insulted by that," Josh said. "I'm not here to beat her up."

"Nor am I," Harry added.

"I know that. But having to replay the whole cycle of events is traumatic and will conjure up all the panic and fear she felt at the time. That's gonna stay with her for years even though she got away."

Janie's mother, Jeanette Frazier, greeted them at the door. Ushering the trio into the living area, she reminded them, "Janie hasn't been herself since it happened. My daughter hasn't stopped shaking for the past twenty-four hours. I'm mostly seeing to it that David is taken care of while Janie tries to deal with all of this. But every time I think about what could've happened to her in that house and to my grandson, I get sick to my stomach and break out in a cold sweat."

"I don't blame you," Skye said. "She got lucky, Mrs. Frazier. And she knows it. But she'll move past this…eventually."

"Call me Jeanette. And I hope you're right, Miss Cree because my Janie is a good person, a good mother even though she has to work and do the parenting for two people sometimes."

"What about David?" Josh asked which earned him a glare from Jeanette. "David saw this guy, too, right?"

"Surely, you don't intend to question a three-year-old, do you?" Jeanette wanted to know, wringing her hands. She sent an accusing scowl toward the detective. "You didn't mention that you wanted to talk to David when you called."

But it was Josh who answered. "Don't worry, we won't talk to David. I doubt he'd be able to tell us much anyway because of his young age."

"Thank goodness for that," Janie exclaimed from the doorway.

Three pairs of eyes stared at their survivor. They hadn't expected the woman to be so petite. The little brunette couldn't have stood any taller than five-three at the most. She looked as if she might weigh a hundred pounds soaking wet.

"So you took down a man who outweighed you by seventy pounds and had you in height by seven or eight inches?" Skye asked, clearly impressed.

Before she replied, Janie turned to her mother and suggested, "Mom, will you go make sure David is occupied while I talk to these people?"

"Sure, honey. You call me if you need anything."

As soon as Jeanette had left the room, Janie sunk down into the nearest chair. She finally addressed Skye's question. "I guess I was able to take down the asshole because David ran into the room and he turned his attention on my child. It was all fear then. I thought he'd hurt my son. And when I saw an opening, I took it. I was afraid he was going to hurt David," Janie repeated, her eyes misting over at the reminder.

"From reading the police report, I'd say you kicked his fucking ass and broke his nose," Skye commented. "Way to go, Janie!"

Janie couldn't help it. That assessment caused her to crack a grin. Her smile broke some of the tension in the room. "You know it wasn't until much later that morning that I realized who tried to attack me in my house. I'd seen the news, never ever considered I'd be a potential victim."

"What can you tell us about him?" Harry wanted to know, getting right down to business. "From the report I read, we already know he wore some kind of a ski mask. We know you wouldn't recognize him again. We're not dragging you anywhere to look at a lineup of suspects. There's no need. So relax here. We just want to see if, by any chance, you can give us something, remember anything that might help us catch this guy."

Janie shook her head and corrected Harry. "Well, for one, I never said he wore a ski mask. That to me means like a knitted cap or something. This was more lightweight and sheer. A stretchy fabric almost like what Spider-Man wears." At that, Janie smiled a little wider. "That's what David asked me after the cops left and I was putting him to bed at Tara's. It was Tara's house I ran to, to get away. Anyway, when I was trying to get David to go back to sleep, he asked why Spider-Man came into our house naked."

"Interesting," Skye mumbled, as if considering the child's take on what he saw. "Could this mask have been homemade?"

"Sure, I guess. It reminded me of one of those masks the wrestlers we sometimes watch on television wear. But instead of ending around the mouth this one covered his entire face and his throat area. It was shiny, too. At least that's what I remember thinking."

Josh exchanged glances with Skye as if keying in on the wrestler angle. "You mean it sparkled or glistened in the light?" he asked.

Janie closed her eyes to try to remember. "Sort of, I guess I'd say it glistened more than sparkled. Huh, that's odd."

"What?" Skye prompted.

"When I fell asleep on the sofa, the lights were on and so was the TV. Oh my God! When I woke up the only light came from my little kitchen, the light above the stove. He must have turned the light on in there." Both of Janie's hands flew to her mouth. "I just realized. He must've been in my house with us for some time before I woke up, long enough to make himself at home. I remember trying to wake up because I could hear footsteps. I don't know how much time passed before I was able to fully come awake. I remembering thinking it was David and hoped he would go back to sleep. Then I heard a dragging sound or some kind of thumping along the floor. I thought David had gotten up to play."

Janie sat there stricken at the realization. "I make sure I lock all the doors and check them every night. Like I said, I'd listened to the news. He got in anyway. I didn't respond to the noise I heard soon enough. I thought it came from outside, a cat or dog. But…how did he get in?"

Harry thumbed through the police report. "The two officers agreed that he made entry into the house by way of the window in the smaller bedroom."

Janie's eyes went wide and she swallowed hard, before her hand moved to her stomach. "David's room? I think I might be sick. I've already told my landlord I can't live there after what happened."

"Anything else, at all, you remember about the guy?" Josh asked.

"He wore Paco Rabanne cologne."

Skye's eyes widened. "You're kidding? How do you know that?"

"I work in a salon all day, cutting hair. Men come and go all the time. I recognize their aftershave. Actually it's kind of a game with me guessing which fragrance they use. His was Paco Rabanne, not exactly cheap either."

"That sells for at least fifty bucks," Josh said in agreement.

"Sometimes more," Janie added. "My ex got it as a Christmas gift one year."

"Mommy!" David shouted from the doorway before he ran and crawled into Janie's lap.

Janie wrapped her arms around his little body and brought him into her. "This is David."

"Hi," David said, not a bit shy for a three-year-old. "Are you gonna catch da naked man wif da dog?"

Skye looked at Harry then at Josh. "What dog? The naked man had a dog?" Skye asked clearly perplexed by that news.

David bobbed his little head up and down. "Right dere," the little boy said, pointing to the upper part of his arm. "The doggie was right dere."

"A tattoo," Skye reasoned. "Just the face, David? Or did the picture have a body with it?"

"Doggie face," David replied.

"What kind of doggie?" Harry said, almost jumping off the couch in the direction of the child.

But Janie gave the detective a hard stare. "Detective, he isn't old enough to know about different breeds of dogs."

"But he could point to a picture if he recognized the same kind, right?" Josh proffered. "Couldn't he?" It was worth a shot. Josh brought out his iPhone, searched the Internet for a website featuring photos of all kinds of dogs. "Would you like to see my phone, David? It has pictures of doggies."

For the next forty-five minutes, Josh took the little boy through a series of websites until David finally pointed to one. "Dat one. It looks like dat one."

Josh glanced at the screen, held up the phone for Skye to see.

"I thought it would be a bulldog," Skye admitted, as she stared at the image. She shrugged one shoulder. "You know, like some kind of fierce dog. That's a terrier, a cute one at that."

Josh turned to Janie. "You didn't see the tattoo, did you, Janie?" Josh asked, hoping for any type of confirmation other than a flimsy lead from a three-year-old witness.

But Janie shook her head. "Sorry, I didn't notice it. I was too shaken and scared of what he might do to my son."

"That's what I was afraid of," Josh mumbled as they turned to go.

Outside as they stood on the street, the three of them went over what they'd learned.

"He wears a mask that looks like Spider-Man," Josh said.

"Or the wrestlers on television," Skye added, biting her lip. "And he has a tattoo of a cute little terrier on the upper part of his arm."

"He wears expensive aftershave lotion and spent time in the house before waking Janie up to assault her."

"How reliable is information from a toddler anyway?" Harry pointed out.

"Reliable or not, it's more than we had before we got here," Skye reasoned, as they headed to the car.

Chapter Eighteen

An eager fourteen-year-old Frank waited for his girlfriend, Denise Holland, at the secret place they liked to meet after school.

The abandoned winery had been closed down decades earlier by his own grandfather back in the seventies. Located a good half mile out of town, down a road no one bothered using any more, the old building was off the main thoroughfare, the spot remote.

They had to ride their bikes to get here. But since the afternoon was warm and sunny, everything a spring day in May should be, it gave the two of them a chance to be alone to talk and to maybe neck. The last time they'd been together here, Denise had let him get to second base. Since then, he hadn't been able to think of anything else.

While he sat in the overgrown courtyard on the concrete rim of the circular water fountain, waiting for Denise, Frank grew impatient. The idea of touching Denise's boobs, what there was of them, got him excited. He hoped she would let him fondle them again today. Of course, hers weren't like any of the others he'd felt. Denise's were small and round and the nipples didn't stick out the way he preferred but they were still breasts.

But as he sat among the weeds and scrub, tapping a stick he'd found on the ground Frank realized this was the perfect, out-of-the-way spot for two kids to meet who had sorta been going steady since they'd gone to the spring dance together back in April. It was now almost the end of the school year when they could spend a lot more time together. That is, if the two of them could manage to sneak away at camp this summer. Since Denise was a member of the same church he went to, his mother liked Denise just fine which was a huge plus. His mother didn't like everyone.

Frank had to admit that bringing Denise around lately had helped him get along so much better with the old bat.

When he looked up and spotted Denise pedaling her bicycle along the dusty road, he became less annoyed with her. Even late, he was glad to see Denise and her long flowing reddish-brown hair. He liked her freckles, her upturned nose, and the innocent way her green eyes always searched his for approval.

As Denise got closer, Frank waved in greeting. But he could tell by the look on her sweaty face that something was wrong.

"What took you so long?"

Winded, Denise almost tumbled off her bike. She rummaged through her knapsack and came up with the ring he'd given her two weeks ago. "I started not to come. But I thought you deserved to hear it from me before Tommy Platt told you."

Frank's forehead creased with troubled lines. He didn't like Tommy Platt who sat behind him in biology class and always gave him a hard time about something. "Tell me what? What's stupid Tommy got to tell me?" Then he saw his ring in her hand, the one he'd taken from old lady Harbison's house. Denise was reaching out to give the jewelry back to him.

"We're...I've...sorta...decided to go out with Tommy tomorrow night to the movies. He's taking me to see Godzilla."

"Why? I thought you liked me. I thought you wanted to spend time with me."

"I did. I do. But your mother never lets you do anything fun. I want to go to the movies with my boyfriend. And you never can go without sneaking around," Denise pointed out. *"Just last week you got in trouble for it when we went to see that comedy, Krippendorf's Tribe."*

"But you belong to the same church as me. You know it's against their rules to watch that filth on the big screen."

"My mom and dad have decided to go somewhere else though."

"Leave? Go to another church, you mean?" His mother wasn't going to like hearing that, Frank decided. She would never let him see Denise again anyway once she got wind of it. "Why? Your parents are making a huge mistake."

"Because they've decided to start going to the one over on Eighth Street."

"You mean the Methodist?"

"That's the one."

His mother didn't like the Methodists. Frank shifted his feet. "So because I can't go to the movies without having to sneak around you're breaking up with me?"

"I'm breaking up with you because you have a temper. You're always on the verge of exploding. Like right this minute, you've got this look in your eyes like you could strangle me or something."

Frank took the stick he was holding and brought it down across her face. "You bitch!" he screamed.

Stunned at the sudden blow, Denise stumbled backward. She felt the sting along with the blood from the nick across her cheek. "What the heck is wrong with you anyway? Why did you hit me?" When she saw Frank take a few more steps toward her, getting closer, she started backing away from him.

Frank saw the fear in Denise's eyes first. That fear fueled his rage. It excited him much more than her breasts ever had. He hit her again with the stick. When she tripped over a patch of burweed, he pounced and took her completely all the way down to the dirt. She struggled but finally Frank climbed on top of her. Before he could stop himself, he found his hands reaching, and then wrapping around Denise's narrow neck. His fingers kept up the pressure, tightening and tightening until he watched as the life slowly went out of Denise's fourteen-year-old eyes.

It wasn't until after when he sat next to Denise's lifeless body that he came back to himself—and realized he'd ejaculated in his shorts.

How the hell did he plan to explain that to his mother? he wondered. And where was he going to hide Denise so no one would know what he'd done?

Chapter Nineteen

Fresh from his victorious bout in the octagon where he had annihilated his latest challenger, Frank decided a celebration was in order. Tonight, he had some time on his hands. He intended to make the most of it. He would treat himself to a road trip, a different community entirely. Before the night was done it would yield a gorgeous blonde. That would make for a consummate week, the icing on the cake, so to speak.

Not for the first time, Frank had decided a change of scenery would spice things up, especially now that he'd left a survivor. Even though the news outlets hadn't used her name, Frank knew that meant Janie Holliman had spoken to the cops.

He'd expected the bitch would talk. But he wasn't worried. What could Janie tell them anyway? That a masked intruder with brown eyes tried to rape her? In Frank's book that didn't amount to very much.

But as long as things were getting a little too hot in the Seattle area to keep tempting fate, he'd decided to switch up his hunting grounds. Besides, new surroundings made for a better game.

Just because he'd driven forty minutes outside Seattle to get to the little city of Snohomish didn't mean he'd changed his methods or his goals.

He hadn't been to the area since last spring. Because of that he might have to refer to his extensive notes to find the house and the target he remembered. But that just meant he'd have to go on the hunt, which was almost his favorite part.

Once he reached the city limits, Frank remembered a town with a charming historic district that included a fair share of antique shops and the usual places that catered to tourists who wanted to buy souvenirs.

But what interested him most was the fact that it had several long and narrow jogging paths hidden among tall trees along the river, that led to the types of houses he preferred—and the single women who lived in them.

The detailed journals he kept would no doubt jog his memory once he applied himself to the task at hand. He checked his map, located the street he was looking for, and drove past the woman's house several times just to be sure he had the right one. He had to recheck the address twice and then the name of the street again. Once he reread his notes yet again, he knew for certain he'd been inside this particular house.

When he spotted the pale blonde with her hair tied up in a ponytail running along the trail at a fast clip, he recognized her from what he termed his "spring break" last March. And just as he had remembered, she met the criteria perfectly.

She would probably fight back. And she would lose.

He parked the Ford pickup and got out, walked to the ridgeline above the neighborhood with a perfect view of all the winding paths. From there, Frank watched her. Familiar now, in stature and build, dressed in sweat pants and a matching top, the runner continued her brisk pace. He kept her in his sights during her entire run which lasted just over an hour.

Once he saw her check the time on her wrist and finally quit jogging, he stared at the way she walked, the sway of her hips, her long, lean legs—and decided she could definitely go at least one round with him.

He continued his vigilance while she caught her breath and drank from the bottle of water she'd pulled from the pouch she wore around her belly.

Excitement raced through him. In a matter of hours he would have what he wanted. As she moved, he began to follow her from the upper pathway, making sure not to let her out of his line of vision while she headed back to her house.

When the greenbelt met up with sidewalk, when she disappeared inside a trendy two-story at the end of the block, he snuck back into the alleyway. There, Frank perused the backyard and the best place to lie low until it was time to make his move.

He took out his phone to snap photos of the area. He removed his journal from his backpack, flipped pages to refer to his entries from last spring...again. The blonde's name was Chanin Crowley, and she was twenty-five years old. She had a yappy little dog he'd have to deal with but he smiled because he realized it would be worth it. Chanin had a toned body and a fondness for plastic surgery. He remembered now that Chanin's lips had been filled with injectable facial filler. According to the receipts he'd found on her desk, she'd also paid for liposuction on her hips and thighs. Her breasts had been augmented to a nice, round, luscious C-cup. She'd enhanced those the previous December, a little Christmas present to herself after a messy divorce.

Before midnight, Frank resolved to make it his mission to see for himself if the surgeon had done a decent enough job on both.

⌁ ⌁ ⌁ ⌁

By the end of October, there had been two more women found brutally slain, bringing the man's grand total, that they knew of anyway, up to double digits.

Single mom Janie Holliman had been the only woman lucky enough to escape from the man's clutches.

Their killer didn't seem to be deterred by state-of-the-art security or new locks. He didn't seem to care if his target had kids in the home, owned dogs, or lived outside the Seattle area. If he felt like the cops were getting close, if he felt their stakeouts might pay off, he simply moved on to another locale.

With each homicide, their killer's rage ramped up.

For his last known victim, an attractive blonde, he'd travelled to Snohomish, where he'd slit the woman's throat before cutting out her breast implants.

Josh had seen it all go down. Chanin Crowley's vicious murder was only one reason his sleepless nights had come back twofold. After the most recent string of homicides, sharp, intense images punched their way into his psyche to stay with him long after he crawled out of bed. The violent outbursts brought him into the chamber of horrors to witness vicious brutality, the like of which he'd never known. Brutality that made him realize this particular madman had a screw loose. How could one human being do that to another? he wondered. When the grisly pictures became almost unbearable, when they wouldn't let up, he had Skye there beside him to walk him through the depth of what he'd seen and the anxiety he felt afterward.

How in the world a thirteen-year-old had been able to handle such vivid savagery at such a young age without going nuts was a mystery to Josh. And it just showed, yet again, what a strong person Skye Cree had been for more than a dozen years.

Since the dreams wreaked havoc on his nights, the disturbing nightmares in turn affected his waking hours, putting a strain on his everyday work schedule and ultimately on his relationship with Skye.

He found he couldn't go without sleep for long before it started catching up with him. Not only was he tired the next day, he found himself distracted during meetings. During the day-to-day stresses of managing his company, many times he caught himself trying to figure out the riddle of *the bones will tell* refrain when he should have been focused on the next upgrade or the upcoming software releases.

As a result, Josh became irritable with his staff. And it had to stop. If he and Skye didn't find a way to catch this guy soon, insomnia proved, once again, that it could and would kick his ass on a daily basis until this case had a resolution.

But if his nightly visitations from the mind of a killer weren't enough, Josh had to deal with the constant knowledge he had to be missing something. At each crime scene, the same message rolled around in his brain and kept coming through loud and clear. *The bones will tell.*

And he didn't have a clue what it meant.

The deaths he saw in his visions were disturbing, as were the crime scenes he got to visit firsthand. But there were no bones spread around to talk to him to tell him anything.

"Maybe you're taking that phrase much too literally," Skye proposed. "Think about it. Maybe these particular bones don't have anything to do with this case at all. Maybe you're getting your wires crossed."

"Has that ever happened to you?"

"Sure. The images merge from one scene to another and they aren't even related. Haven't you ever been dreaming about a tropical island and right in the middle of the white sandy beach while sipping your piña colada you drift into some ugly chore you have to do at work the next day? It's the same principle. *The bones will tell* might mean you need to go visit a forensic anthropologist, sit down to have a heart-to-heart or there might be bones sitting in a box somewhere you need to find or something of that nature. The point is, it could mean you need to keep an open mind, think outside the box. And you won't know for sure what the phrase means exactly until later after you've exhausted all other avenues."

"How much later? That sounds like wasting a lot of valuable time to me."

She huffed out a breath. "That's hard to gauge. It's not one of those hard-and-fast things with a clear-cut indication you have to look deeper. We'll figure it out though. If the phrase is tied to this case, it'll eventually come to light."

"In the meantime, I muddle through and wonder what I'm missing. It's bugging me, Skye."

"Then I guess it must be important, a gut instinct, or in this case a strong, recurring theme which should never be ignored."

"It's difficult to do that when I get the same words over and over again in my head at each crime scene. It's significant, I know it is. Without getting graphic, as horrific as each murder is, let's face it, these victims aren't down to bones. In many instances, the women have only been dead for a couple of hours, like at Tracy's and Julie's house and Kathy Monroe's. I don't think the phrase means current victims."

"Well, whatever it means, if our guy keeps up this pace, we'll have to create an Excel spreadsheet," Skye countered to keep up. She glanced over at Josh stretched out on the couch and caught his reaction, a flinch in his jaw muscle. "You've already done that, haven't you?"

"Why not? It seemed the best way to be able to scan the doc and maybe pick up on a pattern."

"You're kidding?"

"Not at all. His changing neighborhoods all the time is a problem but if you pick up his pattern—"

"Could we predict where he might hit next?" Skye wondered.

"We could try. But it would be damned near impossible because he's so erratic. We know he goes to great lengths to scout for victims, and then stalks them. But if we could ever narrow down his hunting ground, that would be huge."

Skye moved to the map they'd tacked up to a bulletin board near Josh's desk that he used as his home office. There were photos of each victim along with the addresses of each crime scene. They'd added details of each murder so they could track where he'd hit. It was also a way to keep them all straight. She studied each note, tapped the paper. "The thing is he's all over the place."

"But it should be easier than this to pick up the pattern."

"Why's that?"

"Because he's so anal-retentive, obsessive-compulsive, whatever label you want to use to describe him. He feels compelled to go back again and again to the same neighborhood, burglarizing the houses, making sure the people know he's been there. Harry says he's never seen a guy do that before. But maybe we could use that particular trait to lure him into a trap."

"I'm in."

"I know you are. But we have to set the trap first and it has to be something he's unable to resist. We have to control the environment and set up the scene to perfection. As sadistic as he is, he's also smart. Because the bastard is too calm and collected as long as he's in control. Shake his routine and it sets him off enough to take a baseball bat he found under the victim's bed and bash her brains in."

"Or cut out her breast implants. I get your point. But do you get the sense that he's getting more unpredictable? Because that's what I'm getting. Not from any outside influence like Kiya either, but his last four murders have been off the charts in appalling cruelty. How do we even begin to predict when he himself is so unpredictable?"

"It's hard to imagine an unstable killer becoming more erratic. But yeah, he seems to have gone on a tear since he lost control and let Janie Holliman escape. He seems to have taken that personally."

Skye nodded in agreement. "Like he has to prove a point or something."

"Exactly." But Josh had something he needed to say to her. "What point are you trying to prove, Skye?"

She narrowed her eyes. "Don't start on me, Josh. I'm not ready to deal with what Travis did yet."

"And how much time will go by before you are? I know that's the way you feel right now, this moment, but it's a blip on the radar in the grand scheme of things. What about down the road? Because something's been bothering you other than the obvious. It goes well past the initial anger, it's on a deeper level now, I can sense it. Something you haven't been able to shake, and it's the reason you're unable to get a good night's sleep. What's going on with you, Skye?"

She looked away. "I've started to remember certain things from childhood, images really, like snapshots, mostly when I was much younger. They involve Travis and I don't like what it's doing to me up here." She tapped the side of her head at the temple. "I'm recalling stuff that doesn't fit. With everything else that's been going on, I don't want to think about all this right now. I'm not sure I can afford to."

"See, that's where you're wrong. You're already distracted. This thing with Travis, you need to take care of it so that you're able to focus, to fully concentrate on what's at hand. This serial killer isn't a side dish and shouldn't be treated as such. He's the main course. You being unfocused during this time is *not* a good thing." When he realized what she'd said about her childhood, he asked, "What do you mean you remember things? You mean *before* your parents died?"

"Oh yeah. Quite a bit before. Years."

"And it concerns Travis?"

Her head slowly moved up and down. "It does."

"Remedy this, Skye. Take a drive out to Everett and talk to the man. Your ability to get visions might come back for real if your mind is clear of this one thing. That'll only happen when you settle this between you and Travis. Otherwise, you're just spinning your wheels. Look, I'm distracted enough. We don't need both of us to be vulnerable during this time. It might give this son of a bitch an opening. He doesn't need another advantage."

"That actually makes sense."

"Good. Because you don't want to be dragging more excess baggage around for another dozen years, do you?

Why not just settle it once and for all? Either you come to terms with what Travis did or didn't do or you tell the man how much he hurt you, have it out with him and leave it at that. Either way, you get it all out in the open, no more hostility to muddy your mind. What's the worst thing that could happen? You get some resolution either way."

"It may not go well."

"Then at the very least you'll know where you stand with him and can move on. Want me to go with you?"

"No. But you're right. I need to face him about all this stuff and get some answers for my own peace of mind. Otherwise I'll just stew about it for what could end up being years."

"Wasted years at that."

"Okay, I'll drive up to Everett. But I'm not calling and giving him a heads up and I don't want you doing that either. Promise me."

"Who me? I wouldn't dream of interfering," Josh said with a wink.

"Good because the trip will either be a quick turnaround and I'll be back this evening or this hostility between us will take a couple of days to sort out. Either way, I'll pack a bag for overnight just in case."

"Take all the time you need, Skye. Don't let this fester until it rots and there's nothing left to claim for a relationship."

"Okay. But if you should happen to get news of a natural disaster with an earthquake magnitude where the epicenter is located in Everett, you'll know it's nothing to worry about. Just two stubborn Nez Perce butting heads right before they go to war."

Chapter Twenty

Travis's haven from the world was forty acres of ranch land outside Everett that he'd dubbed The Painted Crow. Here he could get away from the hustle and noise of Seattle and spend time breeding, raising, and selling the American Paint Horses he loved.

Among the rolling pasturelands he found the solitude he often needed from running several diverse businesses that usually kept him hopping. Even when he hired the best managers he could find, there were still problems that cropped up. The Country Kitchen offered its share of headaches but it wasn't his only business with a slew of problematic issues. In addition to the greasy spoon, he owned a fishing boat that brought in enough Dungeness crab to supply the Farmer's Market on a daily basis. He owned an office supply store, a design business, and was part owner in an upscale seafood restaurant located in Capitol Hill.

The Painted Crow was his only place to escape from it all.

Hugging the Washington coastline, his spread sat at the top of a majestic cliff where giant Douglas fir and Sitka spruce vied for space to grow tall and strong. The surrounding forest easily turned out hundred-foot-tall conifers that continued, year after year, to dot the peaks and rocky seashore.

Standing in the corral, Travis brushed down his latest acquisition, a feisty, smoke-cream mare he intended to use for breeding. While he worked he could smell the salty sea mist as waves crashed up against the wedge of beach and rock below.

When he heard a car pull in past the iron gate, he recognized the engine in Skye's Subaru. His heart soared with hope. Maybe she'd decided to forgive him. Hell, at this point he'd settle for her sitting down and listening to what he had to say.

Travis watched as Skye crawled out from behind the wheel, watched as she walked up to the wooden fence, all the while boring holes through him. He decided to go with something that wouldn't get him in too much trouble right off. "I hear you have a spirit guide problem," Travis said with a twinkle in his eye. He wanted so much to approach her and give her a hug. Since he wasn't sure that would be a good idea, his feet remained planted where they were. He decided to let her give him a sign of why she was here. It had to be significant that she'd driven out to see him.

Skye smiled. "Turns out, I do. I thought maybe *my father* might be able to help me get her back."

Travis's eyes misted over as he tossed the brush he'd been using into the bucket. He went over, opened the gate and met her with his arms spread out wide. "Come here, honey."

Like a small child, Skye went into his embrace.

"I don't blame you for being upset with me. But you should know by now how much I love you." He kissed the top of her head. "I love you with all my heart. I always have."

"There's something I should probably confess then."

"If this is major maybe we should take it into the house. I made fresh raspberry tea not two hours ago."

Skye nodded. "I could use some of that right about now. It was a long drive up here. But what I have to say, you may want something a little stronger than tea."

His brow furrowed; deep lines that usually weren't noticeable now exposed worry and concern. "Okay, you have my attention."

When they got to the house, Travis disappeared into the kitchen and Skye followed, not content to stay in the living room. But once she watched him take the tea from the refrigerator and fill the glasses with ice, as the silence dragged out, Travis finally turned to her and said, "What gives?"

Skye took a deep breath, let it out. She rubbed her hands on her jeans. "Okay, here goes. When I was about four or five, I know it was around that time because I hadn't started school yet, I saw you with my mother. You were both standing together in the garden. You were kissing. Not like friends, but lovers. So I don't really want to hear your lame excuse or lie that this thing was simply a one-time shot between the two of you where you acted as sperm donor out of the goodness of your heart."

If it was possible every ounce of color drained from Travis's cinnamon face. He dropped into one of the kitchen chairs. Finally, after what seemed like several long minutes passed, he composed himself enough to admit, "It took more than a couple of times for Jodi to conceive."

"Oh please. So this is how you want to mend things with me? With a lie? After your revelation at dinner that night, I started going back in my head to my childhood. I remember times when you were there and Dad was not. He'd go away for long absences. And do you think my math didn't take? What part of 'I was four or five years old' did you not get? You and my mother had an affair. Are you going to sit there and deny it?"

"No."

"I guess that's a start. You want to tell me how you betrayed a man you considered a brother at the time?"

"What I told you the other night was the truth."

"Which part? Maybe you should explain to me which part you want me to believe—this time. Parsing words, Travis, won't cut it with me, not anymore. I want the truth, all of it, from the beginning."

"I saw your mother first. But she wanted Daniel."

"I got that part already. Fast forward to when you first slept with my mother."

This time, Travis got up and went to the cabinet. He reached for the whiskey and poured a generous amount of Jameson's into a stubby glass. He knocked all of it back in one gulp.

Travis turned to face her as if the alcohol had given him the courage he hadn't had before. "Things changed between Daniel and Jodi after you were born. Turns out, Daniel couldn't exactly handle the fact that you belonged to me and not him."

"But he was a loving father. He was always so involved in whatever I did," Skye reminded him.

"Do you want to hear this or not?" Travis snapped. "This is *very* difficult for me. If you want the truth then I suggest you sit down and listen for a change instead of popping off at the mouth at me."

"Very well," Skye said with enough frost in her voice to form ice.

"Fine. After you were born, Daniel had difficulty with the situation. I don't think he'd thought it through very well when he had to look at you every single day and realize each and every day you weren't his, that you belonged to me. You might have gotten your mother's deep blue eyes but Daniel could plainly see you had my nose and mouth. Then for some reason, his bitterness over the whole thing shifted to Jodi. At a certain point, Daniel directed his anger at her. A great deal of that time he and Jodi were at odds with one another. They fought constantly. When you were about two years old, it got so bad at one point that they separated. Daniel moved out. He got a place out near Fort Lewis, Washington, where he worked as a civilian contractor. His engineering job took him out of state quite a bit, and because of that, Jodi and I grew closer."

"I just bet you did," Skye tossed out and earned a long glower from Travis. "Okay. Okay. I'll shut up and let you finish."

"Thanks. But need I remind you they were separated at the time?"

"And need I remind you they were still married?" Skye retorted.

"Point taken. At first, I stopped by to help out with things. I'd sit with you while she went shopping or took a break from all the mommy stuff. But one night I stayed for supper. Afterward we bathed you and put you to bed together. Then we watched a movie. One thing led to another." Skye saw Travis swallow hard and turn to the bottle again. He poured another glass and drank it down before going on, "I ended up spending the night."

Skye's face fell. "You know what? I don't think I'm ready to hear this after all. I'm surprised with all your 'spending the night' I didn't have a brother or sister show up nine months later."

"Why do you say that?"

Skye gaped at the man. "I had a brother or sister?"

He ran a hand over the top of his head. "Jodi got pregnant again."

"Ohmygod. Are you serious? Did my father know? I mean Daniel. Did he find out?" But the look on Travis's face had her wondering why she'd bother to ask. "Of course, he did. Daniel had to be furious with both of you."

"Oh he was. A couple of months went by where he didn't even speak to either one of us. He stayed away from seeing you, as well, didn't come around the house at all for visitation, nothing. But then five months into the pregnancy, Jodi had a serious medical problem. She developed something called toxemia. The doctor admitted her to the hospital in critical condition. Her blood pressure shot through the roof. Her kidneys started shutting down. I was afraid I was going to lose her, Skye, so I phoned Daniel, told him to get his ass to the hospital. He showed up. And for three days we both sat there, either at Jodi's side, or in the waiting room before she finally lost the baby. From there, her condition stabilized. But once Jodi started getting better, her condition improving, she decided losing the baby was some kind of bad omen, some sign that we were not meant to be together. So she persuaded Daniel to give her another chance. Together, they made the decision to give their marriage one more shot."

"Just like that? She sleeps with you. You get her pregnant, again. Then when that doesn't work out for her she shifts back to Daniel. Who are you people? You think you know your parents and then realize nothing could be further from the truth. Wait a minute. Her decision must've meant you were left out in the cold again?"

Travis nodded once and then threw back another shot of whiskey. "I was devastated. That's when I bought this place, The Painted Crow, and moved to Everett. I pulled away from both of them. That time I stayed away. I was determined to leave them both alone to put their marriage back together. Two years went by. I didn't see Jodi and Daniel again until you were about four."

"My God. That day in the garden. You and my mother just couldn't keep your hands off each other—apparently."

Travis poured another glass of gold liquid.

"You keep knocking back enough of that stuff because it's loosening up your tongue. So let's move on. Out of the blue, one day you decide to stop by the house for a visit, find Jodi alone, and make a move on her in the garden."

"No. It did not happen like that at all. Jodi called me."

"Booty call? Isn't that what they call it?"

"Skye Melody Cree, show some respect! If not for me, then for your mother."

"Shouldn't that be Nakota. After all, I'm Skye Melody Nakota, aren't I?"

"Must I remind you that your birth certificate says Cree? Daniel is listed as your father. It's your legal name."

"Should I ask for that DNA test then that you didn't want to take when I was thirteen?"

"I may not be the man you thought I was, but I'll say this again. You will show me some respect. You're a member of the Warrior Society now, act like the warrior you are."

"Screw that. It's a little difficult to show respect, Travis, especially when I'm learning some very not-so-flattering things about the people I cared about."

"We weren't perfect people, Skye. We had our flaws, our issues."

"Oh I can see that. So what happened that day in the garden when Jodi called you? After all that time, why'd she call *you*?"

"She needed someone to talk to. What you saw that day was me trying to comfort her. That's all. Nothing happened between us after I left her and Daniel in the hospital. You have my word on that."

Skye was tempted to toss out another insult about how little she could believe anything he said, when she noted the disheartened look on his face. Knowing Travis wasn't that good an actor, she recognized that sad look for exactly what it was. It could mean only one thing. He'd never touched Jodi again after he made that promise he wouldn't. And he wasn't happy about it. Skye saw the regret in his warm brown eyes. She swallowed down her resentment and finally asked, "Why did she need to talk to you that day, Travis?"

"You won't like what I'm about to say."

Skye spat out in a mocking laugh, "I have news for you, Travis. I haven't much liked anything you've told me so far."

"Fine," Travis said through gritted teeth. "Your mother discovered Daniel was having an affair with another civilian contractor he'd met out at the base. Your mother was naturally upset."

"Naturally. She cheated on Daniel with you. He cheated on her with someone else. You people weren't just flawed, you were weak."

"You're entitled to your opinion. But just remember, you never know what people are going through, what personal issues people are dealing with, or what difficulties they happen to be trying to cope with at any given time. So be very careful whenever you're tempted to hand down a judgment to us lesser folks, us mere mortals. Not everyone can meet Skye Cree's high expectations."

"You're putting this back on me?"

"I'm taking full responsibility for it. I admit I should never have touched Jodi in the first place. What happened after you were born, altered things between Jodi and Daniel, between Daniel and me, between the three of us. We were never the same. Having you changed our lives forever. No doubt about that. But if I hadn't taken Jodi to bed, if I'd kept saying no to both of them, you wouldn't be sitting here giving me a hard time and I wouldn't have my daughter around, my blood kin. I can't regret that, Skye. Don't ever ask me to regret that."

Her mouth opened for a quick comeback but closed at the profound sentiment. The realization hit her then that if he hadn't finally agreed, she wouldn't be here. She reconsidered that path, the options. The man was, after all, her father. At this late date there was only one other issue standing between them.

"Why did you let me go live with Ginny and Bob? The truth now, Travis. You're not that much of a coward."

"After Jodi and Daniel died, I managed to get through the funeral but I started a downward spiral from there. I went into a black hole and didn't come out for months. I honestly believed at the time you'd be better off in Yakima. Every single day, I told myself that."

"But you knew it wasn't true. My mother told you about what kind of people they were and you stood by while I went anyway."

"I know that!" he shouted, right before he closed his eyes as if to block out the memory. It took Travis a while to compose what he wanted to say. When he finally opened his eyes, he admitted, "If it's any consolation, I'll never forgive myself for putting you through those years with them. It was unforgivable. I was your father. But I was afraid of what you'd think. You were thirteen then. Look at how angry you are at me right now at twenty-six. I wasn't sure how you'd react back then and didn't want to take the chance. Look, if you can't get past this, I won't blame you. At all. But if you could see it in your heart to forgive me, I'll make a pledge to you now, I'll always be there for you from this point moving forward. I want more than anything for us to finally be father and daughter. Surely you can give me another chance, Skye. That's all I'm asking."

She blew out a huge breath right before moving across the room and into his arms.

Long after the tears on both sides had dried up, they still had to get past several awkward moments. The biggest one, of course, was the realization that this man had deserted her at the very time she had needed him most. No doubt Travis should have stepped up. He should have been the one to provide his expertise and counsel about what to expect from a spirit guide. His insight would have been invaluable—like how to handle all the disturbing images that started after she got to Yakima. All these things would take Skye longer to get past than she was willing to admit. It wouldn't be easy and it wouldn't come overnight.

But Skye was willing to try.

As the evening wore on, things began to smooth out while Skye helped Travis fix dinner. Slowly over roast chicken and sautéed vegetables, the old friends began to pick up where they'd left off. Knowing each other for years, having a history together worked in their favor. Father and daughter began to find the easy dialogue they'd practiced all those years ago standing in front of the grill at the Country Kitchen, and at the gym where Travis had trained her.

"Do you remember the day Velma and Bill sold me their old Honda Civic?"

"What I recall is the day I begged you not to buy the damn thing because the engine kept misfiring and it needed a new transmission. But someone refused to listen.

Who picked you up on the side of the I-5 when it literally stopped running?"

She beamed and picked up her bottle of Steelhead, sipped. "It was freezing that day with rain to boot. You took me to the dealership, helped me pick out the Subaru. At least that day, I listened."

"It's a miracle," Travis said in jest. "So many times you didn't. Like when you insisted on looking for Whitfield. I won't lie to you, Skye. That was hard for me. Letting you go out at night was the most difficult thing I've ever had to sit by and watch you do."

"And explains you going behind my back to stay connected to Harry."

"Harry was my only link to what you encountered on a nightly basis. And I wanted to stay in the loop. I knew you wouldn't share the details with Velma, or Lena, certainly not with me, so I tried to do the end-around and hope you didn't catch on."

The genuine concern she saw in his eyes was what tipped the scales. Fatherly concern, even then was something Skye thought she understood.

Later as she sat in his living room sipping on another beer, she stared up at one of the large oil paintings done by a local Native American artist named Ty Moon and realized that one of the man's landscapes hung in the lobby of Josh's building. For some reason it reminded her not just of Josh, but the loft—and home. It was the first time she'd thought of his space in that way. When had she started thinking like that?

When she heard Travis clear his throat from across the room, she wanted him to know, "I need your help getting Kiya back on track. There has to be a way for her spirit to be as strong in me as it used to be and is now present in Josh, short of becoming part wolf."

"But you're still getting visions, otherwise you'd never have been able to find York's house and save Kelly Donahue. Even though you did a foolish thing going in there alone when you sent Josh out of town."

Skye twisted up her mouth and harrumphed out, "I knew you'd take his side. And I did not send Josh out of town. NAGA did. They wanted him for keynote speaker and I thought it best he go."

"I call that chop logic, Skye. Besides, I thought that's what The Artemis Foundation was set up for. I thought when a kid went missing you'd call in the troops and we'd rally at ground central. By doing what you did, you didn't just shut Josh out. You shut the rest of us out as well. People who had agreed to help you find the missing."

She puffed out a loud sigh. "Okay. I've been chastised. I've already told Josh it won't happen again."

"Good. Now back to this problem with Kiya. You are still having visions, weak as they might be, correct?"

"Yes, but I have to work twice as hard. I used a paper trail to locate York's address. Even though I saw the house, gray with red trim and thought I might be able to find the street."

"Because you saw Kelly was in trouble."

"I did. And I had to get to her. But after that, I had no clue about anything else. Josh is the one who gets vivid images now." When she saw Travis frown, she added, "I don't begrudge him that, Travis. He's earned it. But what I'm not happy about is losing Kiya...entirely. Why can't Josh and I share a spirit guide?"

"Need I remind you, Josh is not Native. Despite the transformation, Kiya doesn't *belong* to Josh."

"So he's part wolf and they share very strong traits. Whatever you want to call it, they share a connection deeper than the one she had with me."

"Good point. What baffles me is how weak Kiya is with you. How your visions have all but dried up, that shouldn't be happening."

"Really? Even if she has human elements that come from Josh? Because she's very strong within him, stronger than she was with me."

"Even then Kiya should still be connected to you in some way. I'm not sure I understand why your wolf spirit has detached as much as she has."

"Tell me about it."

Travis thought for a minute. "While you're here, let's try a bonding ritual. Just you and Kiya. Without Josh here, Kiya may come back to you. Since you and Kiya were a team long before he happened on the scene." Travis rubbed at his chin. "You know, that might work. It might be the answer."

"Bonding? You mean like a wedding ceremony?"

Travis smiled. "Not quite but it should function as the same in unity and spirit and hopefully give us similar results."

"Then what are we waiting for?"

⁂

During Skye's trip to Everett, Frank had staked out the loft. He'd been there once before waiting for his chance to get inside to look around. When the Cree woman and the gaming geek had headed out in separate cars, Frank knew the timing couldn't be more perfect.

On his first visit to the historic building, he'd already pilfered someone else's card key when he pretended to be from maintenance. He'd discovered long ago that people with money didn't usually spend too much time looking at the lower rung in society. If one wore a uniform and a name tag, they were pretty much invisible to the upper class.

From there, Frank had taken his bounty, the card key, and copied the data. He used the electronic codes to make a duplicate. He'd donned a hideous, royal blue colored shirt and pants with the name "Al" embroidered in white and blue over the left pocket, slid his substitute card through the reader, and waltzed past residents getting off the elevator right into the building.

As luck would have it, the elevator hadn't stopped to pick up any more passengers as he made his way up to Ander's penthouse.

Once inside the upper floor, he did what he always did. Frank set his timer and started with one room, completely going through it before moving on and tackling the next. His fact-finding expedition had him treating the apartment like a grid.

The precision paid off. He got a lot done. After installing several cameras and listening devices in obscure locations in the main room and the bedroom, he moved on to the kitchen. When his watch went off after two hours, indicating how long he'd spent on his little venture, he decided any longer than that and he would likely tempt fate.

As Frank exited the building, he patted himself figuratively on the back for a job well done. How often did one get to stick it to the enemy right in their own backyard and then sit back and watch the film at eleven?

While in Everett, Skye and Travis fasted in preparation for the ceremony.

It was the first time in the months since she'd been with Josh that they'd spent the night away from each other. As much as she missed the man she loved, Travis kept her busy.

Together they readied the in-ground medicine lodge for the ritual they hoped would bring the tradition of Kiya back to Skye once and for all. They worked to cut and stack wood for the fire, prepped the altar and the stones, and gathered the herbs from Travis's garden they required for purification.

At sundown father and daughter made their way down a steep set of steps and into the depths of the earth, twelve feet down. The smooth mellow tone of flutes played and soared while smoke poured out of the smudge pot. Travis dipped a finger into the burned sweet grass, used his thumb to first smear the ash onto his own forehead before moving to Skye's, where he did the same. The gesture, meant to cleanse the mind and prepare the body for acceptance by the Great Spirit, had Skye bowing, for the first time, in respect of her father.

As the music added soft drums and lilting chimes to the sound of the woodwinds, the two dropped down cross-legged on opposite sides of twelve large stones set in a circle. Glistening with the glowing embers, the fire smoldered with fragrant cedar and pine. As the wood sizzled and popped, the smoke trailed upward in soft wisps, making their two shadows seem to float and merge together as one on the dirt walls.

Travis used lavender to heal all past wounds, juniper to protect and ward off evil spirits for the future. To attract the Mother Spirit and her wisdom, he crushed sage and spread it over the low flame.

As the smells grew thicker and stronger, Travis loaded the sacred Chanunpa pipe with fragrant tobacco, a plea and gift to Mother Earth to open the door to the Great Spirit.

Travis inhaled deeply taking in one puff, then two, before handing it to Skye, who did the same. He began to chant. "We call now to Grandfather Sky and Grandmother Earth, our ancestors, our forefathers. We wish for our prayers and questions to be carried to the Great Spirit that we may receive the answers we seek. May they allow my daughter to rekindle the bond with her spirit guide, the wolf, that walks among men."

His hands waved through the air to get the smoke moving. He began to sing. "Ee ah hay, ee ah hay, ee ah, ee ah hay. Oh Great Spirit, we sit before you tonight to help my daughter reconnect to her wolf. Ee ah hay, ee ah hay, ee ah, ee ah hay. Guide Kiya back to her human so that my daughter may continue to walk along the path that is her destiny. Continue to guide her along her path and keep her safe from the evil she must hunt. Ee ah hay, ee ah hay, ee ah, ee ah hay. Renew the connection to Kiya's spirit and return them both as one so my daughter may walk the path of the future. Lead the wolf to the Land of the Spirits so that she may continue to guide and be strong for her human. Ee ah hay, ee ah hay, ee ah, ee ah hay."

While she and Travis alternately smoked the pipe, Skye took up the chant, too.

And suddenly she found herself missing her mate.

By the time the ritual ended, and Travis helped Skye back up the steps to the top, Skye felt drained. The air rushed past her and she fanned her face.

"You okay?" Travis asked as he thrust a bottle of water into her fist, tilted the plastic up to her lips to make her take a sip. "Better?"

She nodded, tried to get her breath back. "Why does that take so much out of a person when it's such a brief ceremony? What was that? Twenty minutes maybe?"

"It's because the heat in there can sometimes raise the skin temperature a good ten degrees. That's why the custom doesn't equate to spending a lengthy amount of time in such a confined environment. It doesn't lend itself to a long, drawn-out event. It's meant to clear the mind and usually does."

As they started walking back to the house, Skye blurted out, "I miss Josh."

Travis smiled. "I'd be surprised if you didn't. You're in love with him."

"He asked me to marry him."

"You don't sound too happy about it."

"I didn't give him an answer. In fact, he got upset about it."

"Ouch. I bet." Travis rocked back on his heels. "Why not? Why didn't you answer him?"

"It's a long story."

"It seems it's a night for such things. And as much as I'd like to hear it, at the moment, you look wiped out. Your experience in the lodge should put you in a meditative state of mind, able to accept whatever you're meant to do. You should take advantage of it and sleep.

Why don't we put this conversation on hold until morning?"

"I think you're right. I'm suddenly exhausted."

Travis showed her to the same room she'd slept in with Josh, which didn't help her pensive state any. After a cool shower, she dug out her cell phone and called Josh.

"Are you surviving without me?" she asked the minute she heard his voice.

"Barely. How'd it go in the sweat lodge?"

"I'm drained."

"Then why aren't you asleep?"

"I wanted to hear your voice before I dozed off."

"Excellent. Are you coming home tomorrow?" he asked.

Home. She was glad he'd used that word. "Yes, I'll be back in the morning."

"Good. When will you know if it worked?"

"Soon, I think. What if it means you won't have access to Kiya?"

"I'm confident it doesn't work that way. But if it does, I'm prepared to go it alone without my wolf."

"You are?"

"I am. But you sound exhausted. Having been through one of these things, I know how much you need sleep right about now. And Skye?"

"What?"

"I love you."

"I love you, too. Josh? I miss you."

"That's my girl. Same here, baby. Drive safely coming back to me."

She'd barely disconnected and plugged her phone into its charging station, before she drifted off into a deep slumber.

The video in her head played like a vacation reel from a travel agency.

Skye found herself in a thicket of woods among giant oaks and redwoods. There was a narrow trail to follow that took her to a trickling creek, barely enough water to wet the surrounding rocks. But when she lifted her head, she realized that up ahead, the stream picked up momentum and became a deeper, babbling brook. It raced faster, winding its way between sandy shores toward rock formations that began to build in height and beauty.

Skye hiked the terrain, trudging up craggy peaks and down valleys. At one point she crossed over the stream just before it widened. Here, she left the forest behind entirely. She trudged along until the landscape evened out and the trail ended in a canyon hidden by lush deep green foliage. The roaring of a waterfall as it thundered over the top of huge boulders had her looking up to watch the force crash into a crystal clear pool of blue at the bottom.

That's when she spotted Kiya. Drinking from the pool, the wolf glanced up. Their eyes met, blue to blue. Here, everything seemed bluer, greener, clear and clean.

Instincts guided Skye to drink from the pool alongside her wolf. She knelt down to cup the liquid, to sip from the cool water. But when she tried to hold it in her hands long enough to drink, it kept spilling through her fingers.

The wolf dipped her head. That's when Skye did the same. Together she and the wolf quenched their thirst and drank their fill until Skye heard Kiya's voice like an old familiar friend. After so long apart, Kiya came alive again inside her head.

Your path is as it once was. From this moment forward, we will be as one again. Nothing will change that.

"What about Josh?"

Josh will always be a part of me and I a part of him. But he is your mate. Stop denying what your heart feels for him and you will be much happier.

Three sharp cracks in rapid succession, like a rifle going off, broke the peaceful silence and had Skye glancing to her right. The tropical scene started to dissipate. The waterfall changed from brilliant blue to blood red. The scene ended slowly, morphing from rich deep blues to bright violet before turning much darker purple, and then fading to black.

For several long minutes Skye stood before the opening of a room or maybe it was a cave.

Whatever it was, the contrast of white came out of nowhere.

Skulls. Three of them. Skeletal remains. Bones.

Be patient. The bones will tell.

Skye knew then that Kiya had taken her down a road until they hit a dead end—a wall of sheer darkness.

The video ended like a long, exhausting journey, leaving Skye out of breath. Coming awake, she wanted to reach for the phone to call Josh, to tell him about the vision, to talk about babbling brooks and tropical waterfalls—to warn him about the bones—the bones that waited in the darkness for someone to find them.

Chapter Twenty-One

Skye got back to Seattle a little past eleven in the morning. When she pulled her Subaru into the space next to Josh's car in the loft's underground lot, she was surprised to find him home at this time of day.

Her senses went on alert.

She'd talked to him less than an hour out and he hadn't hinted at working from home or that anything was amiss. Had he been holding something back while she'd been in Everett?

She considered their conversations while she'd been gone. Josh had stuck to the simple topics at hand, keeping his comments brief. He'd talked about her coming to terms with Travis. She'd responded in kind by admitting she'd done quite a bit of soul-searching while spending time at The Painted Crow. She hadn't gone into detail yet about her vision. She planned on doing that face to face.

It wasn't just the dream she had yet to share with him. Getting Kiya back had given her a different perspective about a lot of things. That included his marriage proposal, such as it had been. She loved Josh. It was time she thought about their future together.

Making her way to the elevator, she rode the car up to the penthouse. When the doors opened and she saw Josh waiting for her, she dropped her bags where she stood and leaped into his arms.

He covered her mouth.

She started to unbutton his dress shirt. When he stilled her hand, she pointed out, "Okay, the day you don't want to make love, something's wrong. What is it? I get this sense you've been keeping something from me this entire time." She put her hands on her hips to challenge him to deny it.

Instead of that though, he kissed her again before stating flatly, "We had a visitor while you were gone."

Skye raised one brow. "Oh really. Anyone we might know?"

Josh strode across the room to his desk, turned his laptop screen around to where Skye could get her first look at their intruder. "Recognize the build? And he isn't wearing his creepy mask this time. What you see is the get-up that matches what the maintenance team in the building wears. Because there was no reason for any of them to be in our home, I asked the building superintendent to take a look at this video. The man isn't one of his."

"Where did you get that? That's not surveillance from the security system here, is it?"

"No. Although he did tamper with the building's security tapes. Luckily I had my own cameras set up around the loft. Something he didn't count on."

"Since when?"

"Since this bastard's been on our radar. He posed as a member of maintenance, somehow managed to obtain a card key—beforehand. So when I tracked the info from the card he used I was able to trace it back to Mrs. Dellingham on the second floor. She's at least seventy-five if she's a day. But she told me she didn't remember giving anyone her card key or losing hers, which means our guy must have been in the building once before to steal a card and duplicate the data."

The realization finally hit home. "Ohmygod. He's been watching us, following us," Skye stated.

"I'd say for a while now. He knew you were out of town and I was busy at work. He saw an opening and took it, simple as that."

As the surveillance continued to play on Josh's computer screen, Skye's heart raced with varying degrees of anger. "But how did he actually know we wouldn't be coming back right away? I could've turned around and come back at any time. You could have, too. Wait. Do you suppose he's been spying on us?"

Josh threw her a disbelieving look. "I took precautions against that from the first time I walked into the home Julie and Tracy shared. I knew he was a voyeur. That he liked to watch."

"That's just one of the things troubling you about this guy. You've been expecting him to do something like this? Look how calm he is, Josh. He walks in here bold as brass without a care in the world. How long was he in our home?"

Josh stifled a grin at the knowledge she'd referred to the loft as home. "Exactly two hours, precisely. He set a timer. See what he does when it goes off, he packs up, hits the road in no short order."

As she continued to stare at the screen, she was mortified by what she saw. "Yeah, but before he does that he goes through everything. Look at him. That son of a bitch is ransacking through my underwear drawer. You caught him in your own safety net, with your own security system, didn't you?"

"That's right. And I have Leo, Winston and Reggie working around the clock, searching every facial recognition database at their disposal to come up with the bastard's name. Skye, this is our guy. And the asshole made a huge mistake when he walked into our home."

"Could he have planted any type of camera in here to keep an eye on us?"

"He did. But don't worry, I got rid of them. The same day he was here. He isn't as clever as he thinks he is."

"He'll miss the live feed. He'll know we're on to him."

"Not if there's a substitute feed in its place."

"God, you're brilliant! What about a listening device?"

"Had the entire place scanned for bugs. Reggie picked up four—one each in the bedroom, living room, kitchen, and the master bathroom."

"Bastard," Skye uttered.

"We're fortunate, Skye. He could have used that card key at any time to come in here at four a.m., like maybe right after you came in from your rounds, dead on your feet, maybe got careless. Think about it. I want this bastard. Bad."

"No more than I do. By the way, I think I know what your *bones will tell* means."

"Your vision showed you that?" He pumped a fist in the air. "And the three of us are back on track. So what does it mean?"

She took him through her dream, trying to describe the brilliant blues of the waterfall in detail and then how it all abruptly changed at the sound of three rifle shots. "The waterfall turned red and then much darker until the whole scene moved to a small black room. I took that to mean it was maybe a cellar or a black hole of some sort. Then I saw this flash of white and saw three skulls hidden in a very dark place. Then I heard Kiya's voice. 'Be patient, the bones will tell.' Josh, there are three victims somewhere with shots to the head. They're waiting for us to find them."

"Then we'll find them."

For the next few days, Josh, Skye, and their crew spent almost every hour of the day and night sitting in front of a computer screen. During that time, the five of them learned every nuance about facial recognition software. In addition to that, Josh and Winston came up with their own personal software app that tracked a cell phone's Wi-Fi usage. They patterned the application on the same premise retail stores had used in testing to track customer behavior while people shopped. But thanks to Winston they were able to soup-up their app to take it to the next level. If their killer happened to use his phone at all to locate any free Wi-Fi network within one thousand feet of the dummy service they had set up, it would capture that person's phone number *and* his ID.

Once the team had that information they could track the location of that specific device within one hundred feet at any given time by going through several different hotspot providers.

The good news was, they had a plan. The bad news, they still had no idea how long they'd have to wait to lure the guy into their trap.

But then, they got lucky.

Chapter Twenty-Two

Skye and Josh met up in a conference room on the third floor of the Cherry Street police station. As they waited for Harry, Josh noticed how edgy Skye was.

"What's wrong?"

"I'm dying to know who it is. After he went through our home, I'm in no mood to play twenty questions at this point or wait for Harry to get here."

"Leo, Reggie, and Winston used every waking hour to scan millions of faces. It finally paid off." Josh removed a copy of a photo that looked like it came from the DMV. "Prime suspect. Frank De Palo, Jr. Twenty-nine, grew up in San Caruso, California."

"Never heard of it."

"Some little coastal town down in Monterey County, south of San Francisco. And get this. Believe it or not, De Palo came from a prominent family with several million in the bank due to old money, that and the ranch land that's been in his family for over a century. It means Frank has unlimited funds at his disposal to—"

"To disappear," Skye finished. "Crap. That's all we need is for the bastard to run. So give me the rest. I'm no good at this waiting game. I want to know what you know. Start at the beginning. I want to hear this Frank De Palo's life story."

"It's fairly colorful. But let's start with the immediate. De Palo lives one block over from the loft. That's right, our loft, in his very own upscale digs. The guy's worth millions, Skye. His parents, Frank Sr. and Elena, still own the ranch land that's been in the family for generations. They also own an extensive string of San Caruso businesses, real estate, and part of a brokerage house in San Francisco. The family even has a wing of the local hospital named after the grandfather, Vincenzo De Palo."

"Where did all this money come from?"

"Vincenzo immigrated to California from Italy in 1901. Once they got to America, the family settled in San Francisco. Then a couple of years later they made their way down to San Caruso where they somehow managed to buy land and a lot of it. At one point, they practically owned the town. They branched out, tried their hand at ranching and apparently made a killing supplying beef to the railroad workers."

"A multi-millionaire serial killer? Unbelievable."

"And then some," Josh said. "Even though his family could've easily sent him to any college in the country, Harvard was begging for him, Frank ended up staying local. Stanford offered him a full wrestling scholarship. "

"An athlete?"

"I'll get to that in a minute. But yeah, it looks like he's able to leap six-foot-tall fences in a single bound."

"I'm liking this guy more and more as our killer."

"There's a lot more to Frank. He isn't just physically fit. He was also considered a whiz kid early on. His placement tests put his IQ off the charts. In high school his teachers deemed him genius material and then in college the same thing. His professors were impressed and echoed that assessment all through his files. A bit of an oddity though. That too, was noted. According to the university database we cracked—he breezed through his core classes, sailed through his major, which ended up being chemistry—to graduate from college in three years. He was twenty at the time and was immediately offered employment at a pharmaceutical company as a junior chemist—in Portland."

"Portland? I knew it. Please tell me this guy was there at the time of the Towson and Valencia murders."

"He was. Work records put him there for the next three years after college. He stays put in Portland where, between his job and whatever other unusual interests Frank has, he earned a Master's Degree in biomolecular science from Oregon State."

Josh stopped, noticed the expression on Skye's face. "I told you the guy was smart. But add to that, he has an attitude problem, a major one. The pharmaceutical company canned him because he couldn't get along with his co-workers, or management, mainly his immediate supervisor who claimed Frank was arrogant as hell and refused to listen to anyone else's ideas. Frank's yearly reviews—which the team managed to locate online and disseminate—show a guy with no ability whatsoever to get along with anyone."

"I'm beginning to love this super team of yours."

Josh nodded. "Leo, Winston, and Reggie are rock solid and so is the info they crack. Give them enough time and they can hack anything, get at any type of info."

"I believe it. What else did they come up with?"

"Frank's employment records indicate that at times he would simply go off on his own tangents. Prodigy or not, he couldn't complete many of his assigned projects, deadlines would come and go, during which time Frank would get more irrational and illogical."

"That says major loner to me. Fits the profile."

"Yeah, but there's more, a lot more. And here's where it gets interesting. After they let him go in Portland, he relocated to Seattle where he took up Mixed Martial Arts or what's commonly known as simply, MMA. He started out fighting locally, soundly won his weight division, moved up to regionals and onto nationals. Up and down the West Coast, Frank De Palo is known as a bit of a celebrity in the sport."

Skye's mouth fell open. "So we have our local celebrity athlete theory confirmed. That's why he wears that creepy mask. Well, other than the fright factor so he can scare the bejesus out of his victims. He's afraid someone will see his face and recognize it."

"Right again. But get this? In high school De Palo was known on the San Caruso high school wrestling team as 'Terrier.' That was Frank's handle because he wouldn't quit or back down no matter how big his opponent happened to be on or off the mat. Reggie found a former teammate listed online, started emailing him. The friend remembered one night in their sophomore year when the wrestlers all got drunk and got tattoos on their upper arms, tattoos representing their nicknames."

Skye gaped right before she started laughing. "Do you realize that means Janie Holliman's son knew what he was talking about? Who would believe that so far our best witness has been a little three-year-old boy? David was right on the money about the picture of the dog that night."

"Who knew? I guess we're learning to accept the clues we get no matter where they come from. And I found out a little bit about Frank's home life back in California."

Skye narrowed her eyes. "While I was gone you and your team talked to the neighbors without me?"

"I didn't. Not yet anyway. But I sent one of the members of the team down to San Caruso yesterday for a road trip and scouting expedition. Leo's still there. Don't look at me like that. While you were busy rehabbing your relationship with Travis, which you needed to do for both of you, I had this."

She huffed out a frustrated breath knowing he was throwing her words back at her. "Travis and I spent most of yesterday on the phone, sorting out a few more things from the past. I got sidetracked. But just because you're right, doesn't mean I'm not upset that you did all this without me."

"How does it feel to be shut out of a plan, Skye?" Josh pointed out.

She made a face. "Okay. I guess I deserved that. I get your point. What else did this Leo find out?"

"So far, Leo's talked to people around the little town who knew Frank as a kid. People the guy grew up with, classmates, longtime business owners, neighbors who knew the parents, that sort of thing. He found out Frank was raised in a very strict environment by doting parents, especially his mother. Not saying either one is a bad thing or something that turns a person like Frank into a serial killer. Parents are allowed to spoil their kids. But when you combine an overly-protective mother with her over-the-top strict, church environment—"

"How 'over the top' are we talking about?"

"Extraordinary. His mother made sure he went to what this group called 'indoctrination camp' where each summer the kids in the congregation would spend time learning the guidelines to stay on the straight and narrow. For three months while he was out of school, Frank acted as a counselor. Not a bad plan to keep kids engaged and busy. But some of the town thought this particular group went a lot too far. The extreme side was a little too radical for most of the residents in San Caruso."

"Okay, so maybe the obsessive-compulsive took a detour with fanatical influences from dear old Mom's group. Could this be the reason he hates women?" Skye wanted to know. "You have only to look at the crime scenes, the photos, to know he can't stand females."

"You've got a point," Josh said.

"Mom's group sounds a little like the same kind of church Aunt Ginny and Uncle Bob dragged me to every time the doors opened."

"I don't think so. This group was led by a guy named Jasper March, who called himself 'the divine one.' According to some of the neighbors Leo spoke with, Mrs. De Palo pretty much thought Jasper walked on water."

"You're kidding? That sounds almost like a cult."

"Exactly. And who do you think contributed the most to Jasper's coffers?"

"Mr. and Mrs. De Palo. But Josh, if Leo found all this out from the people in town in such a short time, are you sure this is all fact? I mean, are you sure the residents don't have some kind of axe to grind against the De Palos?"

"I thought of that. Maybe a little of both, I imagine. Some of what Leo found out is a little hard to believe."

"Like what?"

"Like the fact Jasper made up his own lingo to use in his sermons to the congregation."

"You mean like speaking in tongues?"

Josh nodded. "Using their own made-up dialect, it seems this 'divine one' believed in retribution and preached regularly about the end of the world. And that his followers should do everything to get ready for it. They made up some of their own edicts along the way and preached no tolerance for the consumption of alcohol or drugs in any form. That includes any type of over-the-counter medicines."

"Wait. You said Frank got drunk one night. Doesn't sound like his indoctrination took for real."

"Typical teenage rebellion. Probably."

"I still say parts of that group sound a lot like Ginny and Bob."

Josh gave her a disbelieving stare, ran a hand through his hair. "I guess in some way I can understand your anger at Travis then. Because what you went through with those people must've been—"

"Over-the-top? Extreme? Yeah, it was. And then some. But as you said, I'll have to learn to deal with it to put all of it where it belongs—in the past—because it's ancient history. I need to remember that and move on. So, De Palo is raised by a woman who dragged him to this place where 'the divine one' routinely taught him that retribution was the norm. That it was just a matter of time before the world ended and he'd better be ready to ante up. I'm beginning to think that kind of setting and experiences contributed to his hating women. Somehow." Skye shrugged when she noted the look in Josh's eyes. "You've seen what he does to their faces. It isn't a leap in logic. You add it all up, you have a wealthy nutcase, who thinks he's entitled for some reason. It might explain a few things."

"No argument there. But during his stint at Stanford, Frank got bored with his chemistry curriculum and began taking a slew of criminal science courses."

About that time, Harry came through the door, catching the last part of the conversation. "Wanted to be a cop, did he? Well, that pretty much fits the profile, too. I got your email, Josh. Thanks for the heads up. Sorry I kept you both waiting. But it seems your prime suspect, Frank De Palo, is indeed a mental case, officially. When he was sixteen he got into some serious trouble with a female classmate."

"Rape?" Skye frowned. "Our boy started young."

"You don't know the half of it," Harry stated. "His victim, a fifteen-year-old cheerleader accused him of rape all right. But with a twist. She said De Palo beat her senseless when all she did was question his taste in movies. Bashed her face in so badly, he put that girl in a coma for several weeks. When she finally woke up, and her parents learned who was responsible they insisted on pressing charges. But on the other end of the spectrum, Frank's parents thought the girl was simply going after the rich boy in town out of spite. They didn't believe her."

"So De Palo did time?" Skye asked, sending Josh an incredulous look. "You didn't get to that part yet."

Josh shook his head. "That's because De Palo didn't. He bypassed jail time due to Mommy's and Daddy's influence in the San Caruso community along with several glowing recommendations from Jasper March, Frank's Sunday school teachers, and camp sponsors. No fewer than ten upstanding citizens wrote the judge about what a terrific young man Frank was at the time—some bullshit about what a great youth counselor he'd been—what a terrific role model to the younger members of the congregation he was. To make sure their little darling didn't end up in prison, his parents agreed to a stint inside a cushy, private psych ward."

"You mean like rehab?" Skye noted.

"That's exactly right," Harry replied, tossing a file folder on the conference table. "He stayed there four lousy months and fell off the radar. At some point though his parents, Elena and Frank De Palo Sr., must've known their pride and joy was a little off."

"Because of the rape," Skye reasoned.

Josh traded looks with the detective. It was Josh who answered. "It goes a little further back than that. I told you Leo nosed around some. Turns out the folks who knew Frank best in his old haunt reported that little Frankie showed a dislike for the neighborhood cats. Any time Frankie was around, they disappeared in droves. It seems the little mental case liked to practice dismemberment from an early age. And get this. He frequently spent time on a farm his grandparents owned. He had access to any number of animals. God only knows what the boy practiced on while he was there."

"Ewww," Skye uttered. "That's a Jeffrey Dahmer trait. A lot of serial killers started out that way on animals."

"Bingo."

"Wonder why Frankie-boy didn't go all dissection on his victims here?" Skye wondered.

Again it was Josh who spoke up. "My theory is the dissection isn't what gets him off. While it's gruesome, this guy likes the power, the control of surprising a woman alone as she sleeps, ties her up, rapes her, then strangles her or slits her throat. Maybe he bashes her face in. Maybe he takes out his trusty knife if he really wants to make a statement. *That's* what gets him off. Killing and dissecting animals might've been what did it for him when he was eight, but not as an adult male with certain sexual urges," Josh finished. "The way he treats the women makes me wonder if the guy ever had a normal relationship with one. I'd bet he didn't."

"You're getting better at this, Josh," Skye remarked. "A lot better."

"Courtesy of very vivid dreams," Josh said while taking the time to study Harry's face. "If I were you, I'd check the same type of unsolved murders in and around the university during his college years. Skye's already found two in Portland that fit the same pattern and MO."

"You might've mentioned that, Skye," Harry grumbled. "I would've listened this time around."

"Good to know for the future, Harry. I kept my mouth shut that day we met with the FBI team because I could tell no one in that room wanted to hear about my half-baked theory. They didn't think it was relevant that Bianca and Lisa lived only four streets apart, in identical townhouses with the same floor plans. I found the layouts on the Internet. Turns out, I think you should contact the detectives who investigated their original cases and let them know."

"I'd say Frankie's been perfecting his method for a very long time. He went to grad school in Oregon. So, I'd go all the way back to the area there and then around Stanford where he did his undergraduate work. The man considers himself a brain and superior to the rest of us, even though what I saw him do to Tracy and Julie was more like the actions of a wild animal."

"Not just an animal, he's a coward," Skye said. "He sneaks in to confront a woman at her most vulnerable. Building up all this rage before the attack, then wham, he's armed with a freaking knife," Skye added. "What would make a man that angry? Surely it isn't because he hates his mother."

"Who knows? Who cares?" Harry pointed out, running a hand through his thinning hair. "Whatever it is, we have to catch this son of a bitch before he moves on. As Josh discovered he has the funds to fall off the map anywhere in the world."

"Any idea where we should start looking?" Skye wanted to know.

"He hasn't been seen at his luxury high-rise in over two weeks, which isn't a good sign he's still around. But Seattle PD put out an APB. It'll be on the early news and we've got his face plastered all over the Internet. That's including Facebook and Twitter," Harry added.

"Then let's hope we get lucky."

Skye waited until they got outside the police station. When they were walking to the car parked in the lot, she stopped and said, "Okay, what didn't you tell Harry back there? What are you holding back? You recited all the right things, even shared what you'd discovered about De Palo's background, told him about Leo in San Caruso. But what did you *not* tell Harry back there? And why?"

Josh grinned. "I love it when the mind meld works." He reached for her hand, kissed the palm. "When De Palo got fired from his job and got into MMA, he started training with Mick Hyatt."

"The fitness king? Well. If it turns out Frank De Palo is definitely our guy and Mick is linked to him, the fitness guru might need to find a new turf. But Harry must already know about Hyatt. That isn't what you held back in there, Josh."

"No, it isn't, because Hyatt's been missing now for several days. His wife reported that he left for work as usual and hasn't been seen since."

"You think Frank did something to him?"

"It's entirely possible. Either that or Mick ran off with his longtime mistress. But there's no evidence of that. The thing is, Leo emailed me this morning right before the meeting. He discovered the De Palos, Elena and Frank Sr., haven't been seen or heard from in eight years. Eight years, Skye. They disappeared off the San Caruso scene and no one seems to know where they went."

"Maybe they went back to Italy, Josh. Did you think of that?"

"For that long? I don't think so. Think about the message we've been getting, over and over again."

Skye stopped walking and turned to gape at him. "You think those are *the bones* in question? You think *that* has something to do with Elena and Frank Sr.?"

"Yeah. Are you up for a road trip?"

Skye cracked a smile. "If that road trip means you want to go to San Caruso and poke around Frank's old stomping ground to find these bones, then I'm in. When do we leave?"

Chapter Twenty-Three

Trying to book a flight out to little San Caruso posed a problem. So Josh leased a corporate jet to fly them down to the tiny town squeezed up against the Pacific Ocean. With less than fifteen thousand residents, the nearest airport, turned out to be nothing more than a landing strip. Most of the clientele seemed to be business travelers who either owned small aircraft or their own jets, or leased helicopters to fly back and forth to seven-figure jobs.

Leo Martin was waiting for them outside the one and only hangar.

The programmer wasn't at all what Skye expected. For one thing, Leo couldn't have been more than twenty. Tall and gangly, he had dark, chestnut-brown hair that draped past his shoulders in dreadlocks. Two gold earrings hung from each lobe. Leo looked more like a drummer than a hacker. According to Josh, Leo had been recruited by Todd Graham right off the floor of the Underground Hackers Convention. At the time the sixteen-year-old had turned Todd down cold using the excuse that he'd never been much of a joiner. So Todd had managed to talk the kid into a sometime-contractor gig at Ander All Games.

"I spent yesterday beating the bushes hunting down former neighbors. I didn't have a chance yet to drive out to the De Palo estate. To be honest, I didn't want to go out there alone," Leo admitted.

"I don't understand," Skye said. "Josh said you talked to his neighbors."

Leo traded glances with Josh. "It's a little complicated. The De Palos own about a dozen houses all over the county. Frank still takes care of most of them. Some of them he now rents out. But it wasn't always that way. When Frank was much younger, the De Palos kept four homes for their personal use. I've checked out three of those because Josh had me focus on the ones in San Caruso near all the schools Frank attended—primary, middle school, and high school. But the De Palos' main place of residence is located about twenty miles out of town in an unincorporated part of Monterey County where Frank spent his summers. And because the school district didn't offer bus service at the time that far away, the family stayed in town during the school year so Frank could walk to school. I haven't been out to this other place yet. Rumor has it the place is spooky. People tell me it's been abandoned for years. I'm assuming that's where we're headed now."

"You assume correctly," Josh said. "And you found nothing of interest in the other homes?"

"Not a thing out of place if that's what you mean. I got a realtor to show me around inside one because it's been on the market for at least six years."

Skye turned to stare at Leo. "That's a long time for it to be for sale. Is there something wrong with it?"

"Other than the asking price of just under three million? Not a thing that I could see. But the realtor pointed out all the De Palo houses share one unique feature, one thing in common." Leo hid a grin, waited a beat.

"Unique? How so?"

"Where I come from we call them basements, but around here they refer to what the De Palos added on to each house as bunkers, huge extensions beneath the first floors. All the houses they own have 'em."

"You mean like survivalists?" Josh asked.

"That's the impression I got. Yeah. I did mention the De Palos believed that the end of the world was just around the corner, didn't I?" Leo clarified.

"Interesting," Skye noted as she and Josh started loading up the stuff they'd brought with them, like their laptops and the one suitcase they'd packed, into the trunk of the full-sized Chevy Impala Leo had rented two days before.

Josh crawled behind the wheel while Skye rode shotgun, leaving Leo to settle for the backseat.

Once they got on the road, even with the GPS, Josh had a difficult time locating the rural address. "What is it with this place?" Josh grumbled as he took another detour down one more country road.

"Tax records come up with a three-thousand-square-foot ranch house essentially out in the boonies," Leo explained as he continued to refer to notes he'd taken and saved to his tablet. "According to public records, the property is like a maze to locate. According to gossip the De Palos did that on purpose so no one could easily find them."

"Sounds like they were afraid of something."

"I think the mother was pretty much afraid of just about everything," Leo added.

"Figures," Skye said.

"That's only one reason the family was considered oddities for years."

"I've got news for you, Leo. Their son is one for the books," Skye stated matter-of-factly.

Josh drove for miles and miles, past picturesque hiking and nature trails among the rolling hills and mountains in the distance to reach what appeared to be an agricultural hotspot.

Skye pointed out several thriving farms along the way where strawberries or pumpkins grew. They drove past a field of purple lavender, and noted the apple and apricot orchards laden down with fruit. When Skye spotted a deer gnawing on a field of clover and grass, she made Josh pull the car over to the side of the road until the animal darted off.

"I had no idea this area would be so full of wildlife."

"Well, it might've had a chance to flourish with Frank grown now and not a threat to the local wild kingdom."

"That's a sick thought," Skye uttered. "But probably true. We must've landed in California's fertile growing fields."

"San Caruso and the surrounding areas for about a hundred miles to the north and east are nothing but small farms owned by individuals or a conglomerate of the big agricultural outfits. There's not really an in-between. The De Palo family owns a sizeable chunk in several fruit-canning facilities," Leo explained. "Hence all the groves around here."

"Once you leave the coast, the hot Mediterranean climate and the flat valley coming together make for a perfect environment to grow just about everything from nuts to fruits and vegetables," Josh said.

"But at this point, with everything we've discovered about little Frankie, this part of the county doesn't jibe with the sophisticated millionaire who lives in a high-rise condo and pretends he's better than everyone else. He had to hate it here where he grew up," Skye said. "Even with all that money in the bank."

"I'm sure that's true. Frank's probably ashamed of where he came from, wishes it were someplace else less country, and refuses to admit this is home," Josh said in agreement.

With Skye reading the map and relaying directions, they finally turned down a dusty dirt road that was indeed out in the middle of nowhere. They'd left the valley and the fields behind to reach the only house on the overgrown lane. A one-story, sprawling ranch-style house sat at the end of a cul-de-sac badly in need of some new pavement. The house had obviously once been a showplace, but now required a lot of TLC to bring it back to the way it had looked in its prime.

Rechecking the address against what Leo had found in public records, Skye realized this neglected piece of property had to be the land that belonged to Elena and Frank De Palo Sr. and where young Frank had spent his holidays and summers.

Josh pulled up to the entrance of the sprawling estate. A pair of double iron gates and a rock wall blocked anyone from entering the grounds.

Josh wasn't a happy camper when he had to crawl out of the car in order to deal with the heavy chain wrapped several times around the ironwork. At the end of the links were three rusty but sturdy padlocks dangling from the loop. He picked one up and pointed out, "The elements certainly have taken a toll on these. It tells me this place has been locked up a while, I'd say for years."

"Someone wants to make sure they keep out visitors or the curious," Skye declared. "Want me to distract Leo while you make good use of your super wolf-like strength in order to get us past these locks?" she said with a bob of her head toward Leo who still sat in the backseat.

Josh dazzled her with a smile. He too glanced back at Leo, saw the guy was fixated with whatever his tablet held onscreen. With that, Josh ripped the iron chain from the rusty locks.

Skye shook her head. "That nerdy geek I saved in the alleyway that night has turned into a man of steel. Avoid kryptonite 'cause it's a power zapper for sure."

"I don't think I'm ready to find out what zaps my power for real."

Skye made a face. "I didn't mean…that's a sobering thought," she added and not one she wanted to dwell on at the moment. As they got back into the car to drive up to the house they both got a better view of the place.

Built in 1955, the De Palo estate had been designed with that atomic ranch look so popular during the era. Skye could see the architect had most likely fused California flair with a bold Italian influence to come up with the best use of wood and stone. The long, low roofline, the steep angular eaves, all the glass, the boxy shape, and the two fat fireplaces at each end gave way to classic midcentury style.

As soon as Josh came to a stop, her gaze landed on the double front doors. For the first time since they'd arrived in Monterey County, a funny feeling crawled up her spine. It wasn't the reaction she wanted. Nineteen-fifties architecture aside, there was a "presence" here she could feel, almost taste. And she didn't like it. "There's something not right about this, Josh. I know the tax records show Frank De Palo still owns the property but it doesn't appear anyone's lived here for years. Why would his parents leave their home?"

"It's hard to fall off the radar these days. I can't find any credit card or bank activity for either one of them. Since both aren't yet old enough to receive Social Security, there's no way to track them by the checks they might be receiving at some other address."

"Do multi-millionaires bother to apply for Social Security?" Leo wondered aloud from the backseat.

"Some do. Look, before we go any further, there's something I need to know. Are both of you okay with us breaking and entering to get inside?"

"You know how I feel," Skye answered. "We went over all this on the plane. I didn't make this trip all the way from Seattle to sit in the car and wait while you and Leo take the tour yourselves. We need to know if your hunch is correct. If this is our guy, we need answers now, not wait until another five or six more women have to die before we do something about it." To prove her point, she opened the car door.

For his answer, Leo did the same. He crawled out of the backseat. "I'm in. I didn't wade through the dynamics of this little town for two days to sit on the sidelines now."

"Okay, but depending on what we find inside, it's a whole new ballgame from here if what we suspect is true. If it turns out there's evidence in there that Frank started his killing here with dear old Mom and Dad, we're all in it deep."

"Look, let's just take one room at a time and see what happens. There are three of us. We can spread out and cover more ground or we can stick together," Skye suggested.

"I say we stick together," Leo offered, a little unease starting to creep in.

"Okay, but we still have to get inside first. And we'll need a few things," Skye reasoned as she went around to the back of the Chevy, waited for Josh to pop open the trunk. When he did, she reached in, unzipped the bag they'd brought containing their clothes. She dug around until she pulled out a flashlight. Skye looked at Josh. "You may see perfectly well in the dark these days what with having your '*Lasik surgery*' and all," she said convincingly for Leo's benefit. "But the rest of us require a beam of light now and again."

"You brought a flashlight?" Before she could answer, Josh reached over, yanked her up off the dirt and into a kiss. "I love a woman who thinks ahead and comes prepared."

"Yeah, well, I'm used to perusing dark streets and I forgot the night vision goggles."

He grinned. "Come on, I'm gonna try to find another way in."

"Why don't you just say you're looking around for which window would be the best one to break?" Skye countered.

Josh took her arm and pulled her around to the back of the house. He motioned for Leo to follow. "Maybe we'll get lucky and find one that's already unlocked or a pane of glass that's cracked."

The trio entered a large overgrown backyard with shrubs and vines that didn't look they like had been trimmed or cut back for years. Bugs and spiders hid in the knee-high weeds and underbrush as they pushed their way through to get to more hedges and dense undergrowth.

They finally came to an open area where a lagoon-design swimming pool took up at least half the lawn. The concrete hole hadn't seen water in at least a decade. But algae residue left behind told them what they already knew. The entire property had fallen to neglect and hard times a long time ago.

And nobody had seemed to care.

Getting inside the house though, proved easier than they expected, when Josh located a bedroom window with the screen already removed and a faulty lock that didn't catch because the metal had been worn down.

"Isn't that odd? Maybe someone's already used this window once before to enter when they weren't supposed to be here," Skye suggested.

"That makes no sense. Why would Frank need to break into his own house?"

"Who said it was Frank? Someone could've suspected something years ago and come in through this way to check it out."

"That's a scary thought," Leo tossed out. "How many bodies are we looking for anyway?"

"Let's hope none. But we at least need to check this place off the list first, and see if we can find out what happened to Elena and Frank Senior. Right now, that's what we think. The couple is here—somewhere." Josh pushed up the glass, and went through the frame first. A dank, musty smell hit him almost immediately. "Stay here while I go unlock the back door."

"Not me," Skye said. "Where you go, I go," she reiterated as she leveraged herself up and Josh pulled her the rest of the way through the window.

Leo reluctantly followed by crawling through the opening.

After dusting off her jeans, Skye looked around the room at the lime green and gold décor that looked like it hadn't been upgraded since the 1970s. "Wow, talk about retro."

Josh went over and opened the closet door. "Women's clothing, men's suits, still on hangers."

Skye pulled open a couple of dresser drawers. "Same with the underwear and socks. Wherever they went, they traveled mighty light."

"They never packed. A seven-piece set of matching Samsonite is still stored here in a layer of dust covering the leather," Josh said before picking up a man's Rolex still on the nightstand. "This watch must be twenty years old, ran out of battery life a long time ago."

"That's a brand-new mattress on this bed," Skye pointed out. "It looks as though it's right out of the showroom. Come on. We need to check out the rest of this crypt because I'm beginning to think your hunch is right on the money."

With that, Skye left the bedroom and progressed down a long hallway, checking out each room as she went.

But while the three of them took the tour around the rambling single-story home, a foul odor kept nagging in the air as strong as solid waste. As soon as they reached the back part of the house, the smell grew worse.

The stench was so overpowering, Skye looked around to see Leo's face turn green right before he looked like he wanted to puke.

"Look guys, I hate to bail on you but I can't take this smell. I've always had a weak stomach. I've gotta have some fresh air," Leo mumbled.

"Head outside then," Josh told the kid. "You might as well use the front door. We'll take it from here." Josh turned to make sure Skye was okay with that. "Right?"

She nodded as she watched Leo take off for the front of the house and all but scurry outside. "I might want to gag but I'm not leaving you in here alone. You getting anything?" she wanted to know.

"Oh yeah. That disgusting odor is the same as in my vision, the one I had that night after the sweat lodge. I've never gotten past the way Kiya made sure I could recognize the scent."

"There's something evil here," Skye determined after taking in another shallow inhale of the fetid air. "Let's get this show on the road. Kiya, where are you? Take us to what it is you want us to see."

About that time the wolf began to take shape and then shifted into a physical animal. Kiya sniffed the air and trotted toward the area just off the kitchen, stopped when she reached a door. The wolf pawed at the wood first, and then sat, waiting.

"Please tell me that doesn't lead down to the basement," Skye uttered with a certain amount of dread gathering in her throat making it difficult to speak.

"You mean the bunker," Josh corrected as he turned the handle. The door creaked back to bump the wall. The odor of decomposition hit him in such measures that it devastated the sinuses. Josh eyed the look on Skye's face, the sick green color that matched Leo's. "You want to stay up here? It's fine by me."

"At the risk of being labeled a wuss, I believe I do. But like I said before, I'm not letting you do this alone. Kiya, you take point. We'll follow." Skye hefted the flashlight and said, "Let's go."

Josh sucked in a breath as Kiya took off down the stairs. "Any presence down there has more than likely had the life drained out of it a long time ago."

"That's certainly making me feel better, Josh. Not."

"Sorry. Let's just get this over with."

Josh followed Kiya, then Skye trailed behind both of them, shining the light as she went. But about halfway down, something made her stop. It wasn't that the stairs were scary or that the smell made her gag. That ship had already sailed. But the further down she went into the darkness, the image from her vision flashed into her brain. She knew then, with one hundred percent certainty what lay within the walls, somewhere in that basement. And she wasn't sure she wanted to be a part of it.

Ahead of her, Josh got the same sense and held up his hand. He waved her away. "I get you. Now go back, Skye.

This is totally unnecessary for you to do this. *This* is what Kiya wants *me* to see. For a reason."

"Are you sure?"

"Positive. Now head back upstairs."

"Okay. But Josh?"

"What?"

"Be careful."

"You know I will. I've got Kiya."

Grudgingly she dashed back up the steps. As soon as she reached the top, she yelled back down, "Just because I'm not down there with you doesn't mean you shouldn't feel free to give me the play-by-play."

But Josh had already disappeared into the cavern of the basement and whatever loomed in its dark belly.

Josh followed Kiya into an open area that could only be described as opulent survivalist style. Oak flooring was the first clue. The computer station complete with desk was the second. An eating area consisted of a table with six chairs accessorized in leather seats—something one didn't expect to see in a shelter built for the end of the world.

A generously-sized kitchen had been outfitted with all the home appliances needed during an apocalypse. Storage bins held every variety of canned goods along with a supply of military MREs enough to last a year and maybe beyond through any major natural disaster.

After checking out two bathrooms with working toilets, one on each end of the length of the house, Josh veered off the main room to where three separate sleeping areas had been partitioned off by thin walls for privacy. Each contained a comfy queen-sized bed.

Circling back to the living area, Josh noticed a TV set covered with cobwebs. It had once been designated for double duty—one to get news of the impending doom to come—and two to act as a security monitor.

Outfitting the entire bunker had to cost a cool million, Josh decided as he turned to Kiya. "Where do we look? Show me where you want me to start."

The wolf trotted over to another supply room off the kitchen. In the back beside a crapload of medical supplies, Josh spotted a wire rack. An assortment of animal heads lined the shelves. Some were stored in jars. "No doubt Frank's personal trophy room as a child. Okay, now we're getting warmer."

Kiya suddenly reversed her course to head over to an area Josh had missed. She pawed at a newly plastered section of sheetrock next to a generator and a washer and dryer. This time, Josh could tell it was fresher than the rest of the wall because no one had bothered slapping paint here.

He looked around for anything he could use to bash in the drywall. A sledgehammer would've come in handy right about now, he thought. When he found nothing but a broom, he simply kicked through the gypsum with his foot. It didn't take long for him to realize it was a phony wall. It took him a few minutes longer to completely knock away all the plasterboard.

Behind the jagged panels were three sets of mummified remains, complete with grotesque-looking skulls similar to those one might see in a horror movie.

The skulls stared back at him just like in his dream.

At one time, the bodies had been propped up inside their tomb in a space no larger than five feet across and back. What clothes Josh could make out were in tatters. One body, with longer auburn hair still attached, a female by the look of the hair, appeared to be wearing a flowing blue nightgown. A white shirt and blue jeans hung loosely on the bones of the second set of skeletal remains in the middle. The third skull had graying black hair still visible, a pair of pale blue pajamas draped over the bones.

There was enough difference in the decomposition of the man placed in the middle so that Josh could tell he'd been added well after the other two.

On closer inspection, when Josh leaned his head into the opening, he spotted the bullet holes in each skull. Cocking his head, he noticed a crumpled piece of paper, wadded up next to the feet of the woman. Gingerly, he stuck his hand in and snatched up what was now as brittle as parchment.

Carefully Josh unfolded what looked like a legal document. Reading over the words, paragraph by paragraph, it explained a lot.

❧ ❧ ❧ ❧

Fifteen long minutes went by and had Skye pacing at the top with her shirt covering her nose and mouth. All this time, she'd heard nothing except the house settling. Nerves edged up, starting at her fingertips and ran along her arms. Finally she inched toward the dimly lit landing again. Still met with an eerie, hollow silence, she finally shouted down into the vast darkness, "Josh, come on, answer me."

Skye held her breath, her hand over her nose, trying to deal with the stench that seemed to get worse all of a sudden. As she continued to peer into the basement, she saw no movement, not even a shadow. "Come on, Josh. Don't make me come down there."

"You sound like my mother," Josh finally returned as he climbed the stairs with Kiya in the lead. "Stop right where you are. You don't want to come down here, Skye."

"What's wrong? What is it?"

"Frank's own personal hellhole."

❧ ❧ ❧ ❧

Josh guided Skye out of the house and onto the front porch, describing what he'd seen as he went. "Someone walled up Elena and Frank Senior. Looks like they didn't offer much in the way of resistance. By the looks of their clothes, I'd say they were shot in their sleep. Who the other guy is though, is anyone's guess."

"*The bones will tell*," Skye muttered. "Something definitive, something tangible, that links directly back to Frank. That's what Kiya wanted us to know."

Josh nodded. "Those bones tell us exactly what we needed. Frank's a sick bastard and has been for a very long time."

"How do we explain being here, Josh?"

"I'd like to know that myself," Leo added from the bottom step, his face only a slightly lesser shade of green than it had been an hour earlier.

"The only way we can. We call the Monterey County Sheriff's office, tell them we were looking for the De Palos and suggest they call Drummond in Seattle. Hopefully, Harry will be able to talk us out of this mess."

"Sounds like a plan. But Harry's gonna be pissed when he finds out we held back coming here."

"I love it when you use 'we' at a time like this. But since I'm the one who did the holding back, I'll take the heat for all of it."

"And I love it when you offer to do that. But if Harry doesn't know us both by now, if he doesn't trust us to do the job we're getting paid to do then we have a problem with him in the future. We need to know it now. You *saw* this, didn't you, Josh? All of it."

"Yeah, I did. But this is all still very new to me, Skye. I needed to experience this, the stuff that came to me in the dreams, the visions, for myself, up close and personal. It's a validation. It's what Kiya wanted me to know from the beginning. Just like she did to you each time you saved one of those girls. Besides you, who would've believed me?"

"I know exactly how you feel."

About that time, Josh looked around at just how far the house was from the nearest neighbor. He took out his cell phone only to see he had no service. "Anyone have a signal?"

"Nope," Leo said. "At one point, I even walked down to the gate. Still nothing."

"Nor me," Skye echoed, checking her phone. "What now?"

"Then I guess we haul ass out of here and call the cops as soon as we get one."

"I don't understand," Skye asked the first sheriff's deputy on the scene, a thirty-something guy named Vince Hogue. "Why didn't anyone in San Caruso bother to look for Elena and Frank De Palo Senior before now? How is it no one knew they were dead years ago? You guys didn't even know they were missing."

The deputy narrowed his eyes. "There are reasons for that. For one thing, they were reclusive. After Frank left for college, they stayed out here away from town, never came into San Caruso much. I'll be honest, that was fine with most people. Over the years their attitude had managed to wear pretty thin on folks. They were known to feud with just about everyone in town at one time or another over some silly dispute. Frank Senior even took it a step further a time or two and sued. That caused hard feelings up and down Main Street. In some instances, it caused the townsfolk to lose their paychecks to millionaires who didn't care about anyone else but themselves."

"So we aren't talking about people who were missed?" Josh said.

Hogue nodded. "That's right. To my way of thinking, it was an out of sight, out of mind kind of thing. If Frank Senior and Elena stopped coming into town at some point, I guess no one really cared, hence no one bothered making the trip out here to see what was going on. Besides, if anything was wrong, Frank should've let us know. Now, we understand why he didn't. I think the only other person who ever asked about them over the years was some tax attorney out of San Francisco—a guy who showed up here out of the blue one weekend nosing around."

Josh cocked a brow. "You might want to check to see if he ever made it back to the Bay Area. I'd bet money he didn't."

"Come to think of it, I do seem to remember getting a call that said he'd gone missing. I just assumed he'd run off with a woman or something. Never heard another thing about it, so I thought he turned up. You know those tax attorneys like to live off other people's money. They eventually have to go on the run for some reason or another."

"Maybe this lawyer is the one who broke into the house and used that window we found where the lock had been tampered with," Skye pointed out. "Maybe Frank caught this guy snooping around and killed him, too."

Josh turned to Hogue. "I know Frank got into some trouble when he was sixteen after beating and raping a cheerleader. Do you know if there are any unsolved murders of other young women in the area that go back to say, when De Palo lived here as a teen?"

"We don't get many murders around here," Hogue objected in a defensive tone. But then he cocked his head as if considering the town's history. He scratched his jaw. "Wait a minute, now that I think back to when I first joined the sheriff's department some thirteen years ago, seems to me we do have a couple that remain unsolved. One was a ten-year-old by the name of Cheryl Wittingham. Someone took a baseball bat and bashed in her skull. Volunteers found her the same night her parents reported her missing. She'd been left in a culvert over on Jackson Street. The other was fourteen-year-old Denise Holland. A seasonal fruit picker found her body 'bout a mile from the old winery outside town. She'd been beaten around the face and strangled. Hey, you don't suppose Frank De Palo could've killed them, do you? He'd have been just a kid when those murders happened."

"Did he know either girl?"

Hogue rubbed his chin. "Seems like I remember the report mentioning Frank might've known the Holland girl in school. And little Cheryl lived down the street from the De Palo family on Lawnview." Hogue looked around. "Not this house out here, one of the other De Palo houses they owned in town close to the middle school. Holy cow, wouldn't that be something if we could solve two fifteen-year-old homicides."

About that time it looked as though the entire Monterey County Sheriff's Department pulled down the dusty lane and headed straight for them. Skye watched as several vehicles came to a screeching stop.

Skye, Josh, and Leo stood off to one side and watched law enforcement descend on Frank's childhood home, or one of them.

"If it's been eight years since the parents were alive, that was about the same time Frank lived in Portland, gainfully employed, I might add," Leo pointed out.

"Which means what?" Skye asked. "Josh and I already figured he's probably good for killing Bianca and Lisa while he lived there."

"You might want to include a woman by the name of Meaghan Riddick in that," Leo suggested. "Frank's co-worker?"

"Go on," Skye prompted.

"Meaghan ended up dead while Frank lived there. Co-workers said she often went head to head with Frank over projects they shared."

"This guy's body count is giving me the willies," Skye reiterated. "How did Meaghan die?"

"In Meaghan's case, the coroner said she killed herself, had a lethal dose of meth in her system. Her death was ruled a suicide so it didn't show up, officially, in any police reports you might've found, Skye. But her friends and family disputed that the scientist ever cooked meth let alone ingested it."

"Interesting. What did you mean earlier, Leo? When you said Frank was gainfully employed at the time his parents were murdered? Why is that important?" Skye stressed.

"I think what Leo was getting at is that Frank didn't do it for the money," Josh stated. "He didn't kill his parents for their fortune. If you're thinking that for motive, Leo checked. Frank's never had money problems. He doesn't have an ugly addiction to crack. He doesn't have a gambling problem. In fact, his personal net worth, without his parents around, is probably in excess of eight million dollars in liquid assets. His part of the De Palo family money he got from his grandfather. I'd say his parents didn't have a cash-on-hand problem either, since their net worth totals just under twenty million. Think about it, Frank was their sole heir and yet, he never reported them missing or dead. There was never a probate hearing. Shooting Mom and Dad wasn't about an inheritance."

"You want to fill us in on what else you found?" Skye said. "Because I know you've got something you haven't shared."

"How do you guys keep doing that?" Leo asked. "How do you seem to pick up on things?"

Skye just grinned. "It's a knack. Or Josh calls it our own mind meld trick," she said with a wink.

Josh took out the crumpled piece of paper he'd found in the De Palos' burial chamber from his pocket. "This is a commitment order—from a judge. His parents were about to have their very sicko son committed to a private mental hospital in San Diego."

Skye's mouth fell open. "They knew and were about to lock him up. They knew their son was a sick bastard all these years ago."

"Seems they did. Like Harry said, probably as far back as childhood. Their first clue had to be when animals in the neighborhood began to go missing. More than likely after that, they discovered their son's private stash of trophies and remains. There are jars lined up on a shelf down in one room of the basement. Since the display is right there in plain sight, the parents had to know about Frank's penchant for dismemberment," Josh reasoned.

"Geez, if we don't stop this guy his body count could work its way up to the Green River killer's."

Josh walked over to give the commitment paper to Hogue before turning back to Skye and Leo. "It may be a personal goal to outdo Ridgway," Josh suggested. "And that's why we're going to find a way to stop him."

Skye and Josh and Leo had to hang around San Caruso another couple of days to answer any other questions from the sheriff's department. In the meantime, crime scene investigators descended upon the house out in the middle of nowhere and literally tore the place apart looking for any more victims. They found none except the three bodies in the bunker. It would take some time to positively identify the remains but speculation said it was Frank's parents and the missing lawyer.

Skye communicated daily with Harry and kept him in the loop. But as soon as it became apparent that they were no longer needed in San Caruso, they packed up and flew back to Seattle wondering what the rest of autumn would bring in the way of more victims.

They knew one thing for certain, Frank De Palo would not stop killing on his own. Whether he remained in Washington State or had moved on had yet to be determined. It put everyone on edge.

Frank had not left the country.

In fact, he hadn't even left Washington State but he had scurried off the mainland. He had been forced to go underground since the revelation two days earlier that he was the prime suspect in the murders of his parents *and* their longtime attorney, George Sidwell.

Eight years back dedicated George had made the mistake of leaving his San Francisco home early one Saturday morning to check on the De Palos. Because George hadn't heard from the couple in months, curiosity got the better of him. He'd driven down to San Caruso to find out why the couple had not returned his phone calls.

The thirty-seven-year-old single lawyer had disappeared that weekend. Even though George's girlfriend had filed a missing person report at the time, the authorities had never been able to locate him or his car. No one had ever heard from George Sidwell again after his trip south to San Caruso.

Frank hadn't concerned himself much with his father's loyal attorney until the nosy bastard had showed up on the very Saturday Frank had been tidying the place up. Sidwell had even had the audacity to crawl in through a window.

As Frank saw it, Sidwell hadn't given him much of a choice. He'd taken care of the tax lawyer in the same manner he'd used to get rid of his parents.

It had been a betrayal, pure and simple, when Frank learned his parents had already gone to a judge to get a commitment order. Frank still couldn't figure out how his parents had discovered he'd killed Meaghan Riddick, his bitch of a co-worker back in Portland.

But somehow they had. And on his visit back to California, they'd confronted him with the details which meant they'd probably hired someone to follow him around Portland for months. And not for the first time, Frank realized. They were always sticking their noses where they didn't belong. They hadn't asked him about the mental hospital. They'd *told* him. There was no way Frank would agree to be locked up ever again. The first time he was sixteen, too young to know the ramifications, although at the time it was better than prison. That time he'd let them put him away inside a mental ward to *study* him for four months. But he'd learned then and there how to work the system, how to play the game, what answers to give that would appease the doctors for early release. Eight years ago, he had no intentions of letting his damn mother do it to him again. When his mother said she wanted to put him away for an indeterminate amount of time, Frank lost it. That night, after they'd gone to sleep, he crept into their bedroom armed with his father's own Mossberg, auto-loading, hunting rifle, and put an end to their scheming once and for all.

No one could possibly have blamed him for it.

So for the last two days, Frank had been holed up at the cabin on San Juan Island, the one he'd bought five years earlier for just this purpose, the one on Friday Harbor, using the name James Silver. Since the place wasn't connected to the mainland by bridge, he'd boarded his sixty-foot yacht and motored over in the middle of the night.

At dawn, he'd packed up what he could haul on his back and trekked some five miles over rough terrain to the cabin. He didn't really believe for one minute they'd ever catch him. But like any skilled tactician, Frank always had a plan B to cover "what if" scenarios. Now was no exception. If need be, he could get out of the country using the small plane he kept at the Friday Harbor Airport registered to Marco Silva, another of his aliases. So if that time ever presented itself, if he ever thought law enforcement was closing in, he had his escape hatch at the ready.

The knowledge that the woman and her companion had invaded his family's home back in San Caruso and found out his most personal secrets, discovered his trophies from childhood infuriated him. No woman would ever be part of beating him at his own game.

That meant he'd have to do something about Skye Cree along with that slow-witted, snotty-nosed geek she hung around with.

How the two had ever connected the dots back to his hometown, he didn't know. But he must've missed a step somewhere. It had to have something to do with his entering the Ander loft. The minute the asshole discovered the cameras he'd left behind, from there, things had gone downhill.

His perfect world had almost come crashing down because of them. Not fifteen hours earlier, he'd been positively identified by every local news channel from Vancouver to Portland as the "person of interest" in the string of Seattle homicide cases.

With one newscast, his life at MMA had burned to black toast. He was losing everything that meant anything to him, everything he'd painstakingly put together, built since he left that crappy biotech job in Portland.

For chrissakes, Frank De Palo had fans, a following who adored him in the octagon. He owned two cars, a BMW and a no-frills black pickup he drove when he went out for "death night".

And if he lost everything, it was the fault of that meddling bitch and her fuck-buddy.

He'd wanted a showdown with Skye Cree and Josh Ander, didn't he? He would give them one they wouldn't forget. He could take them both. He was certain of it. No way would he let a computer geek or a female win. Not only that, but Frank had no intention of being locked up in a cell for the rest of his life. He'd die before he let that happen.

So, he'd bide his time. He'd settle the score with Ander and the Cree woman and then head to Canada using the aliases he'd manufactured for himself. Once there, he'd lie low until he could make his way to the Persian Gulf, specifically Dubai, known around the world as the Las Vegas of the Middle East. With a long list of trendy nightclubs, modern buildings that glistened in the sun— and a string of private islands at his disposal—it would be like being on holiday twenty-four-seven.

He couldn't wait to get there.

But first, he would take care of the Cree bitch.

And one thing Frank knew how to do well was track his prey. Once he got a victim in his sights, they rarely got away. Okay, maybe once in all these years, he'd slipped and let it happen. But that was a fluke. He didn't intend to repeat the mistake.

After all, he'd been trailing Skye Cree for weeks. He knew she went out every night. That might be the perfect venue to exact his revenge. Wait in some dark alleyway for her to walk down and surprise her. But it wasn't the setting he preferred. No, when he took down Skye Cree it would be the place of his choosing, a place where he could control the environment—and the woman.

There was no reason to panic, none at all.

Frank knew how to win. He left nothing to chance. And he knew how to make that chance count.

Chapter Twenty-Four

The police may have thought their killer had left the area but Skye and Josh knew better.

Despite Leo, Winston, and Reggie digging into Frank's history as far back as high school, they couldn't pinpoint a financial footprint. They had been unable to track any credit and debit card use. There had been zero activity using any of his million-dollar bank balances. It meant that Frank had likely gone covert using one or more aliases he'd created years before, along with having a string of IDs and other accounts that had no connection to Frank De Palo whatsoever.

"I hate to say this, Josh, but I think we might've hit a dead end here," Reggie admitted one afternoon inside the conference room at Ander All Games where the trio had set up shop. As the twenty-two-year-old graduate of Cal Poly pounded on his Mac's keys, he added, "The three of us have crawled up this guy's ass every which way we can financially and found no activity for the past week. None."

"That isn't to say we won't keep tabs on his accounts. But it appears he's shrewd enough not to leave a trail. He knows we're watching him online, and he's using nothing we can trace," Leo added.

"But remember," nineteen-year-old Winston reminded Josh, as he caught the bug in a line of code and zapped it, "If he gets anywhere within a hundred feet of our dummy Wi-Fi network, and his cell phone is set up to search, we'll be able to track his digital signature without his ever knowing it."

"But what's the likelihood of that really happening?" Josh asked Winston, who'd been coding since he was fourteen. "Let's face it. It's a one in a million shot. I'd hate to hang everything we have on whether or not he searches for a local Wi-Fi network."

"It's a safety net, Josh," Leo countered. "In the event he gets close. It might just be the very thing that captures his location. You never know."

But it was nothing more than a longshot and Josh knew it.

For that reason, he and Skye doubled their efforts to come up with a plan of their own. In order to lure the serial killer out of his lair, they figured you had to give him a good enough reason to crawl out of the hole.

They bounced ideas off each other by brainstorming about it.

"We could do what one of the FBI profilers suggested doing, insult his intelligence."

"Might take too long. What about playing to his vanity?"

"Okay. So we plant a couple of stories on the Internet about how he's too clever for law enforcement and everyone else involved. We'll tell him how much better he is than Bundy or Ridgway. How long do you think that would take? First, he'd have to see it."

"Are you kidding? I bet the guy's spending practically all his waking hours online monitoring every news article and post. But if you don't like that idea, it only leaves one option."

"We challenge the bastard."

"Exactly."

Over the next several days they set up a training area in one of the spare bedrooms of the loft. They replaced all the bedroom furniture with a line of state-of-the-art gym equipment. They protected the hardwood flooring by adding platform mats guaranteed to cushion knockdowns as they went through their workouts.

Once they settled on an approach they could agree on, they revised their angle, and then went over it again and again trying to perfect every facet—until it seemed they were getting on each other's last nerve.

Landing hard on her butt during a particularly difficult maneuver, Skye came up swinging. "You did that on purpose."

"Your timing is all wrong," Josh shot back.

"If you'd stick to what we rehearsed instead of improvising every time I turn around we might make some progress," Skye grumbled. "In spite of all your fancy gadgets, you still can't fight worth a damn."

"Who is it that's sitting on her ass? Maybe if you'd stop criticizing everything I do for longer than ten damn minutes we could get this show on the road," Josh snapped.

"Oh really? So you're saying I'm the reason this stupid idea isn't taking off?"

"An hour ago you didn't think it was that stupid."

"Well, now I do. Besides, if I'm such a nag, then maybe I should pack up my stuff and head back to my own apartment."

"You've been looking for an excuse to do that for months now."

"I have not."

"Yes. You have. You've been dragging your feet for weeks now about making a commitment with me. I asked you to marry me and what did you do? You stood there staring back at me—like a deer that wanted to take off running at the first opportunity."

"You surprised me. That's all."

"Oh I could tell that by the stricken look on your face. It's exactly what every guy wants to see in the eyes of the woman he loves."

"As proposals go, it wasn't the best setting. Plus, your timing wasn't that great."

"I see. So you wanted candlelight, a nice dinner out, a ring maybe? Is that what you're saying? Oh wait, because a guy usually does that when he's at least ninety percent sure he'll get a positive response. Besides, that's a whole lot disingenuous on your part."

"What's that supposed to mean?"

"You know damn well what it means. I'd suggested marriage before and couldn't get you to talk about it then either. As I recall, the last time I brought it up, you couldn't roll off me fast enough before taking that literal step away."

"I'm so glad to know this is how you really feel. I'll just get my stuff and go."

"So who's stopping you? Don't expect me to run after you this time because you certainly don't want to be here with me. Go back to that little dump you call an apartment."

"Fine. At least I'm not a pretentious asshole who has to order all this gear instead of just heading down to Travis's place to work out like any normal person would do."

"You call landing on concrete normal? I'm thinking of you since you spend so much time down there on the mat these days."

"Kiss my ass!" And with that, she stormed off to gather up her things, at least what she could carry. She couldn't wait to get out of the man's house.

෴ ෴ ෴ ෴

There were advantages to being back in her own space, having her familiar things around her. She cooked dinner in her little galley kitchen, making a vegetarian rice dish with ingredients she already had on hand.

After eating, she stretched out on her little sofa to read a book she'd picked up two months earlier at the used book store over on Fairfax near her mother's old ceramics shop.

But she couldn't settle.

After four chapters, she put the book aside and reached for the remote. Surfing the cable, she had trouble finding anything to watch. When she got desperate, she left it one of those DIY channels. The show about gardening reminded her she needed to take care of her plants. She watered, fertilized, and snipped dead leaves as she went.

But that didn't take long and soon she started rearranging her cabinets.

It wasn't even seven-thirty yet when she decided to clean out and organize her one and only closet. By nine, she decided she might as well get ready to go out on her rounds.

An hour later, for the first time in weeks, she walked alone with only Kiya for company. Heading down a seedy section of alleyway between the harbor to her left and Western on her right, she skimmed the vacant lot she passed.

When she thought she heard something coming from one of the ancient manufacturing buildings, she paused long enough to glance down at the wolf. Kiya gave no indication the sound was anything more than rats scurrying around in the night.

Okay, false alarm, Skye thought as she continued to roam, moving from shadow to shadow, gauging her surroundings, listening for anything out of the ordinary.

But the streets seemed strangely quiet tonight.

That all changed around midnight when she spotted two homeless men arguing over a bottle of Two-Buck Chuck. Hoping she could pass by without being spotted, she sighed when one of them screamed at her back, "You. Skye. Stop. You got any money?"

A fifty-something man who already looked like he was pushing sixty-five, teetered over to where she stood under a streetlamp. "Come on, Skye. Just a buck. That's all I'm askin' for. Danny-boy over there won't share. Says it's too cold out tonight."

Skye whirled, came around full circle to see the lined face that had once belonged to a local sportscaster.

William Cannon had suffered an on-air breakdown. As a result he'd seen his illustrious career come to an end over one ill-timed rant. His wife had kicked him out shortly thereafter and the man had slipped into depression. He'd loaded trucks for a brief time but without any permanent place to stay, he had eventually drifted to living on the streets where he'd been since 2001. Recently William had begun to show signs of the early stages of Alzheimer's. Without regular medication, he tended to become confused which made him an easy mark for anyone looking to beat him up. Skye had tried to help him before to no avail, and so had Lena.

"William Cannon, shame on you. You told me you'd get off the street. You promised Lena you'd go stay with your daughter over in Olympia."

William gave her a sheepish look. "I did. Lena drove me over there. But after a couple days, turns out, Karen didn't want me around her kids. Can't say I blame her much."

Skye reached in her pocket, pulled out a five but snatched it back when he stuck out his hand. "Promise me, William, tomorrow night you'll get off the street and head to the shelter. You have to be there early, by four at least to get a bed. Are you listening to me, William? Do you understand what I'm saying?"

"Aw, Skye, you worry 'bout me too much."

"I worry about you because you hang out with Danny Treader who served time in prison and is one mean asshole when he drinks, which is all the time." She reluctantly slapped the bill into William's palm knowing he would either lose it to Danny or he would drink it away—another one of life's sad realities Skye couldn't do anything about. "I come by here tomorrow night, William, and see you here with Danny, I'm gonna get you off the street myself. Understand?"

He nodded but grabbed the money.

Skye shook her head as she picked up her pace knowing full well William was more than likely a lost cause.

She hadn't gone a full block when at Sixth and Wheeler, Skye spotted a group of hookers that included the drug addicted Dee Dee and one of the girls she'd found last spring named Lucy Border. Purposefully Skye veered in the opposite direction. After William, she didn't need the reminder that while she'd saved the little redhead from sex-trafficking bound for Argentina, she'd lost Lucy to an endless string of johns right here in Seattle.

Sometimes the hard knocks in life were too real and depressing to dwell on them.

She and Kiya covered another half mile down yet another back alley until it started to drizzle. The woman met the eyes of her wolf and realized it was time to head home.

"Come on, Kiya, it's time to get warm," she uttered. "Some nights you just need to know when to call it quits."

Frank had never scaled a four-story brownstone before. Even though he'd considered doing just that for about five minutes, he damned sure wouldn't try it at four-thirty in the morning with the rain coming down making every surface wet and slick.

So he slipped into the Cree woman's building the old-fashioned way, through the front door using the key he'd duplicated.

For a few minutes, he stood in the tiny vestibule, rain dripping along his back making a mess on the scuffed wood floor. The foyer was so small and drab, he couldn't help the sense of claustrophobia that wanted to descend along with that feeling he'd landed in a slum. His eyes zeroed in on the cluttered mailbox area to the right. Messy, trashy, it was just another example of how the lower dregs of society couldn't even keep what little they had clean or tidy.

It angered him that such a stunning woman chose to live in this kind of filthy surroundings. But he smiled to himself when he considered how he intended to take care of that tonight. He hefted his bag onto his shoulder, patting the leather. Didn't he have all he needed right here to take care of the bitch?

Frank began the climb up the stairs, trying to avoid the steps he remembered that had a tendency to creak. But in a structure that had been built in the 1940s that was damned near impossible.

He'd given her plenty of time to get to sleep after her ridiculous habit of patrolling her turf. In spite of his admiring her speech that night at the Belmont, if it were left up to him, he never would have allowed her to walk the streets like some common tramp in the first place.

In his experience, some women refused to listen. To him, Skye Cree was another mouthy broad who didn't know her place or when to keep her trap shut. He silently vowed to show her both.

She was up there, hopefully snug in that sorry excuse for a bed she slept in and warm under those hideous handmade quilts she liked so much. Typical woman, impractical and frilly, decidedly ill-informed, he thought now. For that alone, he would give her something special as a send-off.

He knew about her breakup with the geek, knew she'd stormed out of the luxury condo two days earlier. At least she'd shown some sense there in leaving the guy. Ander might've found his cameras, might've thought he'd found one or two bugs, but the jerk hadn't found all of the surveillance devices.

So Frank had listened and learned. He'd waited and he'd planned. And now it was time to act.

Once he reached the fourth floor, Skye's door was only a few steps from the stairs. He mentally prepared for what he'd already practiced. The place was so small, so cramped he'd have to keep to his plan.

Before slipping the key into the lock, he took several deep breaths to clear his mind. Then he stepped into the pitch black. He had to let his eyes adjust to the darkness. It was so much darker than what he remembered. The dammed place was so small and the packed furniture made it seem even smaller. When it took his vision longer to correct than it should, he was tempted just to reach over and flick on the light.

That, of course, he couldn't do. But he could use the penlight he wore around his neck. He thumbed the button to the "on" position and shone the sliver of light around so he could see.

He quickly made out the lump under the covers. In his mind's eye, he knew exactly the spot where he needed to go for his staging area. But first, he needed to remember how far the bed jutted out so he wouldn't bump into it on his way to the minuscule kitchen. From memory, he counted off the exact number of footsteps, his anticipation growing with each stride.

He slipped off his tennis shoes, then his socks, removed his jacket. He pulled his shirt over his head, unzipped his jeans. Just about the time he'd worked them down around his ankles, he felt a sharp searing pain shoot through both knees. He staggered backward before he buckled and crashed into a shelf full of dishes.

Light flooded the room, momentarily blinding him.

"How does that feel you sorry piece of shit? In case you forgot, that was for Sylvia Waterston," Skye shouted as she pulled the baseball bat back around her head for another blow in case he advanced on her. Skye narrowed her eyes at the sight of Frank De Palo crumpled on the floor writhing in pain. Other than his jeans around his ankles, the man was naked.

"Come on, get up, you bastard! So I can finish beating the shit out of you."

"You and what army," Frank spewed out, doing his best to put the pain out of his head long enough so he could stand. Pulling himself upright with the help of the kitchen chair, he balanced himself before he added, "You think that bat will stop me, bitch? Think again. Or are you even capable of intelligent conversation?"

"More than you know. I'm pretty sure this bat is what will bash your skull open just like you did to Julie Freeman. And I'm not here to talk to the likes of you. Normally I don't believe in using artificial means to uh, excuse the pun, bring a man to his knees. But then you, Frank, are no man."

With his right hand, he rubbed his bare genitals up and down in a lewd gesture. "This says I am. You'll never own a pair of these. And without balls you're just something for me to use and throw away when I'm done."

When he tried to make a move toward her, Skye brought her leg up, rammed her knee into his crotch.

Frank doubled over, bumped into the wall so hard he dislodged the stained glass hanging there then went down like a sack of bricks, cupping himself before curling into a ball.

"Aw, did that hurt, Frank? You aren't bleeding even though it probably feels like you are. Try to picture your victims, Frank. Try to picture what they went through when you inflicted so much pain on them. Why don't you tell me how long you've been killing defenseless women? When did you start your little side hobby? Was it with Denise Holland or Cheryl Wittingham?"

At the mention of the two girls, Skye actually saw the fury settle into Frank's brown eyes. She waited for him to right himself again and didn't have to wait long. He tried to stand using the bed this time, swaying a little in the process.

But like any good fighter, Frank still had some game left. He kept up his momentum as he grabbed for his bag and the eight-inch blade he'd brought but hadn't yet taken out. The knife lay within his reach next to the .45. "Fuck you!" Frank yelled.

But before he could get a firm grasp on either weapon, Skye pivoted for a better angle still clutching the bat, and then whacked Frank in the back between his shoulders with a thud. She heard the wind sail out of his lungs as he dropped to the floor, gasping for air. On the wooden surface the knife skidded a little farther away. Frank snuck out his hand, stretched and strained to get to it. And Skye's boot came crashing down on his wrist. There was a loud crack as Skye twisted her boot for effect.

Frank let out a muffled cry of pain. "I knew you couldn't take me in a fair fight," Frank wheezed out as he tried to roll to escape. "I knew you were a crazy bitch," he spat out as he did his best to crawl under the bed.

"Like you ever gave any of your victims a fair fight," Skye pointed out, as she blocked his path and then stomped on his ribs with her boot. She came down so hard, she heard the bones snap. "You want a fair fight, Frank? Then get up," Skye said in challenge as she threw the bat behind her. "Come on, Frank. You know you want to. You want to do to me what you did to Tracy Lewis," she urged and watched him try to stand again. "That's why you brought the cannon with you."

That had Frank throwing out an arm and a punch which Skye dodged. "You telegraph your moves, Frank. I watched every one of your so-called fight videos on YouTube," she told him as she placed a well-timed kick to the other side of his rib cage with the heel of her boot.

When the rib cracked, this time Frank folded like an accordion and struggled to catch his breath again.

"See? Now that time you over-extended yourself like you always do. Is that all you got, pretty boy? Because for some reason, I thought you were gonna be a real badass, a lot tougher, you know?"

With the last bit of strength Frank could manage, he made one desperate lunge in her direction. Skye took the heel of her hand and with an uppercut, landed a blow to his nose.

Frank lost his footing and fell back in blinding pain as the blood spewed forth like Mount St. Helens. Through tear-filled eyes, as if he'd just realized he'd been set up, Frank stammered out. "You were waiting for me? How…how did you know I was coming?"

"Oh Frank, you're the stupidest son of a bitch I've ever seen. Josh and I played you—like a drum."

"You…you…did not."

"Oh yeah, we did."

"You two broke up. I had it planned…all of it…I waited…for the right…opportunity."

"We staged the breakup, Frank. Josh found the bugs you planted, every last one of them. And we set you up like no one before ever has. All we had to do was put out bait a coward like you would never resist. And that bait was me. Face it, De Palo, you got arrogant and that breeds sloppy every time."

With that, the door burst open and Josh came through first, followed by Harry Drummond and then two uniformed officers.

"So this is the brilliant tactician who specializes in beating up defenseless women before he brutalizes them? He doesn't look like much," Josh said with disgust. He stared at Frank in a heap on the floor, still whimpering and holding his balls with one hand, his broken nose with the other. Walking over to Skye, he kissed her soundly on the mouth. "Hello, baby, feel better?"

"Not really, I want to, no, I need to hit him one more time," she said as she made a move past Josh to get to Frank. But Josh grabbed her arm. "It's over, Skye. You beat the crap out of him. Leave it at that."

"I think I better read Frank his rights," Harry determined, dragging a battered Frank De Palo to his feet.

"She'd never have taken me without the fucking bat," Frank grumbled as blood trickled down his face.

While Harry slapped cuffs on the battered jerk, Josh laughed. "De Palo, you're lucky she didn't take that bat and stick it up your ass for scaring the shit out of that three-year-old boy."

Half an hour later, Josh stood outside the building on the sidewalk making sure Skye didn't go after Frank again. It hadn't escaped his notice the way Skye kept watch on Frank while the paramedics treated the guy's wounds, much like a wolf eyeing dinner.

Even the fact that Frank had gladly crawled onto a gurney and let himself be handcuffed to it didn't seem to make Skye feel at ease.

When one of the male paramedics looked at Skye, then up at the half-naked Frank as they loaded the sleazebag into the ambulance, the tech couldn't help it, he laughed. "I'll be damned, I never knew a serial killer before who got his ass wiped by a girl. Not such a tough guy after all, huh?"

That mocking comment brought Frank to a sitting position, his body vibrating with rage. He rose up off the stretcher and shouted, "No one beats me. She got lucky. Do you hear me…lucky! I'll be back, bitch, you just keep watching over your shoulder because you're dead. Do you hear me? You're dead!"

The other EMT, a female, reached over and pushed hard on Frank's broken ribs. "I'd say you're lucky to be alive, tough guy, because she flat out kicked your ass."

"She had a bat," Frank kept saying over and over again.

Harry shook his head as he crawled into the back of the vehicle with Frank. He waved at Josh and Skye before the EMTs closed the doors and said, "Tell the driver to make sure we hit every bump on the way to the hospital, will you?"

"I have to say, that's the longest forty-eight hours I think I've ever spent. I went nuts without having you around," Skye admitted as they made their way back to her apartment.

"Same here. Those two days felt like a week. During which time, I wanted to walk over to your apartment no less than twenty times. I missed being able to look across the room and see you sitting at the laptop, or turning to you in bed."

"I discovered I don't like sleeping alone anymore. I like having you next to me so that when I wake up in the middle of the night, you're there. Besides, I missed that rainforest of a shower you have. Makes me wonder though, what were we going to do if Frank hadn't made his move when he did? What if he'd waited another week?"

With that, she stopped walking and grabbed his shirt. "I'm not sure I could've lasted that long."

"Then our plan would've fizzled. We'd have come up with another one though."

"Thanks for trusting me to handle that bastard."

"You owe me for that. Do you have any idea how difficult it was? I had to watch from another apartment while that son of a bitch went inside knowing what he came here to do to you."

"I know." Skye trailed her fingers down the side of his jaw. "But it's over now."

When they got to the door of the little studio, they stood among the rubble of what used to be her tiny little hole-in-the-wall apartment. She looked around at all the damage to her things. Her colorful Fiestaware that had belonged to her mother was pretty much a memory. Various sizes of broken pieces were scattered all over the floor. She glanced over at the fractured stained glass Jodi Cree had so painstakingly crafted so many years earlier.

"We'll send the stained glass to a professional, Skye. Maybe they'll be able to repair most of the pieces."

"We can try. How did you know he'd break into my apartment that night after my speech? Did Kiya show you that?"

"Bits and pieces. Mostly that and the fact it was evident early on the guy thought he was so much smarter than the rest of us. We had to give him something to make sure he kept fostering that idea."

"At the risk of this going to your head, planting the journals and the computer was nothing short of brilliant. I never would have thought of leaving my old laptop here either. And changing the password so he'd have no problem getting it to boot up was a shrewd move that the jackass never saw coming. And who knew my notes would ever be of interest to anyone but me. Turns out, Frank De Palo found them fascinating enough to keep reading. And setting up the camera in here was an added stroke that gave us a decided advantage." She grabbed his shirt again and pulled him into her. "Tell me something, Mr. Ander. Is your offer still open?"

For a minute he wasn't sure what she meant. But as he studied her violet eyes, he noticed the light come into them. That light gave him sudden hope. "It's still on the table. I never took it off."

"Good. Because I want you, all of you, that includes your family, the swanky address, or a boxy home in the country. It doesn't matter much to me where we live. I guarantee you that wherever you are, I'll be happy. Because I want to marry you, Josh. We'll adopt children. We'll adopt five if that's what you want. Because I love you."

"'Bout time you realized I'm the best thing that ever happened to you since that alleyway."

A laugh sneaked out. "I've known that for months now. I just had to get past some things. I want a Christmas wedding. I think between Lena and Zoe, Velma and your mother, the four of them will be able to put something together that fast. I'm pretty sure Phyllis and Lena will drag me to every wedding boutique in Seattle. And you know what? I'm going to let them. I'm going to look so amazing it'll blow your socks off at the altar."

"You blow me away right where I stand now, Skye. Why Christmas? Why then?"

"I don't know. I like Christmas. It'll be cold out but we'll compensate by going somewhere tropical for a honeymoon. Maybe Maui for Kathy Monroe, how's that sound?"

"Oh, I think I can do better than Hawaii, Skye."

"You can?"

"How about Saint Kitts?" he asked as he went over to a kitchen drawer by her little stove. He pulled out a travel brochure, waved it toward her.

She eyed the paper in his hand. "How long have you had that stashed there?"

"Since I bought this," he answered, taking out a box from his jacket pocket. He flipped it open so she could see the diamond solitaire.

She stared at the rock as she bounced on her toes. "I thought you said you walked out without buying it."

"I lied."

She held out her left hand. "Then slip it on my finger."

He picked up her hand, slid it in place. "Marry me, Skye."

She threw her arms around his neck. "Absolutely. Yes. My answer is yes."

Chapter Twenty-Five

Four days before Christmas, the high predicted for Seattle was a chilly fifty-four degrees. But inside the century-old waterfront chapel on Orcas Island, the one hundred or so guests didn't seem to mind the north wind or the wintery, gray day.

The sun might not have been shining, the sky overcast and dreary, but the mood among those waiting for Skye to make her appearance was positively festive.

At the end of the aisle, a nervous Josh waited for his future wife in front of an arched window overlooking the bay. Co-best men, Todd Graham and Tate Brock, stayed busy as they took turns escorting the few late arrivals to their seats.

As flutes soared in the auditorium, a prelude to the main event, Travis stood in the back in the small vestibule waiting while Lena Bowers and Velma Gentry helped Skye with her long, flowing, feathery veil. At least that's what they had said they intended to do when they went into the room more than an hour earlier.

Feeling tense and overdressed in the tux he'd agreed to put on, Travis adjusted the tie again that felt like a noose around his neck. When the door opened to the dressing room and Lena emerged, dabbing at her eyes and holding onto Velma, Travis knew it was time.

At that moment, realization hit him that this was really happening. Although his role might've been simple, it was far from easy. In a matter of minutes, he had to take his daughter to Josh. He hoped he could get his feet to move.

When Todd appeared at his elbow, holding out his arm for Lena to take her to her seat, Travis watched as Tate did the same thing with Velma.

Travis heard the flutes change to lilting violin strings and the unmistakable sound of "Ode to Joy" by Beethoven. The music brought a hush to the sanctuary as the noise, laughter, and conversation came to a halt.

The bridesmaids emerged out of the same room where Skye had been locked away to get ready. Wearing matching floor-length coral gowns, the girls giggled as they formed a line to wait their turn at the processional. The youngest went first. Eleven-year-old Ali Crandon started toward the altar. Next, it was fourteen-year-old Hailey Strickland's turn, followed by Erin Prescott. Carrying pale pink peonies and a basket of white rose petals, of which each had been tasked to drop their fair share along the way, the girls finally reached the steps to the platform. Like everyone else in the chapel, the teens turned to watch the bride's approach.

Skye appeared in the doorway to take Travis's arm. Wearing a strapless gown in ivory silk and lace with a beaded bodice that met in a contoured fit before flaring out, Skye clutched her own bouquet of crimson stargazers interlaced with white roses—and took a deep breath.

Feeling like Cinderella for real, she glanced around to see all the familiar faces in the pews. Pleased to see her side just as crowded as Josh's, she grinned at Harry and Callie who stood up and smiled at her from five feet away.

She tried not to stare at the crowd before making her way toward Josh. She'd never considered herself a fan of pink— and who knew it came in so many different shades from light to dark? She had to hand it to Phyllis, Lena and Velma. Turns out, the three women had made excellent wedding planners.

At the end of the aisle, Josh got his first glimpse of Skye since they'd parted at the rehearsal dinner the night before. His nerves fell away. The air all but backed up in his chest as he took in the vision walking toward him. He had to remember his lungs needed air.

There was a moment when Travis and Skye reached the altar when his future father-in-law leaned in to him and whispered, "Hurt her and there'll be nowhere for you to hide. Got it?"

Josh grinned, expecting as much. In an equally low voice, Josh answered back, "No need for that. I don't intend to ever hurt her."

"Keep her safe then," Travis said as he slapped Josh on the back. He slipped Skye's hand into Josh's and waited several beats for Chaska Mingan, one of the Nez Perce elders, to ask him the question.

Chaska stared at his friend, Travis Nakota, long and hard. "Who gives this woman in marriage?"

Travis cleared his throat and said, "Her father does."

With that, Josh and Skye looked at each other and mounted the steps together.

But before Chaska began reading from what they had prepared just for them, Josh leaned in, wrapped Skye up in his arms, rested his forehead on hers. "Your path is now mine. We walk in like-minded spirit."

"I know. Two wolves, two hunters, mated for life— running through their own forest and fields of yellow flowers, playing, laughing—loving each other along the way. Forever is the way of the wolf," Skye said softly as Kiya looked on, intent to watch over both of them.

Dear Reader:

If you enjoyed *The Bones Will Tell*, please take the time to leave a review. A review shows others you've liked my work. By recommending it to your friends and family it helps spread the word. Please Tweet/share that you've finished *The Bones Will Tell*.

If you do write a review, by all means let me know via Facebook or my website. I'd love to hear from you!!

For a complete list of the author's other books visit her website.
Want to connect with the author to leave a comment?

http://www.vickiemckeehan.com/
www.facebook.com/VickieMcKeehan
www.vickiemckeehan.wordpress.com/ blog

Go to the next page for a preview of
The Box of Bones
A Skye Cree Novel

THE BOX OF BONES

PROLOGUE

Twenty years earlier
Fort Lewis, Washington

"**Y**ou made soup for dinner? What kind of an idiot woman thinks a man can make a meal outta soup?"

Black-haired beauty Trisha Danes, barely out of her teens, had only been married to the twenty-two- year-old army corporal for six months. But Trisha had already decided it had been the worst time of her life. How was she supposed to know that Milo got pissed off about everything *before* he'd slipped a twenty-dollar ring on her finger? That's what she got for marrying somebody she'd only known a short two months.

She trembled a little at the sound of Milo's angry tone. Lately he always seemed to be mad about something. And tonight was no exception.

In her best Carolina drawl, she tried to pacify him. "It's…not…soup, honey. It's stew and it has lots of meat and veggies like potatoes and carrots and onions, just like you like," Trisha pointed out.

"Well, whatever it is, you made it so damn watery that it looks like soup to me. I can see the bottom of the damn pan," Milo groused.

That was because she'd tried to stretch all the ingredients. But she didn't say this to Milo. Instead she did her best to appease him again and offered, "Okay, okay, no need to get upset. How about I fix you a nice grilled cheese instead? You like those. You can eat it with the…soup."

"I'm not eating a damned sandwich. A man wants a real meal when he gets home from working a ten-hour shift not a bunch of cheese on toast."

Trisha sucked in a nervous breath. It might be different if Milo had an exhausting job loading trucks for the army from six in the morning until four in the afternoon. But he didn't. What Milo did was sit on his ass at a desk inputting data into a computer all day, keeping track of shipments coming onto and going off the base. Not exactly grueling work in Trisha's mind. But she didn't dare mention that at the moment. She didn't want to fight. And because of that she went to the refrigerator and dug out the carton of eggs. "How about I scramble you up some of these?"

"Damn it, woman! That's breakfast food. I want you to fix me supper. What about that don't you understand?"

Now was probably not a good time to remind Milo that they still had another week to go till payday. He could eat a cheese sandwich, or the two scrambled eggs or the watery stew. Honestly though, Trisha was getting mighty tired of Milo's temper flaring like a volcano over the least little thing like what he had for dinner. Trisha backed away from the fridge as Milo stormed over to the same appliance and yanked the door open to see for himself what was inside.

Trisha wasn't taking any chances. She moved three feet away to the counter.

"There's nothing in here but some ketchup, mustard and mayo. We don't even have a hotdog to throw on the stove. Where the hell is the food?"

It wasn't like she'd eaten it up herself. Beginning to shake now with fear that he might take it up a notch, which she'd seen him do lately, she did her best to remind him of their situation. "We have seven dollars in our checking account, Milo. It's gotta last at least another six days before I can go to the PX. We've used up our allotment for food. Look, I've got a can of beans in the pantry I can throw in and add it to the stew. That'll make it a lot thicker."

But when Milo slammed the ice-box door shut and wheeled around with fire in his eyes, Trisha knew she was in trouble. "Don't you dare hit me again! I didn't move three thousand miles all the way across the country to a place where all it does is rain all the damned time for you to use me as a punching bag every single time you get mad about something! I'm not putting up with you hitting me anymore, Milo."

"Oh yeah? Then leave. Get out of my face *and* my house. What good are you anyway? Can't even fix a damn meal the right way," he groused.

But when she reached for the keys, lying out on the counter, to the only vehicle they owned, Milo's truck, he slapped her hand away. "You ain't takin' my pickup. You wanna get out of here? Fine, you walk. You leave with what's on your back."

"That's not right."

"Yeah, well neither is me coming home and finding a crappy meal on the stove." With that, he shoved her through the back door. "Now get your ass out of my sight before I decide to smack you."

"Where am I supposed to go, Milo?"

"Hey, you wanna leave? What the hell do I care where you go?" He pushed her onto the narrow porch and then slammed the door shut in her face.

The minute she heard the lock turn on the other side, Trisha's shoulders slumped. What was she supposed to do now? She took two steps and started pounding on the door.

"At least give me my purse. Come on, Milo. I need my wallet! It has my ID in it."

When the door cracked open slightly, she had hope. But then Milo tossed her handbag over her head and it landed on the wet patch of dirt and weedy grass behind her.

"There. Satisfied now? By the way, I took the checkbook out of it, too. I don't want you writing hot paper all over town that I'll have to cover. Now get out of my sight! You knock on this door again and I'll bash your face in."

Knowing he would do it, Trisha backed down the steps and ran over to retrieve her pocketbook. She brushed off the tan faux leather grain hoping all the grime came off.

It was beginning to get dark and already chilly for October. The sun dipped in the west over the tips of the evergreens as she made her way through the complex heading to the nearest pay phone, a good half mile away.

She didn't even have her jacket. Asshole Milo, she thought, as she tromped off in the direction of the PX. What she had ever seen in the piece of shit, she could only wonder now.

It was time to call her stepmom, Brandy Sue Grainger, collect back in Charlotte. Trisha hoped the woman accepted the charges. After all, it was her stepmother who had tried to warn her about marrying Milo. She wished now she'd listened to Brandy. Not only that, Trisha hoped she could talk Brandy Sue into sending her bus fare to get back home. If that didn't happen, she'd have to hitchhike her way clear across the country. But first, she'd have to wait for Milo to go to work in the morning to go back to the apartment to get her clothes.

As Trisha contemplated where she planned to sleep that night, a jeep pulled alongside her with the windows rolled down. That seemed odd to Trisha because she'd been here two months and not a single soul had gone out of their way to be friendly to her.

When the man behind the wheel brought the car to the side of the road and came to a stop, Trisha stopped walking.

"You need a ride, honey? It's awful cold out here and you don't even have a coat on."

He seemed nice enough and wow was he ever cute, all that dark hair and all. Maybe her luck in the man department had turned.

As she opened the passenger door and hopped into the front seat, Trisha had no way of knowing it was the last ride she would ever take.

Don't miss these other exciting titles by bestselling author

Vickie Mckeehan

The Pelican Pointe Series
PROMISE COVE
HIDDEN MOON BAY
DANCING TIDES
LIGHTHOUSE REEF
STARLIGHT DUNES
LAST CHANCE HARBOR
SEA GLASS COTTAGE
LAVENDER BEACH
SANDCASTLES UNDER THE CHRISTMAS MOON
BENEATH WINTER SAND
KEEPING CAPE SUMMER (2018)

The Evil Secrets Trilogy
JUST EVIL Book One
DEEPER EVIL Book Two
ENDING EVIL Book Three
EVIL SECRETS TRILOGY BOXED SET

The Skye Cree Novels
THE BONES OF OTHERS
THE BONES WILL TELL
THE BOX OF BONES
HIS GARDEN OF BONES
TRUTH IN THE BONES
SEA OF BONES (2018)

The Indigo Brothers Trilogy
INDIGO FIRE
INDIGO HEAT
INDIGO JUSTICE
INDIGO BROTHERS TRILOGY BOXED SET

Coyote Wells Mysteries
MYSTIC FALLS
SHADOW CANYON
SPIRIT LAKE (2018)

ABOUT THE AUTHOR

Vickie McKeehan has twenty-two novels to her credit and counting. Vickie's novels have consistently appeared on Amazon's Top 100 lists in Contemporary Romance, Romantic Suspense and Mystery / Thriller. She writes what she loves to read—heartwarming romance laced with suspense, heart-pounding thrillers, and riveting mysteries. Vickie loves to write about compelling and down-to-earth characters in settings that stay with her readers long after they've finished her books. She makes her home in Southern California.

You can visit the author at:
www.vickiemckeehan.com
www.facebook.com/VickieMcKeehan
http://vickiemckeehan.wordpress.com/
www.twitter.com/VickieMcKeehan